MY KINDA Kisses

USA TODAY BESTSELLING AUTHOR
LACEY BLACK

My Kinda Kisses
Summer Sisters Book 1

Copyright © 2016 Lacey Black
Cover Design by Y'all. That Graphic.
Editing by Kara Hildebrand
Format by Integrity Formatting

Published in the United States of America.

ISBN-13: 978-1-951829-20-9

MY KINDA Kisses

Jaime

It's a Summer sister tradition that on the first Saturday of each month, the six of us get together. We take turns picking the location or activity, anything from margaritas and a movie to wine and painting classes at the small gallery uptown. One thing, though, is as certain as the sun rising over the Chesapeake Bay every morning; there will be alcohol involved.

Always.

Tonight, it's putt putt golf at The Beaver, a local hangout offering a fun, casual atmosphere and a dozen different beers on tap. It's also the home of Harry, the six-foot tall wooden beaver statue that takes up residence right in the middle of the beer garden. You never know what attire that large hunk of hand carved wood will adorn. It can be anything from a t-shirt supporting the local cancer charity to a coconut bra and grass skirt. The best part is, no one really knows where Harry came from. All we know is that he's been in the middle of the beer garden of The Beaver since the 1940's. See, Harry's sort of the official mascot at one of our favorite hangouts in our small Virginian town along the Bay.

Jupiter Bay: Home of eight thousand busybodies who know everything about you, and will still go out of their way to help a friend in need. And since everyone knows everyone in Jupiter Bay, everyone's your friend.

Or so they think.

Right now, I'm about to putt my bright pink ball through the spinning windmill and sink it in the hole for my second birdy of the night. What can I say? Putt putt is my sport. I know my way around the green.

"If you make this shot, I swear I'm never inviting you to play again," my younger sister Meghan grumbles.

"Why don't you shove that straw in your mouth and zip your lips while I sink this putt." My backstroke is smooth, my follow-through precise as I tap my ball, sending it sailing through the windmill, bouncing perfectly off the sideboard, and dropping it straight into the cup. Perfect. Shot.

A round of groans erupt behind me as my five sisters watch my celebratory golf club shimmy. I turn around to face them, all bright eyed and wide smiled, and pretend to buff my fingernails on my shoulder and blow off the dust. This sister is on fire tonight. And I'm sure it has nothing to do with the three draft Heinekens I've already consumed since our arrival a little over an hour ago. No, I can hold my liquor. The beer only helps perfect my putt putt awesomeness.

"I don't even know why we come here. You kill it every time," my oldest sister Payton says.

"Don't be jealous of my mini-golf amazingness. It's a gift. The LPGA called last week and is interested in my skills," I tell her, taking a final drink from my cup.

"I'm just glad to finally see the old Jaime again," AJ adds solemnly. The look on her face lets me know she clearly didn't mean to vocalize the thought. My sisters glance at each other–everywhere but at me, really–before adding discreet little nods.

I can't dispute her statement, because AJ is right. I haven't been myself. Not since my fiancé, Gavin, left me practically standing at the altar. In reality, it was the week of our pending nuptials, but the resulting damage was the same nonetheless. I was wrecked.

The result of the breakup was my return home to Jupiter Bay. I was the only sister to head off to college and not return home. My plan was simple, be married to a successful man by thirty with baby number one on the way by our one-year anniversary. I dreamed of staying home with my brood of adorable little brunette babies with their daddy's hazel eyes. Company dinners, family outings, and PTA meetings. That's what I wanted, and I was one week away from crossing phase one off the checklist when my world came crashing down around me.

I'm a planner by nature. I like to make lists of my daily tasks, my weekly chores, my life goals. Everything and anything can be organized properly on a nice little checklist, ensuring no detail is missed, nothing overlooked. Funny, but never on that list was being dumped before my master plan could fully get off the ground.

My plan essentially stalled the day I received that text. Yep, you heard me correctly. The jerkface pond scum couldn't even break my heart and shatter my dreams to my face. He took the cowards way out and sent an impersonal message as if he were canceling a business meeting with a client.

> **Gavin:** Hey, sorry this is last minute but I can't marry you.

End of story.

And maybe that's all I was: an inconvenience to disregard.

Even though Gavin and I had been together for five years, there never really was that spark, that chemistry that makes you want to rip your clothes off and get it on in the middle of a busy street. We were comfortable, plain and simple. Oh, it didn't start that way. It started as a powerful new love, each one craving the other with an intensity never before felt. Unfortunately, the flicker fizzled and died about as quickly as a sparkler on the Fourth of July. It was all big and bright, and then nothing but the residual smoke.

But even so, I didn't see it coming and was gutted the day he ended our relationship as if I was nothing–meant nothing. Now, I'm the proverbial hamster on the wheel, spinning, spinning, and going nowhere fast. The sister with big dreams of a house, husband, kids, and a cat whose dream never even got off the ground.

"I'm sorry, I shouldn't have said that," AJ mumbles, turning her shining eyes on mine for the first time since her comment.

"No, it's alright. You don't ever have to apologize for speaking your mind. Especially when we all know it was the truth."

"Are you excited to start at the shop Monday?" my youngest sister, one of the twins, Abby, asks.

"I guess." I desperately suck the remaining droplets of beer out of my empty cup. "I don't really know what I'm doing, but I know I can't stay at home any longer. I can't decide if Grandpa walks around in his tighty whities because he likes it casual and breezy or if he's trying to scare me out of the house."

Easy laughter fills the cool, early June night. Five sets of sparkling green eyes of various shades of my own stare back at me. "I think he's just more comfortable in his skivvies. He used to do that all the time when I was still at home," Lexi says. "Remember how we were always terrified to have friends spend the night?"

"Oh, I definitely remember that," Payton adds with a hearty laugh.

Payton is the oldest Summer sister, three years older than my twenty-nine years. While all of us look strikingly similar in appearance, Payton and I have the closest resemblance. Well, if you don't include the twins. Payton owns Blossoms and Blooms in downtown Jupiter Bay where, as of this coming Monday morning, I'll be working full-time, trying to find my next passion in life. No, I don't intend to find my new dream while arranging roses and baby's breath, especially when my thumb is as brown as they come. Lord knows I can't even keep dandelions in the yard alive.

Alison Jane, or AJ as we've all called her since elementary school, is two years behind me. She's the seventh and eighth grade math teacher, as well as the cheer coach, at the junior high. I knew from the moment she was old enough to read to our younger sisters that AJ was our tutor, the nurturer in the family.

One quick year after AJ was born came Meghan. While she wasn't the first Summer sister to get married (that was Lexi), I truly believe Meghan will be the next. Josh and Meghan became a couple three years ago while I was still living in Cleveland with the douche who shall remain nameless. They go everywhere together. Hell, I'm surprised he's not sitting inside on a barstool watching us play mini-golf right now. Josh is a great guy and worships the ground Meg walks on. If it wasn't so sickeningly sweet, I'd almost be a little jealous.

Almost.

Finally, to round out the Summer clan, we have Abby and Lexi. The twins came along when I was just starting kindergarten. They're as identical in looks as you can get, but complete opposite in personality. Where one is outgoing and bubbly, the other prefers books and quiet. Lexi is married to her high school sweetheart, Chris, who is rarely in attendance at any family function, let alone stopping by at the end of Girls' Night.

But one thing's for sure, no one ever miss our monthly sisters' evening.

The gatherings started while I was in Cleveland, but turned into a regular monthly appointment in my calendar when I returned to town. I liked living in the Midwestern city, but, admittedly, never really felt at home like I do in Jupiter Bay. For the longest time, I thought that all I needed was Gavin, and I was content anywhere I went. Unfortunately, he didn't feel the same way.

As we wrap up our game and order another round, Josh finally makes his predictable appearance at the bar. Meghan practically sprints towards him as he steps through the door, the smile on her face radiating delight.

And I'm truly happy for her. I'm pleased for all of my sisters, even the ones who have yet to find love. They're independent, fierce, and loyal. They forge their own way, even when life tries to keep them down. Lord knows we've had enough heartache to last a lifetime, but it doesn't seem to be holding any of them back.

Maybe it's time to take a page from their book and focus on the here and now. I'm here, without Gavin, and that's how my life is going to be. There's no use crying over spilled milk. It's time to pick up the pieces and move forward.

I make a mental checklist of the things I want to accomplish by the time I'm thirty later this year. A *new* checklist. One that doesn't include weddings and babies, but includes simpler things like learn how to grill a steak (something I have yet to master) and repaint my bedroom furniture. Easy tasks that I'll be able to proudly check off, essentially getting myself back in my groove. I also make sure to add a no dating clause to the checklist. The last thing I need is to step into something sticky right now, so fresh out of my breakup. Sure it was six months ago, but that's okay. Slow and steady, that's key.

It's not going to be easy, moving on, but it's necessary. And as I gaze at my smiling sisters, I make myself a promise to help them find their happiness. Even if I don't see mine anywhere on the horizon, I can make sure theirs is within their grasp.

My one chance to live my dream–marriage, babies, PTA meetings–is a thing of the past. But maybe that's okay. Maybe that dream wasn't all it was cracked up to be. Maybe it wasn't for me. Maybe I'll find a new dream that's bigger and better than the one before.

And maybe I'm completely full of shit.

Ryan

2

"What time do we meet with the Hazeltons?" I ask, dropping my tool belt onto the plastic chair across from Mary.

"They're meeting you onsite at four," my faithful office assistant replies with a stern look.

"What?" I ask, following her line of sight down to the tattered remains of one of my only good pairs of khakis.

"I thought the boss wasn't supposed to get dirty when he's 'checking' on a job?" she asks, using air quotes to emphasize the word checking.

"Orlando called in again. His wife's not doing well, so I helped unload drywall."

"You ripped holes in your pants by carrying drywall?" The look she offers reminds me of one my mother used to give me when I was caught doing something I wasn't supposed to be doing. Great. I'm already in trouble, and it's only three o'clock on Monday afternoon.

Pulling a cold bottle of water out of the mini-fridge, I take long, deep pulls before returning my attention to my right-hand woman. "Once we got the delivery truck unloaded, I helped hang a few sheets. No big deal."

"It wouldn't be a big deal, Ryan, if you weren't an hour away from meeting with your largest client yet. You wore khakis and a button-up for a reason, you know." I don't even have time to speak before she continues. "How is Paula doing?" Mary's voice is as sober and wretched as we all feel.

"Not good. They don't think she has much time." I relay the details of my early morning conversation with one of my first hired employees when I moved to Jupiter Bay a little over a year ago. His wife of twenty years is in the end stage of breast cancer. She has fought a long battle, spanning the last two years, but the cancer is winning. "I told him to take as much time as he needed. His job is secure."

"I still can't believe it. She just turned forty last month. Their daughter is going into her senior year of high school." Mary shakes her head, tears filling her wrinkled blue eyes, as she verbalizes the sorrow we've all felt over her fight with this horrible disease.

"Me neither."

"It's good of you to hold his job," she adds, her voice soft and full of compassion.

"It's the right thing to do. The *only* thing to do. Make note to send over some food for them later in the week," I say, Mary quickly jotting down something in her ever-present notebook.

"Consider it done. Are we on track for the Fredrickson family to take occupancy on the first of August?" Mary asks, flipping to the page labeled with the corresponding job site. I've tried to convince her to utilize the computer collecting dust on her desktop, but she refuses to learn. She says her pen and paper are more reliable than the piece of electronics taking up residence in front of her.

"Yep. Drywallers are mudding tomorrow and the flooring should be here by the end of the week."

I watch as she makes notes, noticing the slight tremor in her hand. It's not as noticeable in the morning as it is in the afternoon, but it's there nonetheless.

Mary was one of the first residents of Jupiter Bay that I met when I moved to town a little over a year ago. She was waiting tables at the diner, busting her ass for tips, while on her feet for ten to twelve hours a day. I was immediately drawn to her spunky attitude. Sara, my girlfriend at the time, was taken aback by the quick-witted quips and sassy comebacks from the older waitress. Me? I was fascinated.

After having lunch or dinner in that diner for two weeks straight, I decided that when I got my small construction business off the ground, I was taking Mary with me. She doesn't take any shit from anyone, least of all me. And, honestly, from the very start, I grew to care for the ol' woman, and I was anxious to see her off her feet and bringing home a steady, solid paycheck for her husband and disabled son at home.

Mary runs my office. She answers the phone, is the first contact for potential clients, and keeps me well organized. Not to mention handling payroll, paying the bills, ordering material, and picking up the slack wherever needed. Just the thought of having to do all of this shit without her makes me shudder. Not only does she handle my office, but she effectively handles me. I'll admit it. She makes sure I'm where I need to be, when I need to be there. She's like my mom, but without riding my ass for not calling enough.

Depositing my tool belt in the office I rarely occupy anymore, I gather up my notes and binder with the Hazelton blueprints. Their home will be a massive four thousand square foot Tudor home, with four bathrooms, six bedrooms, and an indoor pool and spa, all nestled discreetly along the Bay. It'll be the largest home I've contracted since starting Elson Developments a year ago.

The first few months consisted of a few small remodeling jobs to help get the word out and bring in a little income. Fortunately, it didn't take too long for word of mouth to spread and my crew of three transformed into a crew of ten. Business grew rapidly, especially with the only other building contractor retiring six months ago and relocating to Florida. We currently have two crews working different projects at the same time, and a list of three new homes, a business expansion, and six remodels waiting in the wings. I've got enough work to keep my guys busy for the next year and a half, and that helps me sleep a little easier at night.

Heading towards the door, I throw a quick wave over my shoulder. "I'll be back after the meeting. Leave whatever checks I need to sign in the drawer and I'll sign them when I get back."

Mary nods in understanding before reaching for the ringing phone.

"Don't forget it's Mrs. Hanson's birthday," Mary hollers, phone cradled in her hand, as I walk out the door and into the bright sunlight.

Mrs. Hanson is my elderly landlord and neighbor. She's the sweetest old lady on the planet and is constantly bringing me cookies or casseroles. Her husband passed away years ago, and her kids are all grown and moved away. I'm pretty sure she's lonely, so I do what I can to stop by every now and again to visit her.

Knowing that I need to run home and freshen up before my meeting, I head towards my truck with purpose. I throw the truck in gear and drive towards my condo, making a mental note to stop and grab something for Mrs. Hanson on my ride back to the office.

ⅹⅩⅹ

It's almost five when I pull out of the lot where we'll soon start construction on the Hazelton homestead. Robert and Carol are ready to get their new home project started. Robert comes from money. His family owns shipping vessels that move cargo from one end to the other along the entire Eastern seaboard. While Robert is still very much a part of the company his family has owned for three generations, he is slowly turning over operations to his son.

The home we're going to build for them is going to be a big project. My plan is to combine my two crews into a singular unit while we complete the foundation and framing, though I haven't ruled out keeping them both going on this one home for the duration of the project. As general contractor, I am also coordinating the installation of utilities, as well as new pipe work. The land they're building on is completely bare. This project is going to be a great test of my capabilities, but I can't wait to get it going.

It's five when I pull into town, and remember that it's Mrs. Hanson's birthday. Groaning in frustration, it only takes me a second to realize that finding a gift at this point could be difficult. Many of the small mom and pop shops close down at five. Sure, there's a Wal-Mart near the north edge of Jupiter Bay, but even I'm not stupid enough to try to find a gift for the woman who already has everything at Wal-Mart.

Spying the small flower shop in downtown, I pull into the first available parking spot and jump out. My watch reads five after five, and I say a quick prayer that I can catch the owner before she closes down for the night.

When I reach the door, I'm relieved to find it still unlocked and I push it open. A bell jingles above the doorway signaling my entrance.

The small shop is brimming with brightly colored flowers, lush green plants and small knick-knacky things that just collect dust. I've only been inside the place once–a long time ago when I was kissing Sara's ass–but I've seen the owner around town. In a place like Jupiter Bay, you can't help but run into someone you know everywhere you go.

Though I don't really know her, she's a striking woman. With long brown hair and deep green eyes, she's a little bonier than I normally like. There's nothing better than the delicate curve of a woman's waist and the seductive arc where her lower back meets her ass. In fact, that's my favorite part of a woman. It's sexy as fuck.

Sara was slender. After the split, I couldn't remember what in the hell I ever found attractive about her in the first place. She was salad-eating, stick-figure skinny with perfectly manicured nails and flawless skin. Her sleek black hair was always immaculate, and her brown eyes sparkled like chocolate diamonds. But her personality was in desperate need of a little work. Sara was a high maintenance bitch who was always out for number one. She was notorious for using people until she got what she wanted or toying with them to suit her game. Then she'd discard them.

Like me.

"Sorry, we're closed."

The woman's voice draws my attention towards the counter in back. Taking long strides, I head towards the voice, determined to buy a bouquet before she can kick me out the door I just walked through.

"I understand that, ma'am, but I'm afraid I'm in desperate need of some flowers. I promise to be quick, take whatever you have already made up, and I'll pay in cash," I offer as I reach the counter.

The woman, who's still showing me her back, is cleaning the work area filled with clippings of greenery and those little white flowers they stick in bouquets for whatever purpose they serve. Her hair is pulled up in a messy knot at the back of her head, revealing the long, slender column of her neck, and for some reason, it turns me on.

My eyes peruse leisurely down the back of her body. A crisp white dress shirt hugs her perfect hourglass waist, tight blue jeans mold flawlessly to long legs, and the swell of her ass is so damn enticing. Even through her clothes, I can see the divot at the base of her spine. The mental image is like a bolt of lightning straight to my dick.

"I said we're closed," she says while she spins around, the last word trailing off and almost inaudible as her eyes lock on mine.

Pale green eyes the color of dewed grass slam into mine so damn hard, the impact forces me to take a retreating step. I'm struck stupid, unable to process a thought let alone communicate words, as I gape back at her. The only thing that saves me from looking like a complete ass right now is that she appears to have the same reaction.

Her eyes hold my attention for what feels like hours. They're expressive and stunning, even when they're wide with surprise.

While she continues to gape at me, I finally allow my attention to pull away from those intoxicating eyes. Smooth, silky cheeks with a hint of a pink blush. A mouth so alluring, lips too luscious for kissing that it's suddenly all I can think about, all I want. To kiss this woman. I swear I could stare at those lips for days, and yet even then, it still wouldn't be long enough.

"Can I help you?" she asks, barely above a whisper.

My gaze returns to her eyes just in time to catch her checking me out. She quickly skims me from head to toe, stopping at my chest on her way back up. She tries to be subtle, sure, but it's futile. I catch her and make no attempt to hide my smirk. I'm a good-looking guy, I know, but there's something about this woman that makes her appraisal that much more pleasing.

"I need flowers for a…friend," I reply, intentionally adding a pause to my statement.

Green eyes slam back into mine as she takes in my words. "A friend?" she asks, trying hard to gather her wits. Unfortunately for her, I can still read how much our meeting has rattled her.

"Yep. A…friend. A *good* friend." Again, I can't help the quirk from the corner of my lips.

"Well, we're closed." Her façade slams back into place as she steels her back and stands to her full height. At six foot two, I still tower over her full five foot eight height. Her eyes harden, those gorgeous green eyes burning into my soul with a fierceness I've never experienced. Stubbornness radiates off her like a furnace, and I'll be completely honest, it's hot as hell.

I know the flowers are for my elderly neighbor, but it doesn't stop me from toying with her. Her reaction to my appearance in the shop, followed by the change in her demeanor when I said they were for a friend, are both unexpected and arousing. I don't know why, but I'm intrigued.

"I promise not to take too much of your time, but I really need some flowers. Don't make me be that guy who shows up at her door tonight without flowers." And with that, I give her the look. I've spent years perfecting it. Part puppy dog, part sexual innuendo. Throw in the full-wattage of my pearly white smile and burning, lustful eyes, and the results are always the same: she melts like warm butter.

Her eyes soften instantly, and I inwardly smile and mentally pump my fists in victory. She offers me a hesitant, shy grin before dropping her eyes to the cleaning cloth in her hand. "I guess I can sell you something as long as it's out of the cooler," she says before returning those eyes back to me.

For the second time since I arrived at the little shop, I'm rendered speechless. Those eyes. They draw me in and refuse to let go. I'm helpless, and that in itself leaves me a little unsettled. I've never felt this magnetic pull towards a woman before.

Beautiful women are everywhere. I've dated a handful and not exactly dated a few more. But this woman, she causes a different reaction entirely. Sure, my pants are three sizes too small right now, but it's more than that. It's in the way my heart rate elevates and my stomach tightens every time she looks at me.

"Though it really isn't my style, I promise I'll be *quick*." I offer a little wink after my sexually-laced insinuation, and struggle to retain my laugh. Her eyes widen in shock and her breathing comes out in little pants. It instantly makes me think of other ways I'd love to make her pant.

Walking over to the cooler, there's a dozen or so premade arrangements ready to go. Honestly, I don't give a shit which one I get. Mrs. Hanson will appreciate any of them, but for some reason, I feel the need to draw out this first encounter, because if I know anything at all, it's that this is just the first of many more to come. I'll make damn sure of it.

"Which one of these do you think says friendly without commitment? The red roses are out, for sure, but what about these bright ones here? Do those give the impression that I love spending time with her day or night?"

God, I'm a bastard. Yes, I'm leading her to think something entirely different than my reality. She has no clue that I've enjoyed sitting on the porch, talking, or playing cards until the wee hours of the morning with Mrs. Hanson. She's more of a second grandma to me than anything else. But something in the way this woman gets worked up when I insinuate sex with someone else leaves me slightly pleased and itching to egg her on a little more.

"Well, if you're looking to say thank you for a wonderful night without having to buy a ring, then I'd go with this one," she says somewhat hastily as she pulls open the cooler door and pulls out a brightly colored fresh bouquet. The most alluring scent fills my senses–hell, my entire being–but it isn't the flowers. It's her. She smells sweet and clean with a hint of floral. It reminds me of the shower. Of water glistening off flushed skin. Of sex. Preferably in the shower.

Turning away slightly, I take a quick moment to subtly adjust the raging hard-on I'm sporting in my pants. "Those are perfect. I'll take them," I find myself saying, even though I'd rather her put them back and get something else. Like a game of cat and mouse, I long for her to reach inside the case and retrieve a different vase. And then another and another. I want to watch her grab every single one of the vases just so I can watch her bend over, those damn pants stretched tightly across her perfect ass. But I know the bouquet she chose for me is perfect. Even though I know shit about flowers, I know Mrs. H will adore them.

She quickly heads up to the counter, the gentle sway of her hips holding my attention the entire way. With her back to me, she begins the process of covering the flowers in cellophane. Her hands hold a slight shake to them. It's a subtle movement, but one I notice nonetheless. The red-blooded male in me wonders if that tremble is a result of my nearness, the same way my body is reacting in my pants to her closeness. That's the effect I'm sticking with right now.

After wrapping up the vase, she turns back to the register. "The card machine is already shut down," she says, those green orbs sliding skimming slowly upward until they land on my eyes.

"I'll pay cash. It's the least I can do since I kept you late tonight."

"It's twenty-four ninety-five."

Retrieving my wallet, I pull out two twenties and hand them to her. I'd be a liar if I said the slight graze of her hand with my own, as she takes the bills, was a coincidence. But it was no accident. I needed to touch her, even just the slightest.

What I wasn't expecting was the impact of that touch. Her gasp is the only sound in the shop. Like lightning, a white-hot bolt of lust strikes our connecting hands, sizzling and shooting heat throughout my body. *Holy shit.*

She pulls back suddenly, as if my touch burned her fingers. I don't even attempt to fight the smile threatening to take over. It feels damn good to smile, as if I haven't smiled in forever. It also feels damn good to feel something–whatever in the hell it is I'm feeling–for my mystery woman.

As she drops my change into my hand, careful not to make physical contact a second time, her eyes dart around the room, refusing to settle on mine. She quickly turns, grabs the wrapped vase, and sets it in front of me as if she's finished with our transaction and with me.

Knowing that our time is coming to an end, disappointment and indecision set in. I know it's time to leave, but my feet don't seem to get the memo. They flat out refuse to walk towards the door. I stand there, watching her, for several heartbeats.

It's a slow process, like the final steps towards the electric chair, but I turn towards the entrance and take a few hesitant steps. Before I can chicken out, I turn back around. Round, light green eyes pierce me, captivating me and drawing me back towards her. "Do you have a name?"

"Yes." That's it. That's all she says.

"Can I have it?" I ask, the smirk fighting to get out.

"Don't you have your own?" she quips with the rise of a single eyebrow, and I know instantly: I'm in lust. Feisty, independent, sassy, and gorgeous. She's the perfect combination.

I don't even attempt to hold back the belly laugh. It sweeps through me in a rush of euphoric bliss. But when she smiles back at me, a beautiful, melt my heart smile, I realize I'm already gone. I'll stop at nothing to see this smile on this woman's face as often as humanly possible. The way her eyes crinkle and light up, the way her cheekbones tinge a soft pink, the way her lips, full and pouty, stretch exquisitely across perfectly straight white teeth, her face lights up with that one simple act. Smiling.

Taking steps, I return to my post at the counter. I set aside the vase, lean down, casually resting my elbows atop the hard surface. "I do have a name, you are correct. What I was hoping for was a name that I could call you when I see you again."

"Oh, who says you'll be seeing me again?" she questions, the sparkle still evident in her eyes. With her hands on her hips, she takes a dazzling defiant stance. But I know differently; her eyes still shine with interest.

"I'm pretty sure it's inevitable. Like the sun rising in the east and setting in the west. I suddenly have the innate desire to buy flowers. Lots of flowers."

She rolls her eyes. "So, let me get this straight. You're going to stop by and flirt with me while buying flowers for your other women?" She says women as if I have a herd of them waiting outside.

I shrug, not denying or supporting her claim. "So how about it? Do I get a name?"

She stares at me for several heartbeats, and I'm sure she's going to shoot me down. Unfortunately for her, she has no idea how persistent I can be. I don't care if I have to buy flowers for every woman in this town, you can bet your ass I'll be back. Soon.

Grabbing the flowers and turning back towards the door, I make my way to the entrance. I grasp the handle and pull, the bell above the door jingling once more. Before I step through the doorway, however, I hesitate. If she's looking at me, I'll come back. If she's not, then I'll cut my losses and move on. It's not like I haven't perfected the art of the cut and run.

Looking over my shoulder, my focus is solely on a pair of alluring green eyes. There's hesitancy in her gaze; it looks both reluctant and relieved. Like she's glad to see me go, but sad at the same time. Her conflict is clear, but it's the memory of her smile that I hang onto and will carry with me. That and the fact that she was watching me go. Hope bubbles in my chest like carbonation in a soft drink.

Shooting her a smile of my own, I head out the door and towards my truck. There's an extra spring in my step as I saunter down the sidewalk and unlock the driver's door. Sliding inside, I set the flowers in the passenger seat before turning the ignition. My gaze returns to the painted brick building, to the woman I see step to the door. Through the glass, I watch as she turns the lock before her own gaze sweeps the sidewalk and street before her.

Even through the glare of the windows, I know the instant her eyes settle on mine. I hold her stare for several seconds, silently conveying a message.

I'll be back.

As I throw the truck in drive and pull onto the street, I keep one eye on the road and one on the storefront. I may not know her name, but I know where she works. Something clearly held her back from giving me her name, more than just to toy with me. I didn't spot a ring, but I suppose that still doesn't mean she isn't taken. That just means the guy is stupid to not publicly declare her as his by putting a ring on her finger. I've never been in a hurry to settle down, but if I had a woman like that, you could bet your sweet ass I'd commit fully and completely as soon as possible.

Determined to find out her story–and her name–I head towards the office to finish up paperwork. Then, it's home and to deliver the flowers to my neighbor. Mrs. Hanson will be thrilled by my Monday night visit, I'm sure, and won't suspect a thing if I slip in a few subtle questions about the beautiful flower shop employee. She's clearly not the woman I've met before who owns the shop, but the resemblance is uncanny. Finding out a little information shouldn't be too difficult.

And once I complete a little recon, it's off to buy more flowers.

3

Jaime

I'm still staring out the front door, even after the taillights on the large truck have long disappeared. I've never felt anything like it. A connection to the way his eyes roamed my body, the way his touch unearthed me. Even with Gavin, I've never felt such a deep, gut-check reaction to a man before.

Sure, his body was amazing. Even in a dark polo, pair of jeans, and work boots, I could tell he's a man who takes pride in his physical appearance. Broad shoulders with a wide chest, trim, lean waist, and a powerful pair of tree trunk thighs. His hair was dark brown with just enough length to run your fingers through it. He's a deadly combination of authority and sexuality. And let's not get into the impressive bulge in his pants that I tried my damnedest to ignore. Holy hell, that man was walking sex.

And that's not even including his eyes. Of course, those deep brown eyes were the first thing I noticed when he stepped into my sister's flower shop at the end of my very first day. Eyes that seemed to devour me inch by inch as they perused and consumed my entire body, lighting me up like the Fourth of July.

Then there's the smile. The one that promised dirty, wicked things with each smirk, each grin he awarded me. It was a beautiful smile that captivated me and left me ready to throw caution to the wind and rip off his clothes.

Who hits on a woman while he's buying flowers for another?

A player, that's who.

But why are players always so friggin' hot?

Can't there, for once, be a hot normal guy? One who *wants* a steady girlfriend, who *wants* to buy her flowers just because, who *wants* to get married and settle down? My thoughts instantly drift to Gavin. He was gorgeous, smart, and charming. And I *thought* he wanted to settle down. Hell, he put a damn ring on my finger, didn't he? But in the end, he walked away without so much as a backwards glance, leaving me in a pile of unusable wedding gifts and satin.

A noise pulls me from my thoughts. "Jaime, are you all right?" Payton asks behind me.

"Yeah, sure. Why wouldn't I be?"

"Uh, maybe because I've been talking to you for two minutes and you haven't so much as acknowledged me."

"Oh, sorry. I was just lost in thought," I respond, turning and looking once more out the front door.

"I'm so sorry it took me so long to make that delivery. The residents were so excited about the lilies that I couldn't get out the door," she says.

Payton donates table centerpieces each week to the residents of Jupiter Bay Nursing Home. When she opened Blossoms and Blooms, her accountant advised her that donations would help accrue deductions. It's also a great way to advertise since she includes the shop logo and phone number on every arrangement. And Payton doesn't skimp on her arrangements either. While some shops may use carnations and daisies, my sister prides herself on delivering cheerful, bold arrangements that are sure to brighten the day of each resident.

"It's okay," I mumble as I head back to finish cleaning the counter. You know, the task I was working on when Mr. Drop Your Panties entered the place?

"You didn't have any trouble? I know it's your first day and all."

I shake my head in answer, my thoughts returning to the last customer of the day. One that I don't plan to think about once I leave work. The same one I don't plan on telling my sister about either. Each Summer sister has a knack for getting the goods from the others. I know she'll start the inquisition, and I'll end up spilling all the dirty details.

If there really were dirty details.

"Oh, you had a customer after closing?" she asks.

Crap.

Turning to face the firing squad, I notice she's looking at the time and date stamp on the top of the receipt. Obviously, I didn't think of that. Do you think she'll buy that the time stamp is off?

"Yeah, we had a customer come in and want something from the case. I figured since it was already made up and he had cash, it would be alright."

"He?" she asks, a perfectly manicured eyebrow shooting heavenward.

"Umm, yeah. I hope that's okay that I sold him the arrangement."

"Of course it's okay. I never want to turn down business. You said he paid with cash? Was he cute?" she asks, scrunching up her pert little nose.

"Umm, yeah, well, I guess. I mean he wasn't ugly or anything. Just some guy. Whatever."

She stares back at me, dark green eyes accessing me, and all I can do is hold her gaze even though I'm dying to look away. The look she gives me reminds me of Grandma. She has this innate ability to see right through you. It was torture when we were teenagers.

"Some guy. Whatever. Hmmmm." She turns away, but not before I catch sight of a grin.

"It was nothing. He needed something for his date. That's all."

"A date, huh? Well, that doesn't mean anything," she says while closing out the register.

"Of course it means something. If he's dating someone, why would he come here and flirt with me?"

"He was flirting with you?" she asks while spinning around, brimming with excitement.

"It was tacky and completely unwarranted."

"Flirting with my beautiful, single sister is unwarranted? Why? Because he had a date? Are you sure it was even a date? Maybe he was buying them for his mom?"

"Oh no, they were definitely for someone special. He kept insinuating that much."

"While he was flirting with you." It's a statement, not a question.

"Whatever. I'm sure I'll never see him again," I state matter-of-factly before turning my attention back to my job.

"Did he give you his name?"

Dropping the cutters in the bin, I turn back towards her. "You can't help yourself, can you?"

"Well, I have to live vicariously through someone! Since you're going to be working here with me and you're the one getting hit on by a hot guy, it's going to be you."

"I'm pretty sure I'm the last sister for you to try to live through, Pay. Look at me. I'm a twenty-nine year old woman with no goals, no future, and who lives at home with her father and grandparents. Not exactly a lot of excitement here."

"I'm proud of you, Jaime. I know it's been a rough six months with everything with Gavin then moving home and all."

"Just because I'm finally working doesn't mean I'm ready to jump into a relationship again with both feet."

"Who said anything about a relationship?" she prods.

I think about those words for several minutes while finishing up the checklist of closing tasks. It has been a horrible six months, many of those days and nights spent crying over a broken heart. I'm certain I'm nowhere near ready for a relationship, but something else? Dating? Am I ready for that?

Exhaling deeply, I face where my sister is finishing up her paperwork. Leaning my hip against the counter, I say, "He was gorgeous. Like cover model for romance novels gorgeous. He had dark brown hair and even darker eyes. He kept staring at me like he wanted to eat me, and...it was...nice. He asked me for my name," I say, whispering that last sentence.

"Did you give it to him?"

Shaking my head, I answer. "No."

"Well, maybe he'll be back and maybe he won't. The point is you felt something. It made you feel good that he flirted a little. And that is step two in Grandma's five step system."

Groaning, I ask the burning question. "Do I even want to know what these five steps are from the woman who still sunbathes naked on a regular basis?"

"Step one is getting out of the house, which you can check off the list, since I know how much you love lists. Step two is to find a guy and engage in a little flirting and conversation."

"What's step three?" I ask, unable to hide my smile. My grandma is the most eclectic woman I've ever known. She's brash and honest and funny as hell. And when you add in my grandpa, all bets are off.

"Step three is to engage in mattress acrobatics," Payton states before bursting out laughing, followed quickly by my own.

"Mattress acrobatics? Step three is sex? Are you kidding? What's step four and five?"

"I have no clue. She never gets past the sex."

Laughter fills the small shop. For seventy-year-old grandparents, ours seem to still enjoy a healthy sex life. I can't even stomach thinking about how many times we've been woken up in the middle of the night by their *acrobatics*. Each of us girls have busted them fornicating somewhere around the house or property. And believe me, it's not a sight you want stuck in your head if at all possible!

"Listen, it's way past closing. Why don't you head home and I'll finish up?" she offers while gathering up the receipts and printouts.

I hang my apron on the hook and grab my purse. Before I reach the back door, I give her my attention once more. "Hey, thank you again for hiring me. I know you could have found someone with some experience, so I appreciate it."

"No one has floral experience, Jaime. I'd either have hired an older woman who thinks she knows everything already or a teenager who's on her cell phone all day and doesn't complain about making minimum wage."

"Well, I still really appreciate it," I say as I start to walk out the door.

"Hey, Jaime?" Payton hollers, causing me to turn back around. "I love you."

"Love you, too." My smile is wide as I slip out the back door and wait until I hear the lock engage.

I slide into my used Honda and head towards home. I can't help but glance at the side of the street in front of the shop where Mr. Handsome and Sinful was parked just a bit ago. I'm sure I'll never see him again, but it doesn't stop me from thinking about him.

I have plenty of things on my list to focus on right now. Nowhere on that checklist is anything about flirting with a gorgeous stranger. Instead, my list comprises of getting a job, saving money for an apartment, and being able to buy my own groceries. All things that I haven't done since I left Cleveland with barely a handful of pennies to my name. Hell, most of those things I haven't done since well before I left Ohio. When I was with Gavin, we shared the same dream. Marriage, kids, house, and therefore he was the breadwinner for the last few years.

At least I thought it was the same dream.

As I pull into the long driveway that leads to my childhood home, I push all thoughts of Gavin and his deceitfulness out of my mind. That ship has sailed, and I'm determined to keep my focus on moving forward, not looking and reflecting back.

Still, it's hard when your entire life was thought to be one way, only to find it wasn't really like that at all. It's a hard pill to swallow.

But, that's part of the past I'm trying to finally overcome. It's what I'm desperately trying to get away from. Something to eventually cross off the list.

I'll get there, one step at a time.

*k*X*k*

Friday afternoon has finally arrived. My first week at Blossoms and Blooms has been a steady stream of walk-in customers, funeral arrangements, and helium filled birthday balloons. I've been manning the counter and working on perfecting my arrangements while Payton handles the deliveries. Of course, when she comes back, she politely explains why you can't put gerbera daisies with freesia, and disassembles my arrangement.

Whatever.

Payton just left for another delivery when the bell above the door jingles. I'm adding the finishing touches to a dozen long-stemmed red roses when I glance over my shoulder. I'm shocked when I see who my next customer is. Pleasantly shocked.

I'm greeted with a warm smile and those twinkling brown eyes. My breath hitches in my throat as his gaze drops to my ass and slowly starts to climb back up. I should probably turn around and nip this in the bud, but I don't. I can't.

"Can I help you?" I finally ask when I find my voice.

His eyes have yet to make their way back up to my face, so I make sure to plaster on my best annoyed look. When brown eyes finally lock on mine, I falter. My well-planned irritated appearance evaporates into thin air. Poof. Gone.

"Just the woman I was looking for. I'm in need of something and I believe you're the only one to give it to me."

Damn him! My heart rate is nearing stroke level and my breathing continually hitches in my dry throat.

"I'm not sure what you mean, but I'm certain I can only help you with flowers." My reply almost sounds foreign, even to my own ears.

"I'd love to get some more of your...flowers," he says with that damn smirk as he leans against the counter.

"Well, I'm sure you could find what you're looking for in the case," I sass, pointing to the display case before returning my attention towards the roses.

When I add the final sprig of baby's breath, I dust off my hands on my green apron. I also realize Mr. Smirks-a-lot isn't over at the case. As if I could feel his eyes crawling all over my body, I know instantly that he's still behind me. But the crazy thing is that I don't feel creeped out by his attention and wandering eyes. Instead, I feel empowered.

Turning around, I return my gaze to his. Sudden need stirs to life between my legs, forcing me to squeeze them closed in an attempt to alleviate the ache. Or ignore it. I could try that, but I don't think it's possible.

"How much for the roses?" he asks.

"These? I thought you didn't do roses. Red roses signify commitment," I tell him as I make my way towards the cooler.

"True, but maybe that's what I'm after this time," he says as he falls in line with me.

"Really? From a colorful bouquet to red roses in only five days? Your friend must really be someone special," I reply, ignoring the taste in my mouth that resembles the bitterness of jealousy.

"Different friend. A *good* friend."

I just get the vase situated on the shelf when his words sink in. Really? Is this man really in here buying flowers for a different woman already? And roses? My gut churns like butter as I gape at him.

"Can I get the roses?" he asks sweetly with that sexy as sin smile.

"Sure," I mumble, retrieving the arrangement I just set in the case not ten seconds ago.

I hit the buttons on the cash register a little too hard, unable to hide my annoyance. I'm tempted to charge the pig double just for spite. It's the least I can do for the other woman.

"Thirty-nine ninety-five."

He whistles as he pulls two more twenties out of his wallet. I try not to, but my gaze automatically drops to his driver's license. Unfortunately, I'm unable to see anything other than a peek at his photo. A nice photo. Dammit.

"Thank you," I reply, dropping a nickel into his outstretched hand.

I'm not quick enough at pulling my hand back, however, and the man's hand snatches closed, grabbing my hand along with his change. I gasp aloud by the sudden movement, as warmth blankets my hand. Fire shoots straight up my arm, sizzling and crackling its way through every extremity.

His hands are large and calloused, and all I can think about is what they'd feel like against my body. An uncontrollable shudder rakes through me. I'm trapped in the heat of his gaze, like gravity pulling me towards him, and I don't even attempt to pull away. It's futile.

After holding my hand for several sexually charged seconds, he finally releases me. I step back, trying to put as much distance between him and the overwhelming desire I feel for him. If I don't retreat quickly, I'm likely to try to climb him like a tree. And since I'm apparently not the only one doing the climbing, he's liable to leave me with a bad bark-burn when I'm done.

Grabbing the vase, I push it towards him. The faster I can get him out of the shop, the better. I have no idea why I can't seem to keep it together in his presence, but I can't. I'm like a teenager with a crush on the captain of the football team, all jittery and stuttery.

It's embarrassing, really. What twenty-nine-year-old has this hard of a time communicating with another human being?

"Thank you." Those two words, deep and rich, are accompanied by another smile. This one's full wattage, as if he's thoroughly enjoying my discomfort.

Oh, don't get me wrong, it's a nice smile. Award-winning, actually. But knowing that he's here (for the second time this week) buying flowers (for the second woman this week) and he's still shamelessly flirting with me, doesn't really settle well with me, you know?

So, instead of smiling back at him, I cross my arms and glare. I'm sure my sister would have a heart attack if she knew I was scowling at her customers, but there's something about this shmuck that ruffles my feathers. A gorgeous shmuck, sure, but a schmuck nonetheless.

He grabs the vase, offers me a wink, and struts towards the door. His jeans are more worn than the last pair and his work boots scuffed and dusty. The polo shirt is replaced with a tight-fitting tee that leaves absolutely nothing to the imagination. I shamelessly watch as he makes his way towards the front of the shop. *Traitorous eyes.*

When I realize he has stopped, I quickly avert my gaze upward, but it's too late. He clearly saw me checking him out. *Again.* My cheeks burn with embarrassment as I focus on anything other than the man at the front door. When he still makes no move to exit, I slowly return my sights on him. His smile is small and almost carries more of a wallop than that damn smirk.

"Goodbye, Jaime. I'll see you soon," he says with a wink before leaving.

I stare at the space he once stood in for several seconds, willing my heart rate to slow down. That man completely causes my world to tilt on its axis, and I don't like it. Not one bit.

It's when I'm straightening up the counter that I realize something monumental. Something that I didn't catch at first, but now shocks me to my core. It's not the fact that he insinuated that we'd be seeing each other again soon. No, this is something bigger.

He called me Jaime as he walked out the door.

He knows my name.

4

Ryan

I'm still chuckling under my breath as I step inside my office, red roses in hand. It took every ounce of control I had to not drive straight to the flower shop first thing Tuesday morning, but I knew that if I was going to continue this little game of cat and mouse with the gorgeous shop attendant, I needed to give it a few days.

When I showed up Monday night at Mrs. Hanson's door with the flowers and cheesecake that I picked up from the deli, she was pleasantly surprised by my visit. I waited until she served coffee before I subtly asked about Blossoms and Blooms. I tried to play it off as just curiosity–you know, since I bought the flowers from there–but Mrs. H has proven to be able to read me like a book in our short year of friendship.

I ended up caving and telling her all about my first meeting of the beautiful brunette with light green eyes and a stunning smile, leaving out the part where I implied that the flowers were for a *friend*.

Over cherry cheesecake, Mrs. Hanson told me about Payton Summer starting the downtown flower business after the previous owners up and closed, relocating to another state. While she was getting her hair done on Monday morning, the ladies were all talking about the second-to-oldest Summer girl, Jaime, moving back home and filling in at the flower shop since Payton was short staffed. So, Mrs. Hanson was already well equipped with information on the happenings in downtown Jupiter Bay.

The look on Jaime's face when I said goodbye, calling her by name, is still branded on my brain. I'm not exactly sure who I'll be buying flowers for next, but you can bet your ass I'll be back there soon.

As I set the vase on Mary's desk, she gives me a look of shock. "It's not my birthday. What's that for?" she asks curiously.

"It's a just because. I was passing the flower place and they had a sale. Thought you'd like some to brighten up the office," I tell her as I drop into one of the chairs in front of her desk.

"Ryan Alan Elson, what did you do?" she asks with a stern voice and even sterner look.

"What'd I do? Nothing. Can't someone bring his favorite person in the world flowers just because?" I kick my feet up on the top of her desk as I say it.

"Humph. If it was anyone else, I might think yes. But you? No, you're up to something. So what is it? Did you spend everything you have? You did, didn't you? What did you buy, Mister?"

Chuckling, I smile over at my friend. "Of course I didn't spend everything I have. You really think I'd want to deal with the wrath of Mary? I didn't spend anything except a few bucks on this gift for you. The jobs are all on schedule. Your job is secure. Everything is fine."

"I still think something is up. I've worked for you for a year, and you've never brought me a random gift other than leftover pie from Mrs. Hanson or that fancy caramel drink from the coffee shop, which you left in your truck for half the day ensuring that it was anything but hot by the time it arrived here. So what is it? Are you sleeping with the florist?"

My eyes shoot towards hers as I realize how close she is to hitting the nail on the head. No, I'm not sleeping with the florist, but I'd damn sure like to be.

"I am not *sleeping* with the florist. I've only met the shop owner once, almost a year ago, thank you very much."

"Then what? Spill."

I consider making up some excuse to get to my office. I'm sure there are several documents and checks that require my signature. But staring over at my first Jupiter Bay friend, I realize I don't want to evade.

"Actually, I stopped in on Monday to get flowers for Mrs. Hanson's birthday. The woman working in there is Payton's sister, Jaime. She's...striking."

It's hard not to get lost in the memory of our first meeting. Her curves, that smile, the way she practically growled at me when I flirted with her after suggesting that I was buying flowers for a fuck-buddy.

"Ah, yes, Jaime Summer. I haven't seen her much since she's been back in town. Her family used to come into the diner when I still worked there. Nice family. Beautiful girl."

I nod my head, acknowledging and agreeing, before standing up and heading towards my office.

"You know, my favorite flower is an orchid. Uncommon, vibrant, and expensive. Every woman has a favorite flower, Ryan," she adds while keeping her gaze on the roses and I return to my office.

Every woman has a favorite flower. Those words repeat in my head as I attempt, unsuccessfully, to read the materials list for the tenth time for an upcoming job. Every woman? That means that Jaime must have a favorite, too. Suddenly, finding out what her favorite flower is the only thing I can think of.

Well, that and the image of dragging said flower across her naked torso.

I'm not the best planner. That's why I have Mary. But there are some things in life that require a man to take the bull by the horns himself and get shit done. Case in point? Operation Secure A Date With Jaime. Even though she gave me the nudge I needed, I can't ask Mary for advice.

Advice. I've never needed help getting a date before in my life–well, if you overlook that time freshman year where I had Billy ask Sabrina if she'd be interested in going to homecoming with me. But that was hypothetical. Today, I'm seeking out a girl that I suspect has as much interest in me as I do her–except there's also clear hesitation mixed in. And that leaves me unsettled and less confident than normal.

I haven't dated since Sara. I tried going out once a couple months back, but the woman wouldn't get her face out of her cell phone long enough to order her meal, let alone talk to me. I've had offers, even so much as one last Saturday while I was shooting pool with my friend Flip, but I just wasn't feeling it. Even hookups seem all wrong right now. I haven't hooked up with anyone since the she-devil herself. Nine long months with no action besides my hand in the shower. That's why my reaction to Jaime is so exhilarating. From the moment I saw her standing behind the counter, I've been hard with a craving that only she can quench.

Jaime. It's time to focus on Jaime and what I need to do to secure a date. Something tells me just flat out asking her isn't going to benefit my cause. I'm going to have to get crafty. Probably mention that all those flowers weren't for *other* women so much as *older* women, both who are like a parent and grandparent to me, respectively.

Pulling perpendicular to the sidewalk, I head towards the very shop in which I purchased flowers for my office manager yesterday. The morning sun is shining and the birds are singing as I inhale some of that crisp Virginia air that I've become accustomed to since moving here, a gentle wind blowing across the Bay. Crossing my fingers that she's working today, I pull open the glass door and step inside.

The familiar bell announces my arrival. Like a magnet, I'm instantly pulled towards her. Jaime's standing at the counter beside her sister and an older woman, each of them wearing matching smiles. When she looks up, the smile on her face falters a little. A bit of shyness and maybe a little embarrassment mix with her warm smile.

"Good morning," Payton says, standing up tall next to the register.

"Hey, Payton. How are you? How's business?" I approach the counter next to the older lady, directly across from the star of last night's dreams.

"Everything's going well. Business is good," she says. I can hear the smile in her voice, but I don't see it because I'm completely transfixed on a pair of light green eyes the color of morning grass after a rain.

A throat clears beside me. "You keep staring at my granddaughter like that and we're going to have to change the rating of this shop to X."

Jaime's eyes widen in shock as she chastises the woman beside me. "Grandma!"

Payton snorts and tries to cover up her laughter with a cough, earning herself a glare from her sister.

"Don't you encourage her," Jaime scolds as she continues to glower at Payton.

"What? It's a good thing when a single man mentally strips a single woman, Jaime. It means he's interested in the horizontal mambo," the woman says casually. Payton can barely stand up straight she's laughing so hard, and Jaime? Her face is darker than the red roses I purchased the day before.

Before either of them can respond, the woman turns to me. "You are single, right? You're not one of those weirdos just trying to get his jollies off with my sweet girl here, are you?"

"Yes, ma'am, I'm very much single. And I am not a weirdo nor am I here to get my jollies off." Liar. I'd love to get my jollies off right now.

Again, a very unladylike snort reverbs through the room as Payton doubles over in laughter. I'm too enthralled with the tiny woman to check for Jaime's reaction to her grandmother's inquisition. But if I know anything about her at all, I can guarantee her face is still beet red and she's doing everything she can to hide behind her long brown hair.

"Huh, that's too bad," the woman grumbles.

"Grandma, this is Ryan Elson. He owns a construction business here in town. We met once several months back," Payton says. I offer my hand to the spitfire old woman, but she only uses it to pull me forward and wrap her arms around me in a hug.

"Please, call me Emma."

The hug lasts a few seconds too long, and I glance over at Jaime and Payton for assistance.

"Grandma, you can stop hugging him now," Jaime says, a hint of a smile drawing on the corner of her lush lips.

Emma finally starts to pull away, but not before grabbing a handful of my ass. I'm startled by her boldness and reflexively jerk forward. Unfortunately, the only thing that does is cement my denim-clad manhood against the older woman's midsection. Thank God I'm not sporting wood right now.

Now who's three shades of pink?

Before Emma returns her attention to her granddaughters, she throws me a sassy wink and a devious little smirk. Something tells me this Grandma is quite the handful.

"Is there something we can help you with today, Ryan? Or did you just come by to get sexually assaulted by a seventy-year-old woman?" Payton asks.

"I'm here for some flowers, ladies." I keep my eyes trained on Jaime as I watch her reaction.

"Well, you definitely came to the right place. Jaime, can you assist Ryan with his order?" Payton asks, her voice dropping with sweetness towards her sister, again earning her a hard scowl.

"That'd be perfect. Jaime, do you mind?" I ask, turning my full attention towards the object of my desire.

"Of course she doesn't mind. Jaime's all about assisting young, gorgeous, robust young men such as yourself," Emma coos with a smile.

"Grandma, stop flirting with him," Jaime mumbles as she follows me towards the cooler.

For the third time this week, I find myself standing beside this gorgeous woman in front of a dozen floral arrangements.

"So, what can I help you with today? Perhaps a bridal bouquet? Engagement flowers?"

"Uh, I'm not quite there yet. I'm thinking something a little more timeless. Something classic and stunning and full of intoxicating fragrance." I lean towards Jaime just a smidge and inhale. She smells like flowers and vanilla and fucking heaven.

Meticulously taking in each vase, I contemplate my next move. "So, which of these flowers is your favorite?" I ask casually.

Jaime looks at me, a questioning and suspicious look in her eyes. "Why?"

"Just curious. I want to make sure I make the best choice...for my friend."

"Friend." It's a statement, not a question. "Well, anything in here would probably be fine."

"And your favorite?" I hedge.

"Is not in this case," she finishes. We both continue to scan the case in comfortable silence. "You could always go with gardenias. They're rich, full, and sweet-smelling," she says, pointing to a large white flower in one of the arrangements.

"That's perfect. I'll take one."

Jaime turns and faces me, her eyebrows pinched in surprise. "One?"

"Yep, only one. Turns out, I'm a one woman, single flower kinda guy now," I add, leaving the smirk off my face. Instead, I call in the heavy artillery and give her my best panty-dropping smile.

It's a proven fact.

She stares up at me for several heartbeats, gauging my sincerity, I'm sure. The room is silent, even though I know we're not alone, which can only mean one thing: We have an audience.

Jaime must realize it at the same time and clears her throat before averting her gaze. "I'll go grab one from the back and wrap it up for you," she mumbles before hightailing it out of the main shop area to the large open workspace and storage just on the other side of a large doorway.

Heading up to the counter where I have an unobstructed view of the room Jaime's in, I pull out my wallet. Two sets of eyes follow my movements like a dog would a bone. It causes me to bounce a little on my feet as I feel their gaze burn into me. I swallow hard and stare straight ahead as Jaime wraps up the white flower.

"So, you do construction, Ryan?" Emma asks, pulling my eyes towards her.

"Yes, ma'am. Home construction mostly."

"Funny you should say that. I'm thinking of doing a little remodeling at home."

"What are you talking about, Grandma? Dad hasn't said anything about remodeling the house," Payton questions.

"Oh, your dad doesn't tell you everything, girl. We were just talking the other day about making updates. He's wanting to start on the second floor, the northwest bedroom."

"Hey! That's my bedroom," Jaime hollers, joining us at the front counter, flower in hand.

"Yes, I suppose it is, sweetie, but you won't be in that room for long. I'm talking your dad into knocking out the wall between your room and the twins' bedroom beside it. If we knock out that wall, we can put in a playroom." Emma gives me the sweetest smile known to man.

"That's so sweet of you guys to want to plan for your great grandkids, but none of us are pregnant, Grandma," Payton says.

"Oh, not that kinda playroom, Payters. I'm talking the dirty sex kinda playroom. Like the one in that movie with the Dom who uses those crazy toys on the virgin."

"Grandma!" Jaime gasps, her hands flying up to hide her eyes.

"Are you talking about Fifty Shades? You've seen *Fifty Shades of Grey*?" Payton asks, but I'm pretty sure she doesn't really want to know the answer.

"Seen it? I own two copies! Your grandpa loves that scene where that cute little millionaire spanks her for the first time," Emma adds with a hearty cat-that-ate-the-canary smile.

"Oh God," Jaime groans. "Wait, and why won't I be in that room for very long?"

"Because I'm working on marrying you off, girl. I have a whole slew of hot, strapping young men who are itchin' to take my granddaughter out on a date!"

Suddenly, I've gone from pleasantly entertained to an uncontrollable need to punch someone as the back of my neck burns with annoyance. If even one of those strapping young men so much as looks Jaime's way, I'll remove their balls with a wooden spoon.

"Look, I'm not looking for a date or to get married," Jaime states pointedly to the elderly woman next to me. "And you," she starts while turning her attention back to me. "I'm sure you have a *friend* to get to. Thank you for visiting us. I'm sure we'll see you again very soon."

And with that, Jaime turns and walks into the back room, essentially cutting us all off and ending the conversation. I watch her go, surprised by how bothered I am that she seems upset. Upset at her grandma or me, I'm not sure, but the thought of her being annoyed or hurt does something to my insides, like someone's twisting my intestines around a butter knife. Like cooked spaghetti noodles. *Pleasant.*

"Wildflowers," Emma whispers, pulling my attention from the woman in the other room.

"Excuse me?"

"Wildflowers. Her favorite flowers are wildflowers you pick along the sides of the road or in the tall grass near the Bay. She's always been a fan of simple beauties over grand gestures." Her green eyes twinkle with mischief, and maybe a little bit of love for her granddaughter.

"Thank you," I reply with a wink before grabbing my gardenia and heading out the front door.

My mind is racing a million miles a minute as I walk swiftly towards my truck, but a game plan is formulating. I'm not sure how I'm going to convince Jaime to go out with me, but I'm determined to make it happen. And thanks to that gem of information that Grandma handed me on a silver platter before I left the flower shop, I have a bit more ammunition in my back pocket.

Now, to sway her into saying yes.

5

Jaime

My first week at Blossoms and Blooms has finally ended. Honestly, I'm dead on my feet after working forty hours standing behind a counter. Even though I'm supposed to be considered part-time, Payton's business is booming enough to warrant my attendance every day. All I can think about right now is a hot bubble bath and a glass of merlot. Of course, knowing that my grandpa will probably be standing outside the bathroom, banging on the door because his bladder is the size of a pea, does dampen my splendid fantasy. In fact, my post-workweek relaxation plans die a slow, painful death.

I slip out the back door, ensuring it's locked behind me, and head towards my car. Something white and fluffy on my windshield draws my attention instantly. As I step closer, I see a flower. And not just any flower. A gardenia.

Carefully, I step towards my car. Glancing over my shoulder both directions, I slowly remove the flower. I examine it, looking for any clue that it could be from someone else, before bringing it to my nose and giving it a tentative sniff. The delicate bloom is aromatic and instantly reminds me of playful eyes and a matching smile. And if I wasn't so caught up in the romantic gesture in this whole thing, I might be a little annoyed with the pesky home construction worker.

"I take it you like my peace offering?" I hear behind me in that deep, rich baritone voice that causes shivers.

Turning around, I come face-to-face with the man I can't stop thinking about. He's wearing the same attire he had on just a few short hours ago, but this time, his hand is filled with flowers. Wildflowers. Bright purple and yellow flowers of all shapes and sizes.

"And why would you be submitting to a peace offering?" I ask, barely able to take my eyes off the gorgeous mix of roadside blooms.

"Well, it turns out I owe you an apology."

"For what?" I ask, still rooted where I stand.

"What if I told you that those flowers I bought this week were for my friends? I mean my real friends, not the kind of *friends* I may have insinuated."

"Why would you do that? Why lead me to believe that they were for someone else?"

He shrugs his shoulders before taking a step closer and setting the new flowers in the crook of my arm. "It was kinda fun to mess with you a little bit. You seemed to get a little flustered and, if I'm being honest, I liked knowing that I rattled you with my presence. But most importantly, it gave me a reason to come in to the shop and see you."

His words hang in the air, honest and rueful. He doesn't smile that cocky smile I've come to expect from him. Instead, his sheepish grin is filled with sincerity. The deep brown gaze holds firm, penetrating my lungs, making it impossible to catch my breath.

"So, you lied to me about who the flowers were for?"

"I might have misled you a bit. The first bouquet was for my eighty-year-old neighbor whose birthday was Monday, and the roses were for my office manager, Mary. She probably deserves fine gems and fancy houses for all that she does for me, but she'll have to settle for the occasional flower arrangement and lukewarm caramel latte from that expensive coffee joint down the block."

"And this one?" I ask, bringing the gardenia to my nose once more.

"That is a beautiful flower for a stunning woman who I was hoping would like to go to dinner with me tonight."

The bloom stills at my nose, my body paralyzed and unable to move. Did he really just ask me out on a date? Do I *want* to go out on a date? It's been a long time since I went out with someone, especially someone new. Besides the fact that I swore I would never, *ever* date again, there's a tinge of uncertainty that I would even remember how to do it. Sure, I made my "no dating ever, ever again" rule as numeral uno on my checklist (writing it in black marker and then highlighting it to be sure it stood out) while I was crying in a pint of Moose Tracks ice cream, but it's been so long since I even considered this step, I probably wouldn't remember proper dating etiquette.

"Did you just confess to misleading me to get my attention, and then ask me out on a date? In the same statement? What are we, in sixth grade?" I ask when I finally find my voice.

"I agree it might sound a tad bit juvenile, but I assure you my intentions were solid. I just wanted to get close to you a few times without freaking you out. You're too beautiful for your own good, but looked like the kinda girl who freaks out easily."

I squint my eyes at the handsome man. *Is that a compliment?* "So you bought flowers to get close to me? Why not just ask me out?" I ask, taking a defensive stance.

"Would you have said yes?" he asks.

"No." It's automatic. There's no way I would have said yes to a strange man coming into my place of work and asking me on a date. But that doesn't mean I wouldn't have been tempted.

"Listen, I'm not that bad of a guy. I feel bad for deceiving you. Why don't you let me take you out to make up for it?"

"Smooth change of tactics, Ace. Do all the women fall for this line of crap?" I ask, incredulously. Yet, when he smiles that half smile, my panties are suddenly a little damp and my breathing a bit shallow. And I realize how easily women would fall for that very line of crap.

"Probably not as much as I care to admit," he says sheepishly. And there he goes again with that damn half smile. "One date. That's all I'm asking for. I'll pick you up at six."

"I'll meet you there," I reply without even thinking. The words just fly from my lips like an aircraft taking off from the carrier.

Ryan's face lights up like he just won some sort of prize. His eyes twinkle and his mouth turns upward in a devilish grin. Realizing what I just said, I open my mouth to retract my statement, but he won't let me.

He steps forward and places a single finger against my mouth. Having his skin touch my lips sends blood rushing through my veins. My body is alive with want, reminding me, not so subtly, that it's been a long time since a man has touched me. Six months ago, I swore off men–all men. But right now? I'm ready to throw my inhibitions, and maybe my clothes, straight out the window. The thought is frightening and invigorating at the same time.

"Don't say it. Don't take it back. Go out with me." Then he goes in for the kill. "Please?"

It's a losing battle. Hell, it's a battle I didn't even really show up for. He has me whipped from the beginning, my pulse battered without even really trying. I know what my answer is going to be, and it's not the same as the one I *should* give.

"Okay."

One minute I'm blissfully alone, living with my dad and grandparents, hating all penises for life, and the next thing I know,

I'm being seduced into a date with a sexy, smooth-talker wearing work boots and tight jeans.

I'm afraid my panties might be in trouble tonight.

k}{}{k

I changed my outfit three times before finally settling on a black maxi dress with thick straps, black ballet flats, and a pink sweater. Nights in Jupiter Bay are still chilly, even during the summer months. Average highs for June are eighty degrees with lows dipping down to the upper-fifties, but for the residents of Jupiter Bay, well, we're all accustomed to the cooler, milder weather.

Fidgeting, I do my best to not pace in the living room while I wait for Ryan to pick me up. We argued for five minutes solid before I ended up caving, allowing him to pick me up for our date. It's not that I didn't want him to come to my house, except that it really isn't *my* house. If I lived alone and not with my dad and grandparents like an almost thirty-year-old loser, I wouldn't have fought his chivalrous act tooth and nail. Instead, I repeatedly proposed that I meet him there.

And you see where that got me, right? Standing here–with my grandparents pretending to play Gin Rummy and not completely eavesdropping in the kitchen nearby–while I wait for my first date to pick me up at this house since I was seventeen and heading to prom.

Don't get me wrong, I've decided to back out at least a dozen times since I got home, and I probably would have if Ryan would have given me his phone number. The jerk probably did that on purpose so that I couldn't cancel.

I'm in no way ready to date, am I? I mean it's only been six months since I was dumped via text from the man I was a handful of days away from giving all of my happily ever afters. It's too soon. And besides, I'm still not a huge fan of the penis population.

Sure, I'm being unreasonable. One bad breakup doesn't constitute labeling every male on the planet as a lowdown, dirty heartbreaker, but that one act of misery is enough to construct walls around my heart so tough, it makes Fort Knox looks like a Chuck E. Cheese on a Sunday afternoon.

These walls are thick. I've spent plenty of days and nights doing yoga for my relaxation and flexibility, and then following it up with a pint of ice cream. And after I consumed my cup of sugary deliciousness, I'd reinforce my heart, brick by brick. It's better than any self-help video you'll find on the internet, let me tell you.

Brown eyes the color of smooth, rich chocolate flit through my mind. *Damn him.* Yes, damn him, because I've known him for all of six days–spent less than a half hour in his presence–and I can already tell he has the ability to break me. Ryan Elson, with that charming, boyish smile and a body that makes me want to beg for mercy, has the complete capability to chisel away at my carefully fashioned barrier. He's a smooth operator, this he has already demonstrated, which means I'm just going to have to be extra vigilant where he's concerned.

The front door opening snaps me out of my self-inflicted pep talk. My dad walks in, his graying hair disheveled and his green eyes reflecting fatigue. Yet, for as drained as he appears, as soon as his eyes land on me, he smiles that same wide, lopsided grin that I've always known and remember. The same one that accompanied him in every photograph of our family, clear back to the wedding photo hanging in the hallway.

"You look nice, sweetheart. Are you going out?" he asks, setting his hat and briefcase down on the chair.

I glance down at my dress, wondering for the ten-zillionth time if it's the right choice for tonight. Ryan wouldn't tell me where we were going so I had a hell of a time picking something that could work in a casual diner or a nicer restaurant.

"Yeah, I'm...uh...I'm going to dinner." My dad's right eyebrow rises. "With a guy."

The surprise is obvious, though he tries hard to cover it quickly. "Really? That's great!"

"Is it? I mean, is it too soon to be going out? On a date?" My voice trails off until it's almost inaudible.

"No. Absolutely not," Dad says while stepping forward until he's directly in front of me. "You've been home for six months now, Jaime. There's no mandatory waiting period that deems when it's appropriate for you to start dating again. Only you can say when it feels like the right time."

There's a pregnant pause as I let his words sink in. Going out on one date doesn't constitute a relationship. In fact, I could easily play the field and enjoy a few free meals while getting back in the game. Of course, that doesn't really sound like me either. I've never been one to jump from guy to guy, keeping it light and breezy. Casual was never my thing. Long term, commitment was the path I chose.

Maybe it's time to add casual dating to the checklist.

Before I can say anything, a hard knock sounds at the front door. Air catches in my throat as I quickly smooth out my wrinkleless dress, one of the many nervous gestures I've become accustomed to whenever Ryan Elson is in the vicinity.

Dad steps back and opens the door before I can even think about moving. As if I've stepped into a time warp, not only am I aware of the fact that my dad has on his Dad-face and is staring down my date, but my grandparents have conveniently appeared at the kitchen doorway, both pushing the other to try to get into the room first. This is far worse than prom.

"Good evening," Ryan says, eager eyes anxiously searching me out.

"Hi," I croak out through a dry throat.

Ryan is wearing a pair of dark denim jeans with a navy blue Henley shirt. It's tight and accentuates the definition in his arms and chest and instantly causes warmth to rush to my core. His worn boots are replaced with a newer pair; these free from scuffs, dirt, and everyday wear. Who knew work boots could be so sexy? *Good God, this man is potent.*

My brain skids to a stop of its mental undressing, quick to catch up to the fact that we have an audience. A quick glance over my shoulder confirms that my grandparents are both grinning like they know a huge secret that they're dying to share, while my father's eyes dart between Ryan and me.

"Ryan, this is my dad, Brian Summer." Ryan quickly steps forward and shakes my dad's hand, exchanging courteous small talk.

"This is my grandpa, Orval, and of course, you've already met my grandma, Emma." My voice flutters with nerves that I'm sure everyone on this side of the Bay could hear.

"Of course he remembers me," Grandma says, stepping forward and wrapping her slender arms around Ryan's broad waist. "Who can forget Grandma," she quips while hugging him a bit too long. Again.

In true Grandma fashion, I'm horrified when she not so subtly reaches down and pinches his butt. Mortification snakes up my face and down my chest, burning me until I'm left wishing I would actually burst into flames.

There's no way this could get any worse, right?

"Emma, quit copping a feel on the poor young man. If you're wanting to feel something firm, I've got just the thing," Grandpa remarks.

I was wrong. It can get so much worse. My face surely rivals the color of a fire truck as I gape, wordlessly, at the people who helped raise me.

"It's such a nice rear, though," Grandma says brightly as she finally steps away, releasing her hold on my date's ass. "That's important, Jaime. Your grandpa had the best rear end this side of the Atlantic Ocean when I met him."

To my utter humiliation, Grandpa sticks his ass out just enough to give Grandma an unobstructed view to ogle, then he starts to move. It's an odd twerking motion combined with some sort of leg stretching. But when she smacks it, that's when I know it's time for Ryan and I to get the hell out of dodge!

"Come on," I mumble, taking Ryan's warm hand in mine and pulling him towards the door.

"It was very nice meeting you all," he says as I drag him towards freedom.

Grandpa gives a friendly wave. "You too, son. Oh, you have protection, right?"

That stops us both in our tracks.

I'm terrified to turn around. I send up a silent plea that Ryan suddenly developed acute deafness and totally missed the statement.

"Uh," he starts, his hand tightly squeezing my own.

"Let's just go before he offers us one of his and feels the need to demonstrate," I whisper, both of us staring at the exit just inches away.

Robotically, Ryan opens the screen door and waits for me to walk through first. I'm stunned speechless, sure that our first date is over before it even began. I mean, really? Who would blame him for suddenly developing a stomach virus or a severe case of bronchitis? Not me, that's for sure. If I were in his shoes, I'd be tearing out of the driveway right now, not bothering to look back.

When we reach the porch, I steel my back, ready for the brushoff I'm sure is about to come. But as I stare up at the clear sky, I'm greeted with only silence. Ryan, still gripping my hand, starts to laugh. Before I can ask what in the world he could ever find funny about this situation, the door behind us opens.

"Take me with you?" Dad asks as he steps outside, his voice laced with humor.

"That was so embarrassing," I mumble, still unable to meet Ryan's eyes.

"They're like this all the time. It's like living with newlyweds." My dad turns towards Ryan. "I apologize for the behavior of my in-laws, Ryan. I'd like to think that old age affected their filters, but I don't remember either of them ever having one."

Ryan laughs again, and my dad smiles. It's a genuine smile, one that I don't see near as much as I used to. Oh, he masks it well and puts on a good show, but it's not the same. Not since my mom died.

"You kids go have fun," he says as he sticks his hand towards Ryan once more. "It was a pleasure meeting you, Ryan. I hope to see you again soon."

I hold my breath, trapped in the trance of their conversation.

"It was a pleasure, sir. And I really hope to see you again, as well. In fact," Ryan says, turning and smiling at me. "I'm sure this won't be the last time."

The sincerity and honesty in his words strike me like a bolt of lightning. His insinuation that he'll be seeing me–and my family–much more isn't lost on me. In fact, it warms my chest and sends butterflies fluttering in the pit of my stomach.

My dad nods his head and steps back. "Call me Brian."

On autopilot, I'm pulled along by Ryan's hand towards his awaiting truck. The fact that he still wants to spend time with me is far more shocking than the awkwardness that my grandparents just bestowed upon me.

When we reach the vehicle, Ryan opens the door, but doesn't let go of my hand. I finally find the capability to make eye contact, and when I do, I'm greeted by brightly shining brown eyes. They twinkle like stars in the clear night sky.

I'm pulled from his gaze by the feel of his calloused thumb running along my knuckles. Tingles of awareness race through my body while goosebumps speckle my arms, even beneath my sweater. With a wink of his uber-sexy eyebrow, Ryan finally releases my hand and heads around to the driver's side of his Chevy.

We're heading into the heart of Jupiter Bay before he finally speaks. "Your family is amazing."

"Are you kidding me? They're so wildly inappropriate. I'm so sorry about all that. I mean, God! My grandma felt you up." I drop by gaze, unable to hold eye contact.

Ryan's laughter fills the cab of the truck. "They're great. I wish my grandparents were still alive," he says wistfully. "But, I'll be honest, even if they were, I don't recall them ever acting like that. Your family is unique."

"Unique. That's a polite way of saying batshit crazy."

"It is not. I liked them." He draws his attention away from the road for just a second. "Honest."

"Then you must be a little batshit crazy yourself," I add humorously.

When I'm greeted with more laughter, I finally allow myself to smile and relax.

"You might be a little right, but I've discovered that sometimes a little crazy is just what you need." He looks over once more and winks before returning his attention back to the road.

The ride is filled with pleasant silence as we make our way towards our destination, which he has yet to share with me. All of the shops in downtown are closed up for the night, with the exception of the occasional bar or restaurant. We bypass all of them though, and head towards the east edge of town.

Lights reflect off the Bay as we pull into one of Jupiter Bay's finest steakhouses. It's situated along the water with floor to ceiling windows along three sides. A large wooden deck spans the entire length of the building and butts right up against the coastline. It used to be one of my favorite places when I was younger, but since my return, I've only eaten here once. I'm surprisingly excited for dinner.

With Ryan.

He comes around to the passenger side and helps me down from the truck. I'm glad I settled on the dress. Even though it's casual and the atmosphere laid back, it's the perfect fit for dinner along the Bay.

Hand in hand, we make our way to the large wooden front door of Helena's. As we approach the hostess, I take in the low lighting and the busy dining room. Even the outdoor deck appears to have several occupied tables, though it's in the upper fifties.

"Reservation for Elson." His smooth, velvety voice rockets through my body, sending tingles of awareness to settle directly between my legs. His voice is an aphrodisiac for the hormonally challenged.

"Right this way, sir."

The older woman leads us through the dining room to the back area. An empty table is situated in the corner, surrounding us with glass on two sides. The tables are just far enough apart that you can hold a private conversation without everyone around you knowing your business.

Ryan's hand on my lower back shocks me. Not in surprise, but in comfort. Natural. It's intimate and does even more damage to my frayed and neglected lady parts than his voice.

"I didn't get a chance to tell you yet, but you look beautiful tonight," he says after taking his seat across from me.

"You didn't get a chance because you were being grilled about protection from my grandpa," I state with a smile. I'm rewarded with one in return as I add, "And thank you. You look very nice yourself."

Truth is he's frickin' hot! But I can't say that. Not today, not ever. He's just the type of guy I should be avoiding. Gorgeous, cocky, one who will evoke the desire to throw caution to the wind, along with my panties.

I squirm a little in my seat as we order drinks and an appetizer. Ryan's attention is one hundred percent devoted to me, which is a pleasant change from Gavin. His nose was always in his phone or attention given to someone around us. Even when he was sitting right in front of me, it always felt like he was only there in body, not in mind.

"Tell me a little about yourself," he encourages as he takes a drink from the beer bottle the server just delivered. "I know you work at your sister's flower shop, or have for a week."

"Yes, it was my first week and it was harder than I thought it'd be. I'll have to stop teasing Pay so much about the simplicity of working with flowers." There's a long silence at the end of my statement as if I don't quite know what to say next.

"That's it? That's all you're gonna give me?" he asks, a single eyebrow arched upward.

"What do you want to know?" But I really don't want to hear the answer to my question.

"Well, let's see. You live with your inappropriate grandparents and dad. There's more there, I'm sure."

Twisting my wine glass between my fingers, I contemplate how much I want to reveal. "I'm the second to oldest of six, all girls. My mom died when I was fourteen from ovarian cancer. My dad, who's a pilot, was gone a lot for work, and when my mom died, he needed help. Her parents moved across town and into our home to help raise me and my sisters so my dad could still provide for us."

"That's very admirable of them. I'm sure your dad appreciated it."

"Oh, he did. He changed jobs, though, about a year after she died. He went from commercial airlines to private jets. The pay was better and he wasn't gone quite as much."

"I'm sorry to hear about your mom."

"Thank you," I whisper, trapped in the sincerity in his eyes.

"So six girls, huh?" he asks, taking another drink from the bottle.

I chuckle. Everyone seems to get hung up on the fact that my parents had all daughters and no sons. "Yeah, six girls in eight years. I'm pretty sure they kept trying for the elusive boy. I think when she got pregnant the fifth time and it was twin girls, well, I guess you better take what God gave you and just be happy."

Ryan whistles and shakes his head. "Damn. Your dad was trapped in the house with all you women? No wonder he traveled so much for work," he adds with a grin.

"What about you? Where's your family?" I ask after we order dinner.

"My parents are in upstate New York, as is my little sister Dena. Plus I have two brothers on the west coast, Brock and Trent. I talk to them all whenever I can, but it's never enough for their liking, ya know?"

"Yeah," I reply, recalling how much my sisters and I talked while I was in Cleveland. I spent the entire five years of my relationship with Gavin talking to my sisters because they were more accessible than he was. He was always in a meeting or prepping for a client. Always something *other* than me.

"What's with that face?" he asks, pulling my attention back to him.

"What face?"

"You looked lost in a memory for a minute."

"Yeah," I reply again.

"Wanna tell me about it?" he hedges.

Now it's my turn to chuckle, though mine sounds hollow. "Well, that's more of a third or fourth date conversation."

"So it's about a guy?" There goes that damn eyebrow again.

"Isn't it always?" After a pregnant pause, I try to steer the conversation back to safer waters. "What brought you to Jupiter Bay?"

"Would you believe me if I said a woman?" That cocky smile slides easily across his full lips. I chuckle at the irony of the fact that I ran home to Jupiter Bay to escape the memory of a man, while Ryan evidently ran towards this place, chasing a woman.

"Isn't it always?" I ask, revealing my own smirk.

"Touché," he replies with the tip of his beer bottle.

"Tell me about it," I encourage as our server delivers sizzling prime rib and twice baked potatoes.

"Let me get this straight: You can ask about my past, but I can't ask about yours?" Ryan asks while cutting a chunk of meat off his juicy steak.

"Exactly," I tell him with a smile before savoring the rich flavors and seasonings on my own slice of steak.

"Her name was Sara. We met in New York and dated off and on for a bit. She was a little fish in a big pond there, and well, she didn't like it. She requires a lot of attention. So, when she decided to move back to her hometown, I moved with her. The relationship was good at the time, but unfortunately, it didn't last more than five minutes after we moved here."

"But you stayed?" I ask, finding myself surprisingly interested in Ryan's story.

"Yeah, I stayed. I kinda fell for this small town. I met Mary, who is my office assistant, almost immediately after moving. She's a hoot. I'll have to introduce you soon." Ryan's eyes sparkle under the low lighting as he goes on to tell me about how he met Mary, as well as his neighbor and landlord, Mrs. Hanson. Of course, Jupiter Bay being the small town that it is, I've met both ladies before on numerous occasions. Mrs. Hanson has played bridge with grandma for years, and Mary Simons worked at the same diner I waited tables at my senior year of high school.

"So, this woman…Sara. She broke your heart?" I ask, my gut tightening with something I'm not really liking. Jealousy.

Ryan smiles a broad, sexy grin. "I wouldn't go that far. She eventually showed her true colors almost as soon as we set foot in town. It might sound cruel, but I'm relieved to have discarded the excess baggage."

I look at him for several seconds, contemplating whether to ask more questions or not. I'm curious, sure, but I don't want to seem too pushy for information. Especially on a relationship that appears to have ended somewhat badly.

Glancing over his shoulder, my eye catches on someone familiar. As I watch my brother-in-law, Chris, sit down at the booth, things start to click into place.

"Ryan?" I ask. "Would your Sara happen to be Sara Sullivan?"

His forehead creases as he shoots me a puzzled look. "How'd you know?"

"Because she just walked in and is sitting with my brother-in-law."

My heart rate spikes as I watch Sara fawn all over my youngest sister's husband. While my first reaction is to walk over there and give Chris a piece of my mind, I know his job has required him to wine and dine prospective clients from time to time. As a financial consultant, he's been known to. I just wish it wasn't Sara Sullivan.

Chris seems to notice me about the time Sara rubs his forearm. He quickly pulls back and offers me a polite wave. Sara, seeing his attention drawn somewhere else, turns and follows his line of sight. When she sees me—and her ex—she quickly stands up and heads in our direction, a bit of extra swing added to her approach.

Sara freaking Sullivan.

My arch nemesis.

And Ryan's ex-girlfriend.

Just who I wanted to deal with tonight.

6

Ryan

As soon as I see Sara heading this direction, the wood I was sporting under the table while watching Jaime enjoy her food dies a quick, painful death. Out of all the restaurants in town, why in the hell does she have to be in the same one I'm in on my first date with Jaime? I've been fortunate enough to barely run into her since the break-up–it's not like we run in the same circles–so why in all things holy is she strutting up to my table now with a Cheshire cat grin and a gleam in her eyes that scream *trouble.*

"Well, look who we have here," she coos as she closes the distance until she's standing close enough that I can smell her expensive perfume. "If it isn't my friend Ryan Elson. How have you been?" she asks, bending down and offering me a cheek. It's tempting as all fuck to ignore her gesture, especially when she's dropping four inches of exposed cleavage in my face.

Been there, done that. Wasn't worth the t-shirt.

I give her a polite, chaste kiss on the cheek out of courtesy to the patrons around us. I'm not one to cause a scene, especially while on a first date with a woman I had to work my ass off at securing in the first place. When she lingers a little too long while bent over me, I clear my throat and pull back. My eyes lock on the shocked green ones of my date.

"Sara, it was very nice to see you again." Lie. "But as you can see, I'm enjoying dinner tonight with a friend."

Sara turns and stares at Jaime for several heartbeats as if trying to place her. "Oh my gosh! Is that James? I haven't seen you since graduation!" Sara screeches in that fake, overzealous, completely irritating and overly exaggerating tone that makes my skin crawl.

My eyebrows shoot skyward. The mortification mixed with anger is written all over Jaime's face, instantly pissing me off on her behalf. Obviously, these two know each other, and if I'm reading the scene accurately, I'd say it wasn't a pleasant knowing.

"Sara," Jaime mumbles through gritted teeth.

"Wow, you look good! So, like, you're back in town now, right? I heard all about your episode. I'm so sorry," Sara purrs sympathetically as she drops her hand onto Jaime's forearm. But I see the malice lying just below the surface. It wasn't something I was able to define for the first part of our relationship, but towards the end, I was always able to see the bitchy, condescending side that she tried to hide.

"Episode?" Jaime asks, the hand holding her glass stopping halfway to her mouth.

"Yeah, the breakdown. I heard all about the guy who left you at the altar and stuff. I can't believe that happened to you. I mean, who does something so mean?"

It takes everything I have not to crawl across the table and wring Sara's boney little neck. Jaime's eyes drop to her plate and refuse to move. Her chest rises drastically, as if she's fighting off her emotions. Could be anger, could be despair. Could be a little of both.

Either way, I'm done with this conversation.

"Listen, Sara, we're enjoying dinner right now. I'm sure you don't want to keep your friend waiting. Thank you for stopping by the table." I don't say a word about it being nice to see her, because it wasn't. Not after the stunt she just pulled with Jaime.

"I'm sure I'll be seeing you both around town. It's not like anyone can hide in a small town," she smirks before wiggling her fingers and flitting away.

For the first time, the silence is awkward between us. Jaime still refuses to look up from her plate, and leaves me uneasy and filled with uncertainty. I don't like it.

"Can I ask you something?" I finally ask, her beautiful green eyes finally looking up for the first time in several long minutes. Her slight nod encourages me to continue. "Are we getting dessert here or over at Ice Cream Emporium?"

My question seems to shock her as the surprise registers on her gorgeous face. She opens her mouth, but no words come out. I don't hide my grin. Jaime probably thought our date was essentially over when my ex showed up, but she'd be wrong. If anything, I'm invigorated to discover more about this complex, shy woman, if not completely determined to peel away each individual layer until I discover the real woman beneath.

Dropping my napkin onto my plate and a few bills on the table to cover the check, I extend my hand towards her. She's hesitant at first, but her eyes flash grateful as she takes my hand and stands up.

Sharing a booth, I dip my spoon into her hot fudge sundae while she steals a bite of my strawberry shortcake. The way she licks and sucks on her spoon causes a stir in my pants once more. I never thought eating could be so damn sexy until I've watched Jaime Summer lick melted ice cream off a spoon.

"So, aren't you going to ask me about what Sara said at the restaurant?"

"No."

"No?"

"I figured if you wanted to tell me, you would," I say as I take a big bite of strawberries.

Jaime's silent for several seconds as if contemplating whether or not she wants to speak. "James was a stupid nickname I was given early in high school. I don't remember who started it, but Sara was the one who latched onto it and made sure everyone used it."

"What does it mean?" I ask.

"I was a late bloomer so they called me James because I resembled a boy. It didn't matter that I had long hair. I had no boobs, no butt, and was as curvy as a two by four."

I hear the words she's saying, but I don't see it. My eyes devour her ample chest, the arc of her hips, and the lushness of her body. Jaime is one hundred percent all woman. "Well, looks like you had the last laugh," I state bluntly.

When my eyes crash into hers, her cheeks are a sexy shade of pink. "I guess," she adds shyly. "Anyway, they called me James up until I left town for college."

I study her from the corner of my eye as she finishes off her own dish of vanilla with fudge. She seems pensive as she looks down at her empty bowl. Her eyebrows arch and little wrinkles furrow around her eyes. Even when she's deep in thought, she's stunning.

"And just so you know, there was no breakdown."

I smile over at her to try to ease her worry. Jaime seems like the type who carries the weight of the world on her shoulders, but doesn't seem to be recovering from any sort of mental breakdown. "Okay."

"Okay? You're just going to take my word for it that I didn't go crazy and freak out?"

"Yep. Do you know why?" I ask, moving my bowl away and reaching for her hand. She shakes her head, so I continue. "Because I trust you."

"You do?" Her words are full of surprise and happiness.

"Yep. Even if you did, it's not my place to judge. Maybe someday you'll feel comfortable enough to tell me the story about the breakup. Until then, I'll take as much of your time as I could get from you."

And that's the God honest truth. There's something about this woman that does it for me. I'd never admit this aloud, but she has me picturing white picket fences, three kids, and a cat. It's scary and exhilarating at the same time. Especially because I don't like cats.

After ice cream, we enjoy coffee and plenty of conversation right there at our booth. We talk about everything: my business, her work at the flower shop, some of our college stories, and even a bit of our childhoods. She's easy to talk to, and if it weren't for the ice cream shop reaching its closing time, we could probably sit and chat for the better part of the night.

We visit for a little more while we head back to her house. I'm not ready for the night to end, but it's after ten, and I don't want to push my luck. Jaime's quiet as I pull into her driveway and shut off my truck. With leaded feet, I head around to the passenger side and help her from the big vehicle.

Neither of us says a word as I guide her up the walkway, my hand protectively and possessively resting on her lower back. Standing on her front porch, the night air wrapped around us as the crickets chirp and the waves crash in the nearby Bay, I long to wrap my arms around her slender body and lose myself in a kiss.

But I won't. Not tonight.

The gentleman's rules of dating state that making out like school kids shouldn't come until at least the second date. Of course, this is a rule I've never followed up to this point. At all. But something tells me, with Jaime, I need to take this nice and easy. No need to ram my tongue down her throat and risk scaring her off for good.

"Thank you for going to dinner with me. I had a great time."

Eager green eyes stare up at me as she answers, "I had a great time, too."

I step forward and give her a polite kiss on the cheek. It's nowhere near enough to tide me over until date number two, but it'll have to do. Her cheek is warm against my lips, and a slight gasp echoes through the night. Her fresh, floral scent tickles my senses and causes all blood in my body to one concentrated area in my pants. It's that moment that I long to throw her over my shoulder, carry her off to the nearest bed, and have my wicked way with her.

Again, but I won't.

"I'll call you," I state.

With herculean strength I didn't realize I possessed, I step back. Slowly, I move and start to descend the stairs. Jaime remains rooted in place as I slide into the cab of my truck. I watch as Jaime slowly turns and opens the screen door. She gives one last glance over her shoulder towards my truck before slipping inside.

The look on her face was a mixture of disappointment and longing. Sitting in my truck for several minutes, I replay a fast-forwarded version of the entire evening, right up until I said goodbye. My gut tightens painfully as realization sets in. I put that look there. She thought I was walking away, clearly not aware of my attempt at politeness. Knowing instantly that I made what could clearly be one of the biggest mistakes of my life, I pull the keys out of the ignition, dropping them on the floorboard, and jump out.

My legs move swiftly as I all but sprint up the sidewalk and head towards the front door. Before I reach the top of the stairs, the light flips on and the door opens. Jaime looks concerned as she hesitantly pushes the screen door and steps back into the night.

"Is everything o-" she starts, but my lips cut her off.

My hands dive into her long, brown hair, as my lips taste hers for the first time. I feel her slender fingers grasp my side as I run my tongue along the seam of her lips, seeking just a little taste of her sweet mouth. When she opens her mouth, I slip inside, reveling in the feel of her warm, wet tongue sliding against mine. I fight off the groan that threatens to erupt from my soul.

Jaime burns my flesh through my shirt as she wraps her hands around my back, gripping my shirt and hanging on for dear life. I maneuver my hands down, holding her firmly by the jaw and lacing my fingers into the hair behind her ears. The angle is perfect to deepen the kiss, so that's what I do.

Fingers flex against me as I pull her body flush against mine. Jaime purrs like a cat as I frame her legs with my own. She's soft and curvy to my hard and unforgiving. And I'm not talking entirely about what's happening in my pants. Her body melts into me. The slide of her tongue, the nip of her teeth, and the taste of her mouth are like lightning that rips through my bloodstream. I'm consumed like never before, and I want nothing more than everything this kiss promises.

And it does.

This kiss is the start of something. Something great.

But now isn't the time for all of that. As much as I'd like to see where this kiss goes, I just can't let it.

Keeping contact between her lips and mine, I start to ease back. I'm in desperate need of a little distance between her soft body and my own. I caress her swollen lips and crack my eyes open. It only takes a few seconds to completely memorize the euphoric look on her face: her bee-stung lips, her rosy cheeks, and the way her eyelids flutter, combined, it's a memory I'll happily carry with me to bed tonight.

"I'm sorry I didn't kiss you earlier. I wanted to. God, I wanted to so damn bad, but I was trying to be polite."

Her eyes flutter open. They're hazy and dilated as she focuses on my face. "I'm glad you came back."

The words are soft and lust-infused and do dangerous things to my body. They're full of heat and desire, and I'll be damned if I don't want to start that kiss all over again.

"I should go. Thank you for tonight. I'm going to call you, Jaime."

"Okay," she whispers.

With one final kiss, I pull back and head back to my truck, this time with a little extra spring in my step. As I slide back into the cab, I find the keys I dropped on the floor and start it up. Jaime remains on the porch, her arms wrapped around a post as she watches me back out of the driveway. I sit at the edge of the road for several seconds as we both gaze through the darkness at each other.

A smile spreads across my lips as I pull away and head towards my place, the memory of that amazing kiss still playing through my mind. That was my kinda kiss. It's a memory I'm sure to relive multiple times as I end up taking my dick in my hand to relieve the ache.

Yeah, it's definitely going to be a long night.

Jaime

Monday morning is busy as I finish up a cheerful bouquet of daisies and roses to be delivered this afternoon to a receptionist at a law office. Payton, finished up with her morning deliveries, comes barreling through the back door at the same time Lexi comes swinging through the front.

"Tell me all about it!" Lexi exclaims as she tosses her purse up on the counter.

"What?" I ask, feigning indifference.

Honestly, I'm surprised that the news of my date Saturday night took this long to make its way through the Summer women. Usually when anything major happens in our family, word spreads faster than athlete's foot in a locker room.

"Don't play dumb with me, Jaime Marie Summer. You know exactly what I'm talking about." The look Lexi gives me is stern. I can tell she's not leaving without getting a detailed play-by-play of the entire date, start to finish.

"I heard she was making out with him on the porch," Payton chimes in.

My face burns with mortification as I turn to face the oldest Summer sibling. "Where did you hear that?"

Even as the words leave my lips, I already know the answer: Grandma.

"A fairy told me," Payton sasses with a grin that lights up her dark green eyes.

Lexi snorts a laugh. "A fairy. Right. You mean a seventy-year-old woman with eyes as sharp as an eagle. Come on, Jaims. You didn't really think Grandma wasn't waiting up to snoop on your date, did you?"

Of course I suspected Grandma would wait up to eavesdrop on my date, but when I returned home and didn't see a single light on besides a lamp in the living room, and the rest of the house was quiet, I figured she went to sleep. Lord knows she's not the spring chicken she was ten years ago when she was crashing our slumber parties and making surprise appearances when our dates would bring us home at night.

"Well, I had hoped," I mumble.

"So? Tell me all about it!" Lexi exclaims once more.

"We went to dinner at Helena's. It was nice. Your husband was there, by the way," I mention to Lexi.

"Yeah, he mentioned he had another work thing," she says, almost sadly. Her eyes match the tone in her voice, and I make a mental note to ask her more about that later.

"Anyway, after dinner, we went to Ice Cream Emporium and talked until they closed. That was it."

"That was it? What about the make out session on the porch?" Payton asks.

"It was just a kiss," I reply. My cheeks instantly turn a fabulous shade of embarrassment as I focus my attention on the bouquet I just completed.

"Just a kiss? According to Grandpa, Grandma thought she'd have to turn the hose on you," Lexi giggles.

I thought she might have to as well.

"Are you going to see him again?" Lexi asks, her blue-green eyes sparkling with excitement.

"I don't know. I mean we just went out three days ago. He said he'd call me, but I'm not holding my breath or anything." I try for casual, but inside, I'm a ball of nervous energy.

I'm nowhere near ready to admit it out loud, but after the date Saturday night, I'm definitely hopeful that Ryan calls me and asks me out again, which in itself is just crazy thinking. I didn't want this. I didn't want to want him, to like him.

My lips tingled for hours after he left, while I lay awake reliving that kiss over and over again. It was, without a doubt, the single best kiss of my life. The way he dominated me, took control of the moment and my body, left me with shivers of delight from head to toe, even now, three days later.

"Oh, he'll call. You should have seen the way he was looking at her, Lex. I'm surprised the smoke detectors weren't set off. Grandma is certain she's already pregnant."

My sisters giggle behind my back as they carry on as if I'm not even standing here. I busy myself cleaning up greenery clippings and stem pieces, silently wondering if Payton is correct. Will he call? Lord knows I shouldn't want him to.

But I do.

In desperate need of a redirect, I turn back around and focus on my youngest sister. Lexi's long, brown hair is full of honey highlights and tied in a messy knot high on her head. It's her standard look, yet there's something different about her. Her green eyes streak with shades of blue and lack the brightness they normally hold. Instead, they appear distant and filled with a sadness I'm not used to seeing from the baby of the family.

"Lex? What's wrong?" I ask, unable to mask my own concern.

I know each of my sisters well. She tries to hide it. She tries to push the weight of her problems to the back so that I'm unable to see it. But it's there, buried deep. "Nothing," she replies with a forced smile.

"I don't buy it," I tell her, stepping forward until I'm directly in front of her. Reaching forward, I extend my hand and wait until she places hers against my palm.

Lexi sighs, resigned to spill whatever is causing the light in her eyes to dull just a bit. "I'm...well, I'm worried."

"Worried about what?" Payton chimes in, coming over and standing next to me.

"Why can't I have a baby?" she whispers so quietly that I almost can't make out the words.

"A baby?" I ask, my heart rate kicking up a few hundred beats per second.

"Yeah," she confirms. "Chris and I have been trying to have a baby for almost two years. I've been thinking about going to see someone. You know, to figure out why."

The dejection I see in her eyes all but knocks the wind out of me. It's a sadness I see so clearly and know all too much about. It's devastating when your dream is there, so close, and yet still so far out of reach. Like a butterfly, beautiful and alive, fluttering high in the sky, just out of your grasp.

"You think there might be a problem? With you?" Payton asks, her face pail with worry.

"I don't know. Maybe me. Maybe Chris. There has to be something, right? Some reason why we've been trying for twenty-two months and still haven't gotten pregnant."

"I'm sure it'll be okay, Lex. Call Doc Simpson and see what he says," I add.

"Uh, Jaime, Doc Simpson retired three years ago," Payton replies with a snicker. "Apparently you haven't needed a reason to see Doc since you returned." Again, my sisters laugh at my expense.

"No, I haven't needed a reason to see Doc, but that's beside the point. Call whoever took Doc's place and make an appointment. I'm sure everything is fine, but you should still get both of you checked out," I instruct to my youngest sister.

Her eyes seem to lighten right before mine. As if speaking to us, saying the words out loud has somehow helped lift the little weights settled on her shoulders. The Summer sisters grew up in a large family, overflowing with tons of laughter and plenty of love. It's no wonder that many of us have kids at the heart of our own dreams. Lexi is no exception. Even at only twenty-four years of age, I can see that Lexi was destined to be a mother.

"I will," she replies. The smile she gives is small but real. "Thank you."

I step around the counter, Payton hot on my heels, and engulf Lexi in a hug. It's warm and familiar and floods my body with love. My sisters and I have always been on the touchy feely side, and I don't see that stopping anytime soon.

"Keep us posted," I whisper as the bell above the door chimes, announcing the arrival of a customer.

Stepping back, I turn and offer a bright smile to the newest arrival. My smile falters on my lips as my eyes clash with warm, dark brown ones. The smile that spreads across Ryan's full lips is sinful. Flashbacks of our kiss Saturday night flood my mind, while warmth floods another part of my body.

Ryan must be able to sense my body's response to his sudden appearance. Wearing his standard work boots, a pair of worn jeans and a dark gray tee that accentuates a pair of well defined, toned arms, Ryan saunters towards me like a wolf stalking its prey, that breathtaking smile spread widely across his wicked lips. Lips that I'd love to feel explore my oversensitive body.

"Good afternoon," he says towards my sisters, yet keeps his focus entirely on me.

Unable to find words, I just grin back at him, pulled into an alternate universe created by his rich, chocolate brown eyes. A world where only he and I exist.

"Hi," I squeak in an unnaturally high pitch. The kind of pitch that only dogs respond to.

I'm rewarded with yet another delicious arc of his uber-sexy lips. Caution is millimeters away from being thrown to the wind.

Suddenly, all I can think about is whether or not Payton's work counter is strong enough to withstand the weight of my rear perched upon it, Ryan's tall, thick body positioned between my legs.

"See? What did I tell you? They're going to set off my sprinklers." I hear Payton's words permeate the lust-induced fog that only Ryan evokes.

Startled, I take a step back and walk into the counter behind me. Ryan winks at me, but still doesn't focus on anything other than me.

"So what brings you to Blossoms and Blooms today, Ryan? Here to pick out flowers?" Payton asks. Without needing to see her smile, I can feel it in the way she asks the question.

"Not today, ladies. I was hoping to speak with Jaime for a moment."

The smile he turns towards them is pure panty-wetting wickedness. I feel the impact of it all the way over here, and it's not even aimed at me. And my sisters are helpless to combat the potency of that beautiful smile. Of course, he knows that too. He knows exactly how much charm he's inflicting on my poor, defenseless sisters. It's the same charm and charisma he wields at me every chance he gets. This man is devilish.

"Oh? What about?" Lexi chimes in, leaning closer so that she doesn't miss a single word.

Turning his full attention to the two panting dogs beside him, he feeds their need for information. "About Saturday night. I was going to ask her to have dinner with me again. Do you think she'll go on a second date with me?"

It's as if I'm not even in the room anymore.

"Are you kidding? She's talked of nothing else," Payton says with a mischievous grin.

"Hey." I gently slap my oldest sister's shoulder as my eyes bounce back and forth between the three of them.

"Really? That's a good sign, right?" Ryan asks, feeding off their over-dramatics.

"Oh, really. It's been Ryan-this and Ryan-that since the moment she stepped foot inside the shop this morning." This from traitor Payton.

"And she has been beaming and talking about how much she wants to see you again ever since I arrived just a bit ago." And of course, conspirator Lexi chimes in beautifully as if on cue.

"I'm right here," I remind my pesky siblings.

As expected, neither of them acknowledges my statement at all. They're as bad as Grandma. Only with less butt grabs and talks about sex toys.

"So, you're saying I have a shot?" Ryan asks while my sisters practically drool on the smooth counter before him.

"Definitely," one says, while the other replies, "No doubt!"

"Excellent, ladies. You've been most helpful, but if you don't mind, I'm going to steal Jaime away for just a few moments and do this officially." As he reaches out his hand, which I readily drop my hand into, he throws them a final wink before turning his full attention back to me.

Ryan leads me towards the corner by the display case, just out of direct earshot of the two eavesdroppers. He never lets go of my hand and stands directly before me. I can feel the heat radiating off his large body, stirring to life the same desire I've attempted to squash–unsuccessfully, mind you–over the last three nights.

"I have to be honest. I almost picked up the phone at least a dozen times to call you since Saturday night," Ryan confesses in a low voice.

"Why didn't you?" The words are out of my mouth before I can even slide the protective wall into place around my heart.

And that's the problem here. Ryan catches me off guard. I'm completely unprepared for the reaction my body has when he's near. How can I properly protect my heart from the devastation and destruction this gorgeous man will surely inflict if I'm swooning like a teenager every time I'm around him? It's unsettling, really.

"I didn't because I'm a dumb boy who's trying to abide by the 'three days with no contact after the first date' rule."

"There's really a rule?"

"Maybe not so much a rule as it is a suggestion. Boys are stupid. And that rule is stupid, so I'm done with it. I haven't been able to stop thinking about you. From the moment I pulled away from your house, you're all I've thought about. It's so bad that I missed a nail and smashed my finger with a hammer this morning."

Bringing his hands up to inspect further, I see the fingernail on his left thumb a tad purple. Moving it to my lips, I place a gentle kiss on the discolored nail. "Poor finger."

"Lucky finger," Ryan murmurs, his breath hitching in his throat.

The air crackles around us as heat begins to spread throughout my body. My cheeks feel flush suddenly as I gape up at him, realization setting in that I'm still holding his bruised finger to my lips.

"I was hoping that you'd be available Saturday to have dinner with me."

My heart pounds wildly in my chest. "You want to go out again?"

"Of course I do. I have a great time with you and am hoping to get to know you better."

"Really?" I choke out over my too-parched throat.

Ryan chuckles in response. "Yes. I love spending time with you. So what do you say? Dinner Saturday night?"

"Okay." The words are automatic and spill freely from my lips.

I'm rewarded with another breathtaking smile, which I can't help but reciprocate. "Excellent. How about I cook?"

"Wait, you cook?" I don't know why that would surprise me so much. I mean, he's a single man who lives alone. If he doesn't want to eat fast food every night, of course he knows how to cook.

Again, he chuckles. "Yes. I do my own cleaning and laundry too. Come by my place around six. I'll text you the address."

"Okay." You know for someone with a bachelor's degree, I seem to suddenly lack decent communication skills.

Ryan smiles widely before leaning forward and placing his lips against my cheek. The kiss is sweet and chaste, but still packs a hearty punch of lust to my overactive libido. Just over his shoulder, I hear collective "aww" from the meddlesome duo. Ryan's lips curve into a smile against my skin, which sends another flutter of something decadent in waves through my body.

"We have an audience. I'll text you later," he whispers.

Before he pulls away, I hear a sharp inhale in the hair behind my ear. Unable to formulate a response, I stand there, wide-eyed and mouth gaping, as he turns and heads towards the door. When he reaches the doorway, he throws a wink over his shoulder to me and a wave to the gossips at the counter before slipping out the door.

"Holy moly, Jaime, that guy is smokin' hot. I've seen him around town a few times, but never really noticed how gorgeous he is. Please tell me you're going out with him again?" Lexi asks.

"Of course she is! Look at her face! You couldn't wipe that smile off with a putty knife and a two-by-four. She has that 'I'm going to get laid soon' glimmer."

"Payton! You've been hanging around Grandma too much. You really need to find yourself some friends," I retort while walking back up to the counter.

"I don't need friends," she says casually. "I have you guys."

And that's the truth. The six of us are more than sisters. We're best friends. Confidants. A team. We've been through hell and back together and, miraculously, came out smiling on the other side. My sisters are my lifeline; always have been and always will be.

Smiling, I finish out my workday, anxious for my second date with Ryan this weekend. I can try to deny it all I want, but that would be fruitless. I want to see him again. And again and again. I definitely feel something powerful when we're together, and as much as I want to fight it, I just can't. I just need to remember to keep my heart out of play here, and I'm sure I'll come out unscathed on the other side. If I don't involve feelings and all that other mushy stuff, I'm sure I'll be fine when he walks away.

Because if I know anything, it's that he *will* eventually walk away.

Therefore, the only possible solution to this entire Ryan scenario is to have fun, but keep it light and my heart from getting involved. Mentally, I make a list as if to cement my plan in place. Fun–check. Keep your heart from getting involved–check.

Should be easy enough, right?

Ryan

The week crawled by at a snail's pace, but it's finally Saturday. Date night with Jaime.

I've been looking forward to this night all week. I spent Thursday night cleaning the entire condo, top to bottom, and last night shopping for dinner supplies. I'm not exactly chef material, but I can grill a mean slab of meat. Hell, it's practically written in my male DNA: Must be able to master the barbecue.

I'm expecting Jaime any minute, and if I told you I wasn't nervous to have her here, I'd be a damned liar. I'm very nervous. Jaime is edgy and jumpy when it comes to dating and relationships, this I figured out practically the first time I met her. But I don't give up that easily. As long as I remember to take it slow and not scare her off, I'll be fine. She'll come around when she realizes there's something real brewing between us. I know it–*feel* it.

A soft knock sounds at the front door and my entire body suddenly takes notice. Jaime's here. Hell, even my dick knows when she's close by. He's standing up, ready to greet her too. And if I'm not careful, he's liable to claw his way through my pants just to get to her.

Adjusting myself and willing my hard-on into submission, I step to the door. Jaime is standing on my porch wearing a light pink dress that hits just above her knees. Her arms are covered in a sweater, giving her a wholesome look. But I know the fire that breathes to life when I kiss her. It's a fierceness I wouldn't mind revisiting later this evening.

"Welcome," I tell her, opening the screen door and dropping a light kiss on her cheek.

"Hi," she says shyly. "I brought a bottle of wine."

"Thank you," I reply, taking the bottle from her extended hand. "Come on into the kitchen with me. You can sit at the counter while I finish getting the meat ready for the grill."

Jaime's hot on my heels as I make my way into the adjacent kitchen. She takes off a sexy librarian sweater and sets it aside as I point to a barstool and grab a wine glass from the cabinet. Thank God my sister got me a set when I moved into this place, otherwise she'd be liable to drink white wine from a plastic Star Wars cup.

"This place is great," Jaime states while glancing around my space.

Like the rest of the place, the kitchen is small but practical. "Thanks," I reply as I add sliced onions and carrots to the potato mixture. "My neighbor, Mrs. Hanson owns it. She tried to hire me right after I moved in to fix the place up, but I wouldn't hear it. I couldn't take any money from her, you know? She bought the supplies and I installed them. I did it at night and on weekends so that I didn't have to run it through the company. She's the sweetest old lady and I enjoy spending time with her. She makes me dinner and brownies and stuff; it's the least I could do."

When I'm greeted with silence, I turn towards Jaime. She's staring at me with a small smile. Our gazes lock for several moments. My heart rate kicks up a few hundred beats per second with one look. Jaime has a shine about her, a lightness that breathes happiness and serenity. The crazy part is that when I'm around her–hell, when she's in my mere thoughts–I feel that shine spilling over on me. I smile more than I have in God knows how long, and it's all because of her.

And I just met her.

That's terrifying and exciting all at the same time. Like diving headfirst into the blind water without having a single clue as to what dangers really lurk just below the murky surface.

"That's very sweet of you to do. I've known Mrs. Hanson most of my life. She's friends with my grandma. She's the kindest woman. She used to always bring over homemade angel food cake with fresh, sliced strawberries. My sisters and I used to fight over the last piece."

"Her angel food cakes are amazing. She made one for me a few weeks ago for taking her garbage out to the curb," I say as I gather up my grilling supplies. "I think I'm ready to step outside. Care to join me?"

Jaime stands up, grabs her glass and the pan of potatoes, and follows me towards the back door. Holding open the door, Jaime slides beneath my arm, careful not to knock into the platter of meat, seasonings, and grilling tongs in my other hand. I can't help dipping down and catching the briefest hint of vanilla coming from her hair. Her smell is intoxicating and, as always, causes things to happen in my pants.

Outside, the air is brisk filtering off the Bay. I'm several blocks inland, but it doesn't matter what part of town you're in, you can still smell the salt in the air and feel the cool breeze swept from the sea.

Sitting down on a lawn chair, Jaime sips her wine while watching me throw the foil packet containing the potato mixture and the pork loin on the grill. The gas is set to a low heat as I spread a honey glaze over the top of the loin. I can't help but notice that she's watching me intently. When I'm finished, I grab a can of beer from the fridge and join Jaime on the deck.

"You seemed very interested in my cooking skills. I promise you I've done this before."

"Actually, I was making mental notes," she says. "I've never really been able to master the grill. Everything I cook is either charred to a crisp or is still clucking when I pull it off."

I try not to chuckle at her admission, but it slips out. "Grilling is an art. It's not to be taken lightly."

"It's on my list of things to learn. Maybe, someday, you can help teach me."

"I'd be honored," I tell her honestly. We stare at each other for several heart-pounding moments before she breaks eye contact, looking around.

"This is a nice area," she says, the sun's just starting to drop below the trees.

"It is. Mrs. Hanson plants and maintains the flowers around the trees and I mow."

"Do you always call her Mrs. Hanson?" she asks, a smile playing on the corners of her lips.

"Not always. Sometimes I call her Mrs. H." I take a drink of my beer, fighting the smile that threatens to spread across my own lips.

"Funny guy," she says with a grin.

"Truthfully?" I ask with a serious look. As soon as she nods her head for me to continue, I add, "I have no clue what her first name is."

Jaime stares at me stunned for several heartbeats before laughter bursts from her sweet lips. I'm helpless at the impact of that simple gesture. "Seriously?"

"Yep. When I moved here, I was referred to her place by one of the local realtors. She called her Mrs. Hanson, and every time I spoke with her, I always spoke to her more formally and politely. I'm pretty sure she knows that I have no clue what her first name is and she's playing me now."

"I bet she is." More laughter fills the evening as Jaime's sparkling eyes lock on mine. "It's Patricia, but she goes by Pat," she offers, throwing me the life raft.

"Good to know," I whisper, giving her a wink and a smile in return.

I relax in my chair, content to just sit beside her. The crickets start to chirp as the breeze starts to pick up a bit. Jaime runs her hand up her arm as if attempting to warm her cooling skin. Quickly, I jump up and slip back inside my condo. I could step further into the kitchen and grab the sweater she arrived in, but a hoodie sweatshirt is folded atop the washing machine by the back door, so I grab it instead and slip back outside. At least it's clean and not a random work shirt.

"Here," I say as I step before her. "Stand up."

Jaime's several inches shorter than I am and petite compared to my broad shoulders and long arms. Placing the sweatshirt over her head, Jaime fits her arms through the sleeves, which easily hang about five inches longer than her fingertips. She giggles as she whips her hands around, the loose material of the sweatshirt flopping around like a fish out of water.

"Come here," I say as I roll the sleeves up to her wrists.

"Thank you," she whispers, gazing up at me with those big green eyes.

Angling her face upward, I trace her jaw with my thumbs, gently pushing the loose strands of her hair behind her ear. The slightest touch of her skin against mine seems to cause instantaneous reactions to both of us. Jaime's breathing becomes labored, her lush mouth opening to form the perfect little O. My reaction is more visible in the crotch region, but it's a painful reaction I've become accustomed to with her.

And because I'm weak and unable to resist her, I bend down and brush my lips against hers. I can taste the wine on her lips and feel the heat of her mouth as I do everything I can to keep the kiss somewhat platonic. The last thing Jaime needs is for me to turn into a caveman on her, throw her over my shoulder, and carry her off to my lair where I'm sure to ravish her from head to toe for hours on end. Days, even.

"Dinner should be ready soon," I tell her.

"Okay," she replies, her eyes clear and bright.

"Do you want to eat out here or go inside where it's warmer?"

"I'd love to eat out here. Unless you're cold and want to go in."

"I'm good. If you're comfortable in the sweatshirt, then we can eat out here," I suggest which earns me a head nod.

Thirty minutes later, we're sitting around the small table on my small deck. The pork loin is perfectly tender and the vegetables crisp. Jaime switched to water when I took the meat off the grill, and I figured it was probably wise to follow suit. Last thing I want to do is get buzzed up and alter my state where Jaime is concerned.

"This is so good," she moans with a mouth full of food.

"I'm glad you like it."

"Where'd you learn to cook like this?"

"From my mom, actually. She used to cook like this daily when I was growing up, and she always made sure that my siblings and I learned how to cook. We each had a job in the kitchen nightly."

"That's awesome. My mom tried, but there were so many of us that it was kinda just a free-for-all." Jaime smiles, but gets a far off look in her eye like she's reliving a pleasant memory of her happy childhood.

"I'm sure it was poetic chaos in your household," I tell her, finishing off my potatoes.

"Most days, there was nothing poetic about it. It was just chaotic and dramatic. There was always bickering, crying, fighting over makeup and boys. But it was also amazing," she adds. "I've become extremely close with all five of my sisters. We're best friends as well as sisters."

My only response is a smile. She doesn't need words. Every word she speaks is the truth if the way she glows is any indication. I was close to my siblings, but nothing like the bond she shares with her sisters. I've only met two of them, and I can see it. In fact, I'm pretty sure they all feel the same way.

"How about a few getting-to-know-you questions?" she asks.

"I'm game. Ask away," I advise, leaning back in my chair.

"Favorite color?" she starts off.

"Blue. You?"

"Red. Favorite food?"

"Mexican. You?"

"Does chocolate cake count?" she asks with a smile. "Chicago hotdogs are my favorite."

"Hotdogs? Really?"

"Yep. The ones loaded with all the toppings including a pepper. They're the best. Favorite movie?" she asks.

"Easy. *Shawshank Redemption*. You?"

"*Radio*. Cuba Gooding Jr. was outstanding in that role. It still makes me cry every time I watch it."

"I've seen it. Good movie. Now, my turn," I say, straightening up in my seat.

"I already know your favorite flower, so how about favorite sport?"

"Hockey. Those tight pants are great to look at on television," she replies, fighting her smirk. "You?"

"Hockey. I used to play street hockey as a kid, and when I was in college, I joined a club at a community center and played ice hockey during the winter. It was fun."

"Huh. So, we have something in common."

"Oh, I think we have more than *something* in common. I think it's safe to say we have a lot of things–important things–in common," I say.

"Like what?" she asks.

"Like the fact that you like spending time with me as much as I like spending time with you."

A small smile spreads across her face as she nods her head. I reach over and squeeze her hand, unable to keep my own smile off my face. When I let go, we each dive back into our dinner, each one silently lost in our own thoughts.

After dinner, I gather up the dishes and run them inside. When I return, Jaime is curled up in a chair, her long brown hair gently blowing in the breeze. She looks casual, but deep in thought.

"Penny for your thoughts?" I ask as I move my chair so that it's butted against hers.

Jaime looks over at me, her eyes guarded slightly. My heart stalls in my chest at the sight. She looks scared. Like she's about to choose flight when having to decide between fight or flight.

"Five years ago, I was living in Cleveland where I went to college. My degree was in hospitality, and I was working full time at a travel agency that specialized in cruise trips. It was fine, but not really what I wanted to do with my life."

She pauses for a moment. I almost ask for more information about what she wanted to do with her life, but I decide against it. My job right now is to keep quiet, listen, and offer her friendship if she wants it. Something tells me that Jaime revealing information about her past is a big deal for her. Therefore, I sit still and keep my mouth shut.

"I met Gavin when he came into the agency to book a guys' trip with some of his friends. He was good looking, charismatic, and flirty, and I was smitten."

My gut tightens with a foreign emotion that I haven't experienced in a damn long time. Jealousy. Just the thought of some asshole with his hands all over Jaime, kissing that same place on her neck that I've been fantasizing about, makes me see red.

"We dated for almost two years before we moved in together. He was working a lot of hours, and I was at home, taking care of the household. We wanted the same things and seemed genuinely happy, or so I thought. That's why when he left me the week of our wedding, I was devastated."

Her eyes drop to the clutched fingers on her lap. She's wringing them nervously, and all I want to do is make it all go away. I long to erase that wrinkled frown. I want to take away the hurt in her eyes. I want to eradicate her heartache and make her whole again.

"It wasn't a breakdown the way Sara mentioned in the restaurant last week, but it was shocking all the same. He sent a text message. A text message. Who sends a text message to break up with someone? Especially an engagement."

"I'm so sorry, Jaime. Clearly the guy's an idiot. But the question isn't who breaks up with someone by text, the question is who's dumb enough to let a woman like you slip through their fingers," I say, my voice husky and deep, even to my own ears.

"Wow, that was pretty smooth," Jaime teases, feigning seriousness.

"Thank you," I reply. Turning my chair once more, I lean forward until we're almost face to face. Or more accurately, lips to lips. "I only speak the truth, though. I'm serious, Jaime. Who's stupid enough to let you go? You're funny and smart and gorgeous with your big green eyes and sexy brown hair. I think about kissing you every moment of every day. And my dreams? Well, they're full of kissing too, because ever since I met you, feeling your lips against mine is all I can think about."

"Really?" That one word comes out just above a whisper.

"Really. When I saw you standing in the flower shop, my first thought was that your lips were the most lush, perfect lips I had ever seen."

As if by gravity pulling us together, Jaime leans in the rest of the way and her lips meet mine. It's a tender kiss filled with question and longing. Unspoken questions fill the night air. What will happen if I deepen this kiss the way my body craves? Is she ready to move forward? Is she as attracted to me as I am to her? Will she keep an open mind if I ask her to consider a relationship? Can I convince her to take the chance?

But I'm not going to think about the answers to any one of them. Not right now.

Instead, I rejoice in the way her mouth molds to my own, the way she tastes. Her tongue slides alongside mine, causing my cock to tighten painfully in my pants. I should probably adjust it for comfort, but I can't seem to remove my hands from her hair.

Taking a few final nips at her swollen lips, I pull away to gauge her reaction. Her eyes are cloudy with lust and her breathing labored. She looks stunning with her wet lips and slightly tussled hair.

But when her eyes clear, I see it. No hesitation. No question. No fear.

Only desire.

Standing up, I extend my hand towards hers. It's a simple gesture, but the meaning behind it is mountainous.

"Come inside for a drink?" The question is spilled from my lips before I can consider it, though there's no way I'd take it back.

If she comes inside with me, there's a good chance this relationship is advancing to the next level. If she decides to head out, then I'm right back to square one, fighting to slay the ghosts of her past. At least this time I know what I'm up against. I know the damage caused by some douchebag who threw her away like yesterday's takeout.

I know which route I'm hoping she takes, but I'm even more surprised when she actually chooses.

With her hand resting firmly in my own, Jaime offers me a smile and says, "I'd love to go inside and have a drink with you."

Best answer ever.

Jaime

I follow him back inside the condo, my hand tucked securely inside his. Even though I was invited in for a drink, I'm certain that this night will lead to other things. Naked things. The lustful look in his eyes is unmistakable. It's a look that has been there since I stepped onto his porch when I arrived. His eyes are filled with desire and need, and I'm all too worried that mine have reflected much of the same.

I'm nowhere near ready to jump headfirst into the deep end of a relationship, but that doesn't mean we can't enjoy something casual, right? I mean, sex doesn't equal love and marriage. Sex is fun. Sex is great. And it's been a long time since I've indulged in the spontaneous side of dating.

The living room is little and quaint, and decorated far better than I expected. Remembering what Gavin's place was like before I moved in, a small spaced filled with clutter and worn furniture, I'm pleasantly surprised by the cleanliness and style of Ryan's place.

A large bookshelf adorns one wall, and I'm drawn to his selection of paperbacks. Mostly mysteries or thrillers, I'm shocked when I find a copy of one of my favorite books, "The Notebook" by Nicholas Sparks.

I turn to find Ryan's sheepish eyes diverted and the corner of his lips turned upward. "My sister. It's her favorite book so for my birthday this past winter, she sent me a copy as a joke. Said it would help me find someone who was worthy of my time. In other words, someone *not* like Sara."

I return my attention to the paperback, and gently remove it from the shelf. The spine is crinkled just a bit, proving that this copy has been opened, and probably read, several times. "It looks well read. You read it, didn't you?" I ask, looking at him over my shoulder.

"I cannot confirm nor deny your claim," he states, walking over and gently taking the book from my hands.

"Why not?" I ask, huskily, when I realize he's standing close. So very close. His front is almost touching my back in an intimate way, and I catch myself before I can sway backwards just a fraction of an inch until I feel his body pressed against mine.

"Would you think less of me as a man if I told you I read it?" he asks, his sexy voice deep and gravelly.

"No."

"Then I've read it five times. When they die together at the end? That gets me every time." He gives me a pointed look before continuing. "But if you tell my sister that, I'll have to kill you," he adds with a wink and that slight upturn of a single corner of his lips.

Ryan turns me around and tosses the paperback onto the couch. His fingers thread into my hair, the movement both sensual and possessive. Beautiful, full lips hover directly over mine. Neither of us speak yet completely conveying our thoughts and intents with our eyes. They're hungry and full of passion and devour me whole.

"I want to kiss you," he whispers, his lips slowly inching towards mine.

"I want you to kiss me."

The words are barely past my lips when he makes his move. The kiss is greedy and hungry, sparking a fierce desire within my body, leaving absolutely no room for thought to enter my mind. I'm lost, completely gone, in this one, perfect kiss.

Keeping one hand firmly entangled in my hair, he slides his other hand down to my lower back, pushing up his sweatshirt. His fingers dig gently into my skin as he pulls me forward, flush against an unforgiving wall of muscle.

His tongue urges my mouth open by sliding against the seam of my lips. Reflexively, I grant him access and moan when his warm tongue slides seductively against mine. My fingers grip the back of his shirt, rooting me into place while I hang on for dear life.

And in a way, I am.

This kiss is powerful. Uncontrollable.

"Jaime, I want you. I want you more than I've ever wanted anything before in my entire life. I want to take you to bed more than I want my next fucking breath of air." Ryan's teeth gently nip at my kiss-swollen lips, drawing me further into his spellbinding gaze. "Please say you feel the same way."

His voice is raspy, his eyes cloudy with longing and lust. His self-control is slipping, right before my eyes, and it's a powerful feeling, knowing that I'm the cause of such a strong reaction for a man like Ryan Elson.

I don't even think, I speak. "I want you, too. Just as badly."

Before I know it, I'm lifted off the ground, my legs automatically wrapping around his waist, and I'm lead backwards, presumably towards his bedroom. His hands are wrapped around my rear, holding me in place while he steps into a darkened room.

Guess we're passing on the drinks.

Ryan's lips devour mine in a bruising kiss as my fingers work overtime to remove the clothing barriers between us. Craving the feel of his skin against me, I'm clawing at his polo, anxious to rid him of the offending shirt. Unfortunately, with the shirt tucked into his jeans and my body wrapped around him, that stupid shirt is going nowhere.

Sensing my eagerness, he gently sets me down. My legs are wobbly and my heart is tripping over itself with excitement as I watch him untuck his shirt and remove it quickly in one fluid motion, that sexy ability that only men seem to possess.

With the shirt gone, I'm finally able to ogle my fill at the broad chest and hard, muscular planes of his amazing physique. He's perfection. I've never seen a chest like Ryan's. Shoulders, pecs, and abs so gloriously firm that my mouth literally hangs open as if my jaw is hinged. This is a man who works manual labor every day, not someone who spends hours in a gym.

He stands still for several sexually tense filled moments letting me look my fill before smiling and reaching for me. First, he removes his sweatshirt that I've been wearing, followed quickly by my dress. Pulling me into his arms, he slowly slides the zipper downward, the skim of the teeth echoing through the room much louder than normal.

"I feel like I've been waiting forever for this," his voice pushes through the sexually charged haze in my mind. "For you."

And with those two little words, my entire world ignites into flames. His eyes hold my gaze and are filled with more passion than I've ever experienced. My heart leaps in my chest at the simple meaning of those words. Something wonderful and equally terrifying happens in this moment. Something I'm nowhere near ready to dissect.

Before I'm able to consider the meaning of his words any further, Ryan's lips find mine once again. This kiss is slow, sensual. With his lips still sliding seductively against mine and the zipper of my dress at the base of my spine, he slowly slides the dress down my body. Cool air caresses my skin and goosebumps pepper my exposed body.

When the dress pools at my feet, Ryan releases my lips and steps back. His greedy eyes devour my body, from my turquoise lace strapless bra to the matching thong panties and on to my orange painted toes, he leaves no part of my body untouched by his hungry gaze.

Giving in to the need to feel his skin beneath my fingertips, I run my fingers down the ripples of his chest. The muscles tighten against my touch, telling me that I affect him as much as he does me.

My fingers continue their downward course, blazing a trail of molten heat with each caress. When I reach the waist of his pants, I zero in on the lone button fastening them together. Keeping my eyes locked on his, I release the button and skim a single finger across the top of the waistband of his briefs. Ryan's eyes are fire as he wraps one arm around my waist and pulls me against his body.

"God, you're driving me crazy," he groans as my finger dips behind the band.

"A good crazy, I hope?" The teasing and flirting is something new to me. Even in the throes of passion, I've never been someone who's forward and playful in the bedroom. I kinda like this new Jaime.

"The best fucking possible kinda crazy there is," he growls as he grinds the hard ridge of his hard-on against my stomach.

I'm point two seconds away from climbing his leg and humping him like Grandma's Chihuahua, Sparky, used to do to the mailman when we were younger.

Fortunately, I'm saved from such an embarrassing act when he picks me up in his arms and carries me to his bed. The dark comforter is cool, yet plush beneath me as he lays me down. I wrap my arms firmly around his neck, ensuring that he's unable to run away from me. Not that I think he would.

My lips are greeted with another kiss, this one fierce and possessive. Large, warm hands grip my waist and glide to my bra. He tugs on a cup, releasing a single nipple. Without removing his mouth from mine, he tweaks and caresses my tight little bud until I'm writhing underneath him, using his body as my own personal scratching post–or in this case, a rubbing post.

"I need to taste you." His words are almost orgasmic in themselves. My body practically levitates while my head silently screams *Yes, please!*

Ryan rises up so that he's resting on his haunches between my legs. His eyes roam freely once more while his right hand searches for the clasp at my back. Releasing the closure, my breasts are freed. Air lodges in my throat as I take in the greedy way his eyes consume each one. If my body were a possession to be had, Ryan Elson would own it and rule it effective immediately.

Dipping down, I'm shocked when he runs his nose up the center of my panties, inhaling deeply as he goes. The groan is throaty and comes from someplace deep inside of him. I've never experienced anything so erotic in my life. Gavin never wanted to go down on me, always complaining about the taste. He seems to crave it, need it. Warmth floods the little scrap of material ensuring that they're completely and effortlessly soaked.

"God, you smell fucking amazing," he groans as he pushes the wet material to the side.

I hold my breath as I wait for what's to come next, but nothing happens. Anticipation pours through me, wild and reckless as I risk a glance up at him. He's staring at my center, his eyes full of hunger. It's as if he's stuck in some alternate universe, lost in a trance where it's only him and me. Of course, the fact that he's staring at my crotch has nerves shooting through my body at an alarming rate.

Reflexively, I try to close my legs, which basically just frames his head with my thighs.

"Don't," he whispers as he gently pushes my thighs back open. "You are so beautiful. I could stare at your perfection for the rest of my life and still want more."

Ryan runs his hands up my thighs once more, parting them as far as they'll comfortably go. Holding my legs a part, he dips his head forward and swipes his tongue across my swollen flesh. Time stands still, air fails to move, my body burns with desire as he licks me, long and leisurely, all while keeping his eyes firmly locked on mine. I practically levitate off the bed as he dips his tongue inside my wet heat.

A loud moan fills the room. The noise sounds foreign, even to my own ears, and I'm startled to realize it's coming from me. Snaking my fingers into his lush brown hair, I hold on for dear life as his tongue tastes and worships me. He plunges his tongue deep and hard inside of me, his pointer finger zeroing in on the little bundle of nerves just above my entrance. I'm teetering on the edge of orgasm, inching closer and closer with each swipe of his finger or flex of his tongue.

My clit is pulsating. He gently circles his finger over the top before lightly pinching, and the combination throws me headfirst into a total star seeing, white-light blinding orgasm. I have no shame as I grind against his hand, riding out wave after wave of earthshattering bliss.

The orgasm seems to go on for hours. Shockwaves of pleasure consume me until my body is nothing but uncontrollable shudders. I'm spent and boneless, a heap of nothing atop a down comforter.

"Geezus, I've never witnessed anything more spectacular than that," he says as he moves up my body. My tired eyes are suddenly struggling to keep focus on his handsome face. "In fact, it was so fucking fantastic that you're going to do it again." He stretches over top of me, his jean-covered erection nestled tightly between my thighs. "But this time? I want you to do that while my cock is buried inside of you," he whispers moments before his mouth claims mine once more.

And just like that, the heat of his words and the fierceness in his kiss has my body sparking to life and craving more. How that's even possible, I don't know. I've never felt raising desire consume me almost immediately after an orgasm. Hell, I've never even experienced an orgasm like that. Intense. All-consuming. Epic.

Ryan. It's the way my body reacts to him.

I try to slide my hand between our bodies to reach the button of his jeans, but it doesn't work. My hand is stuck between hard muscle and soft skin. I feel his smile against my lips moments before I lose contact with him. He's standing before me, illuminated by the soft light spilling from the hallway, and reaches for the zipper.

Time stands still as he slowly lowers the zipper and slides his jeans down powerful thighs. Tight white briefs barely contain the impressive bulge threating to burst through the material. My mouth waters at the prospect of getting my hands–and maybe my mouth–on his erection.

He quickly strips, never taking his eyes off mine. The moment is raw and sexually charged, and before I know it, he's standing before me, gloriously naked like a work of art that should be displayed in a museum. His eyes are hungry, his jaw clenched with tension, and his hands shaking as he reaches into his nightstand for a condom.

With stealthy hands, he covers his hard erection with latex and makes his way back towards me. I'm shaking with anticipation. He steals my breath as he covers my lips with his own once more, his body canvasing me from head to toe. Warm, rough hands skim my flesh from my shoulder, down my chest, and towards the junction of my legs.

No surprise, I'm wet and ready for him. His fingers slide easily through my folds, teasing and caressing me until I'm panting against his lips.

"Please, Ryan," I beg, nipping at his full bottom lip while my fingernails bite into the tender flesh of his shoulders.

"I love to hear you beg. So hot," he confesses as his lips skim across my neck.

Rising above me, he positions himself at my entrance. Our eyes remain locked as he slowly pushes forward. My entire body burns with desire as he stretches and fills me completely.

"Holy shit." Ryan groans the words as he closes his eyes, seeming lost in this wonderful moment. He's still and appears to be struggling to maintain his composure right before my eyes. It's exhilarating.

"Please move." My words come out a plea once more.

Opening his eyes, he pulls back gently and drives forward, hard and wholly. With each powerful thrust of his hips, I'm steadily pushed closer towards another orgasm. I feel it building clear down to my toes, spreading through me like an uncontainable wildfire.

Grabbing my hips and raising me up, he changes the position ever so slightly. The angle causes his dick to hit that magic place inside of me that so few ever reach. I know it won't be long now. There's no way I can control what is coming, no way to stop the inevitable. My sights are filled with white light once more, and I'm unable to catch my breath, as I feel every stroke he makes within me.

"You feel so fucking good," he growls as he pistons inside of me and grinds against my swollen clit, hard and unforgiving.

"Ryan," I holler as the orgasm sweeps through me, this one just as intense as the first, if not more.

My body clenches around him as he slams into me a few more times, eagerly riding out the waves of my release. Finally, he follows me over the edge into complete oblivion. My body pulsates, gripping the steel length of his cock, as my name slips repeatedly from his lips. I've never heard a sweeter sound before in my life.

Exhaustion seems to hit us both at the same time as we both fall into a heap of sweaty, tangled limbs. Our mixed breath comes out in harsh pants. My entire body cradles him as if he's the most priceless thing ever, him still firmly seated within me.

Shifting his weight, Ryan rains tender kisses across my face. My cheeks, my forehead, my nose, my lips, nothing is left untouched by his lips. With one hand cradling the back of my neck, he slides the other down my arm and links his fingers within mine. In just a few simple gestures, we're quickly taking the moment from hot and steamy to intimate and cozy.

"Please stay with me," he whispers, his breath fanning against my neck.

"Okay," I say without giving the meaning or the ramifications of my reply a single thought.

Because the simple fact of the matter is: I want to stay.

Here.

With him.

And so I do. He excuses himself to take care of the condom while I snuggle against his pillow. It smells so distinctly like him: woodsy, musky, and clean. Manly. The scent lulls me towards sleep.

I barely register the dipping of the bed, but feel the warm washcloth against my most sensitive area. After only a few seconds, the washcloth is gone and I'm encompassed in strong arms and pulled into the crook of his arm. Ryan's body is warm and hard, and I'm surprised at how comfortable it really is.

"Good night, Jaime. I had a great time tonight," he whispers, running his hand along the side of my head.

"Me too," I reply, the honestly and simplicity of the words warming me.

With my head nestled against his shoulder, my hand resting on his chest, and my leg thrown over his, I drift off to sleep.

10

Ryan

The banging on the front door pulls me from a sex-induced, heavy sleep. It might very well have been the best night of sleep I've ever had. Hell, can you even call it sleep? There sure as hell wasn't too much sleep going on. The images of Jaime splayed beneath me, naked and moaning, was enough to cause my dick to stir to life all over again. Three times I took her throughout the night, and I still haven't had my fill. In fact, if the tent I'm pitching with the sheet is any indication, it's safe to say I'm ready to go another three rounds with the lovely Jaime Summer.

Right now, however, I'm in need of getting rid of my insistent knocker.

Gingerly, I slip out of my bed and grab a pair of running shorts from the dresser. I'm still hard as granite as I take in the sight of Jaime sleeping on my other pillow. Her long, brown hair is a tangled mess and her breathing is still deep and steady. The desire to ignore my guest and climb back into bed with her is great, but I can't do it. I'm sure the knocker is Mrs. Hanson, who often stops by for morning coffee on the weekend. While I'm not willing to just ignore her, I'm very anxious to get rid of her and return to the woman warming my sheets, so the quicker I get out front and answer the door, the quicker I'll have Jaime's long legs wrapped around me. Preferably my neck.

I don't bother with the t-shirt. Another loud knock rings out just as I reach the living room door. Fearing that Mrs. H is going to wake up Sleeping Beauty in my bed, I rip the door open with a bit too much force, anxious to get on with the rest of my morning plans.

The faces I'm greeted with aren't the ones I expected to see on the other side of my front door. Two of Jaime's sisters are there, and their eyes are wide with shock and indignation, presumably at my lack of clothing. The shorter, younger sister's eyes light up with laughter as she giggles. When she runs her eyes up and down my body in an appreciative way, I mentally kick myself for not grabbing that damn shirt. She doesn't seem the least bit put out by my attire–or lack thereof. Payton, on the other hand, shies her eyes away and blushes a not-so-flattering shade of fuchsia.

"You must be Ryan," the sister I don't know says.

"I am."

"Ryan, this is Alison, or AJ as we all call her. AJ, Ryan Elson."

I take AJ's offered hand and give it a gentle squeeze. Stepping back, I motion for Jaime's sisters to step inside.

"Is she here?" AJ asks, the smile never leaving her face.

"She's here. She's sleeping," I confirm.

Lexi turns to Payton who is casually browsing my DVD rack. "I knew she'd be here. *I'm* not the one freaking out."

Before I can ask *who* she is referring to, I hear another car pull up, quickly followed by several doors closing. Stepping back over to the door, I see two women and a man practically running up my front walk. When I open the door, they're already there, breaching the threshold only a moment later.

"Did you find her?" The twin sister that I haven't met yet asks, her panicked face bouncing from AJ to Payton.

"She's here," Payton confirms.

"Oh, thank God!" another sister says.

I'm quickly starting to lose track of who is who. Payton must sense my confusion and introduces me to the three newcomers.

"Ryan, this is the other twin, Abby, as well as Meghan and her boyfriend, Josh."

Josh steps forward to shake my hand, careful to keep his eye contact. More giggling ensues, once again reminding me that I'm severely underdressed at this little family gathering.

"Nice to meet you," I tell him before giving waves to Meghan and Abby.

"Sorry it was like this," Josh says sheepishly.

"I'm just gonna run…" I point towards my closed bedroom door before rubbing my hand along the back of my neck, "back there and…"

Before I can finish my sentence, a series of honks pierce the morning sunlight. Stepping back to my front door, I'm not surprised in the least when I see another sister get out of the car, followed very closely by Grandma.

"I tried to call her," Meghan says, nodding towards Grandma. "But she didn't answer."

Yet to find out what in the hell is going on, I open the door and let the two newcomers in. Grandma gives me a stern look at first, but then her eyes change into something else as she slowly scrutinizes my exposed body. It's delight and appreciation and eagerness. It's slightly unsettling.

"Young man, is my granddaughter here?" she asks, her eyes still focused down on my shorts.

"Uh, Jaime? Yes, ma'am."

"Oh thank God! I thought she was lying dead in an alley somewhere!" Emma exclaims dramatically.

"Stop it, Grandma. We all knew exactly where she was." This from Payton.

Without acknowledging her granddaughter, Emma grabs her cell phone and dials. Since she put it on speakerphone, we're all treated to the sound of the phone ringing.

"Hello?"

"Orval, good news. You can call off the National Guard. We've found her. She's over fornicating with that handsome construction worker."

Now, it takes quite a bit to embarrass me. I don't blush very easily. But when Jaime's sisters all gasp or snicker, and every pair of eyes in the room focus on me, I can honestly say I feel my cheeks start to burn.

"She's fornicating? Right now?"

"No, not right now, Orval, but the boy just answered the door practically naked and he's sporting a hard-on bigger than that maple tree you cut down last winter."

Again, all wide, horrified eyes return to me. Or more accurately, on my crotch.

"Grandma! You can't say that!" Abby gasps, humiliated on my behalf.

"Oh, hush, child. I'm married, not dead." Then her eyes dart down to my shriveled up manhood. He may never want to come out and play again.

Dropping my hands to my groin, I take several retreating steps until I feel the wall at my back. Even though I'm not sporting wood, I feel like my junk is on display. You know, one of those exhibits featured at a museum? Everyone just stands there, motionless and gawking.

"I'll, uh, be right back. I'll just go grab Jaime," I mumble before slipping down the small hall and ducking into my room.

I slip inside the bedroom, careful to make sure the door is latched and locked properly. I definitely wouldn't put it past that crazy ol' lady to barge into my bedroom to have a peek at the goods. What I'm greeted with when I turn around steals the very air I breathe. Like a thief, Jaime Summer has snuck into my life and stolen something from me. Something I didn't realize I was so anxious to give until this very moment.

Jaime stands before me wearing my shirt from last night. Her hair is tussled and wild, reminding me all over again of the many ways I spent giving her pleasure throughout the course of our evening. Her lips are slightly swollen and her eyes tired, yet still shining brightly.

All of a sudden, I'm ready to say screw it and ignore the houseguests anxiously waiting on the opposite side of the door. Screw them (figuratively) and screw her (literally). My dick is fully engaged in this new plan of operation.

"Is everything alright? I heard voices," Jaime says as her eyes feast on my exposed chest. The combination of her lustful eyes and her sexy morning voice instantly rouses a possessive growl from my chest.

Dammit with her family's shitty timing!

"Actually, I think you may want to get dressed. We have company." I say, stepping closer until I feel her body heat against mine.

"Company?" she asks, snaking her warm arms around my waist.

"Yeah, apparently you not letting anyone know that you wouldn't be home last night was cause for a bit of concern amongst the natives."

"Concern with the natives? What are you talking about?"

"Your family is in the living room, and they won't leave until I provide proof that I didn't haul you off to my lair and murder you." I chuckle now, the magnitude of the situation finally settling in.

"My family?" she whispers, bringing her hand up to her agape mouth. "They're here? Oh my God."

Pulling her into my arms once more, I say, "It'll be alright. Let's just head out there and make sure they know I didn't dismember you and store you in my freezer. Then we can come back in here and hang out. Naked." I wiggle my eyebrows and offer a cheesy grin.

Her laughter sends my blood flowing southward and my heart beating faster.

"I didn't think I had to check in with them after I decided to stay here last night," she says sheepishly, pulling away and reaching for her clothes.

"I imagine once we get this initial incident out of the way, they'll know you're with me if you should happen to not come home again." At least she better be with me, because after last night, I'm sure as hell going to get her in my bed as much as possible.

"So, there's going to be another sleepover? You're awfully confident there, champ," she sasses.

"Hell yes, there's going to be another sleepover. And another after that, and one after that too."

Jaime turns a beautiful shade of pink as she blushes from the top of her chest, clear up to her forehead. She tries to hide it by turning her back to me, but I saw it. I also couldn't miss the way she fought to keep a smile from crossing her sweet lips.

I dress quickly in the first pair of dark jeans and t-shirt I can find, while Jaime dons last night's dress. She looked stunning yesterday with her styled hair and makeup, but today, in the morning light with her bedhead and her face makeup-free, she's gorgeous. She's simply the most beautiful woman I've ever laid eyes on.

"I can't believe I'm about to do the walk of shame. With my entire family here. This is so embarrassing," she mumbles as she attempts to tame her wild locks by finger-combing them. It doesn't work.

"At least SWAT isn't here. Or the National Guard. I heard your grandma tell your grandpa to call them off."

"Oh God," she groans loudly, dropping her head to her chest to hide her face.

Before I can reassure her, there's an insistent knock on the bedroom door, followed quickly by the jingling of the doorknob. Thank Christ I locked that thing.

"Jaime! Now is not the time for a quickie. Your entire family is out here waiting to make sure you're breathing, and all you're interested in doing is another quick ride on the bologna pony! You and 'Oh God' need to get out here right now!" Emma hollers through the doorway.

Jaime practically flies across the room and throws the lock. When she opens the door, Emma is standing there with a smirk and eyes full of laughter. "I wasn't...we weren't..." she tries to defend to her grandma, but can't seem to get the words out.

"Come on, sweetie. Grandpa just pulled up. We're going for breakfast." And with that, Emma turns and walks away, leaving a stunned Jaime gaping in the doorway.

kXXk

It's easy to get lost in the shuffle when you're seating twelve at a table in the middle of Fran's Diner in downtown Jupiter Bay. If the restaurant was quiet before we arrived, you wouldn't know it now that we're here.

When Lexi and Chris pulled up, with Grandpa in tow, the entire family convened upon my small living room until she and I were both ready to go. There was no getting out of breakfast since the entire Summer clan was wide awake and had been scouring the town, looking for Jaime at seven in the morning.

So here we are. I managed to throw on a clean pair of jeans and a t-shirt, while Jaime is sitting next to me, beautifully mussed up and with a slight glow to her face that screams sex. And, hell, if that thought doesn't make my chest puff out with some sort of male pride. Her bedhead is tamed into a messy bun, she's make-up free and wearing last night's dress, all while sitting in the middle of a busy diner, surrounded by Sunday churchgoers and her massive family.

She's still the most gorgeous woman in the room.

I come from a larger family, growing up with three siblings, but I don't remember it being as noisy as it is with the Summer group all vying to speak over the person sitting next to them. And the laughter. I've never seen so many bright smiles and heard so much jovial laughter in my life.

I like it. A lot.

"Sorry that this is happening. My family doesn't quite understand the idea of boundaries. You shouldn't have been subjected to the early wake-up call or interrogation." Jaime sets her hand down on my thigh as she speaks, not close enough to be suggestive, but close enough to cause a rise in my pants.

"Don't worry about it, beautiful. Your family is great. They care about you a lot," I remind her, thankful that she has such a big, loving family.

"Is this your first run-in with the family?" Josh asks on my left side. I've visited with him off and on throughout breakfast, and I've discovered I like the young banker.

"Well, as a whole, yes, though I met Emma and Orval last week."

Josh must pick up on my facial expression because he laughs quietly, as to not draw attention from the rest of the table. "Oh, I remember my first run-in with them. I'm pretty sure Orval slipped a condom in my coat pocket."

"I'd believe it. He asked me about protection that first night, too."

"Crazy ol' man," Josh mumbles with laughter in his eyes as we both glance across the table where Orval is feeding Emma eggs from his fork.

The look the oldest member of the family gives his wife is full of love and causes a hitch in my breath. I realize that I want that. Someday? Now? The sooner the better if you ask me, but I'm definitely ready for that all-consuming, powerful love those two have shared for decades.

And I might want that with Jaime.

That thought would usually cause me to laugh uncomfortably, but not today. Today, I relish in the idea of becoming something more, something great with her. I feel it in my soul that she's special, and I plan to take full advantage of discovering the depth of the connection.

"He's great," I tell Josh with a hidden grin.

"So, Jaime, are you and Ryan, like, dating now?" AJ asks from across the table.

I feel Jaime tense beside me, her hand clenching my leg where she's left it resting for the last several minutes.

"Of course they're dating, now. A girl doesn't bed a man like that and then let him slip through her fingers. I mean, look at her! She's glowing in that post-sex way that I always get with Grandpa." Gasps are heard on both sides of the table.

"We're all so glad to see you out and living your life again, Jaime. Especially with one who makes you scream 'Oh God' with a house full of family. That must be some trouser snake he's carrying," Emma chimes in with a wink.

I don't have time to let mortification settle in that Emma just referred to my penis as a trouser snake. My focus is pulled to Jaime. I can feel her retreating away from me immediately, and it only gets worse as the breakfast winds down. She sits beside me, ramrod straight, but appears miles away, lost in thought. I wish I could see what's going on in that beautiful little head of hers, but at the same time, I'm kinda glad I can't. I probably won't like it.

When it's time to leave, I attempt to contribute towards the bill, but Jaime's dad won't hear of it. Instead, I drop a few extra bills on the table for the tip, and escort Jaime outside. She hugs each of her sisters, as well as her dad and grandparents, before stepping silently towards my truck, yet to say anything to me.

The ride back to my place is quiet, and not in a comfortable sense. Something happened between the blueberry waffles and now, that has caused her to withdraw from me. We went from playful and touching to distant and apprehensive in a matter of minutes, and I don't like it.

Not one bit.

Jaime

11

How in the world do we go from light and casual to labels and relationships?

That's exactly what happened in a matter of moments at breakfast. One minute I'm sitting down, my hand comfortably resting on Ryan's leg, when one of my sisters brings up dating. I know AJ meant no harm in asking her blasé question, but it struck a nerve and rocked me to the core.

See, this is why I didn't want to date. I'm not ready to think about anything more than a few casual dates. And *that* is different than dating. At least it is to me. I'm all about maybe having a little fun with Ryan, because he is that–fun. He proved that over and over again last night. I have a great time with him, and if I wanted to, I might even be weak enough to admit I feel the chemistry he keeps referring to. But the fact is, I'm just not ready for anything serious.

Clearly, it's time to nip this whole pre-relationship thing in the bud.

Cut my losses, and all that.

Get out while I still have possession of my heart.

Pulling into the driveway, Ryan cuts the engine and comes around to the passenger side. Still, without saying a word, he places his hand on my lower back and steers me towards his front door.

"I should go," I whisper, averting my eyes, before we get to the front door.

Ryan's hand stills just before his key reaches the doorknob. "Jaime -" he starts as he turns to face me.

I don't let him get any further. "I had a great time last night," I start, retreating just a few steps backwards. "Thank you for having me over for dinner last night. And…the other…thing."

One eyebrow shoots heavenward "Thing?" he asks, a slight smirk playing on the corners of his lips.

"You know what I meant," I mumble, ready to cut tail and run.

My breathing is shallow and my pulse beating a steady stream of Morse Code against my throat. My heart is telling me to run before Ryan has the chance to destroy it like a paper shredder, but my body is the ultimate traitor, pulling me back towards Ryan.

As Ryan's long legs eat up the porch between us, I sway in his direction, drawn by some sort of magical pull that only he seems to possess. Strong arms wrap around me, and I don't fight it. I'm helpless against it.

My hand holds a slight tremor as Ryan links his fingers around mine. Deep brown eyes focus entirely on me, burning into my soul with their honesty and hunger. "I know this is new and terrifying, but I'm not letting you push me away. I get that you're scared, and that's okay. I wasn't looking for anything right now either, but shit happens. It did happen. I met you, and you're the best thing to happen to me in a long damn time."

Oxygen evaporates completely from the air. As if he could read my mind, Ryan confirms that he is ready to go to battle against every insecurity and demon I have. My fear of falling for the wrong guy, only to get my heart broken again, is put right out there on a silver platter. What more, Ryan seems unfazed by his revelation. Instead, he's taking it as a challenge, a minor detail to overcome.

"So here's the deal: I'm going to let you get into your car and head home. I'm going to give you a little space to sort through the crap you're dealing with in that beautiful head of yours. But know this: I'm not going anywhere. I will fight for you-*for us*-because I believe *this* -" he gestures between the two of us, "is worth fighting for. Already I know it. I feel it. I believe deep down at the bottom of my soul that what we have is the start of something special. That we are worth it, and I'm ready to find out if that feeling is right."

Ryan places a firm kiss on my lips before stepping back, allowing me the space to leave. I'm breathless-from the kiss *and* from his declaration-as I make my way to my car. Dropping into the front seat, my legs quiver and my hand trembles as I attempt to slide my key into the ignition. After the third try, I finally hit pay dirt, and my Honda fires up.

I feel Ryan's eyes on me as I back out of his driveway and pull onto the street. Before shifting to drive, I risk a glance back up to the porch. Ryan is standing there, his hands resting on the handrail. I almost throw the car in drive and pull back in the driveway.

Almost.

Instead, I slowly release the break and move forward. Ryan watches me, our eyes locked on each other until I'm forced to look ahead to the road. Even then, I still couldn't miss the grin that consumed his full lips a split second before I turned away.

It's that grin that keeps me company on my drive home. That smile and those eyes and that incredible body that won't quit. But as I pull into my own driveway, it's his words that finally cause my body to sag in defeat. Because if I've learned anything about Ryan Elson, it's that he won't let this go-he won't let *me* go. At least not yet.

Oh, he'll be back. He'll give me the space I need, but then he'll come for me. You can bet on it, because he wants me. I see it in his eyes and feel it in his touch. We're two separate magnets pulled together by a natural force. It's absolute. Final.

Closing my eyes in resignation, I realize one thing; I'm not strong enough to fight it.

⊁)(⊁

"What do you say to coming over and watching a movie Friday night?" Payton asks while we tidy up the worktable the following Wednesday afternoon.

I haven't heard from Ryan yet, but I know his radio silence won't last much longer. He offered to give me space so that I could work out my concerns when it comes to him and dating. I go from wanting to run as fast and as far away as I possibly can in the opposite direction to willing to jump in with both feet, and every possibility in between. I've been over this every which way in the last three days numerous times, but I keep coming back to the same thing every time: I want him.

That doesn't mean that I'm not scared to death of getting hurt again, which is why I'm willing to date Ryan casually. Keep it informal, and keep my heart safe. A few friendly dinners, followed by more mind-blowing sex. Walk away when it starts getting personal. Easy peasy.

"Um, yeah, that sounds good. I'll bring the popcorn and beer. You get the pizza," I tell my older sister as I grab my purse.

"Have you heard from him?" she asks, standing just over my shoulder.

"Not yet." But I will. I know it. "I'm heading home to help Grandma peel peaches for pies. She says she has to make them tonight because it's the only night she's not watching *Sex And The City* reruns. How about you? Any big plans for this evening?"

"Wish I could join you, but I have an appointment with McIntire and Associates. I guess Roy is retiring and he's assigning someone else my business taxes. I have to meet them tonight to go over the second quarter." Snapping her fingers, she adds, "Which reminds me, I need to print off a profits and losses worksheet."

Absently, Payton starts to make a list on a loose piece of scratch paper.

Payton has occasionally complained about the stresses and headaches associated with being a business owner. Being single is for the best, or so she says. She's not pulled between running her business and raising a family. There's no guilt when she's required to work late and no closing down the shop when the kids are sick.

Even though I see her resolve to her single ways, I can tell there's something else there. Something that she keeps buried deep.

Longing.

She often changes the subject when marriage and kids are brought up, but I can see it. Maybe it's because of my own disastrous relationship that I can so clearly see Pay's mask that she keeps firmly locked in place so that no one can see her pain. Sure, I've brought it up before, but she refuses to talk about it. I won't push her on it, though. At least not yet. When she's ready to talk or explore a relationship, then I'll be there for her, eager to discuss all the details. Until then, I'll wait.

Stepping out through the back door, I'm not surprised when I find Ryan waiting for me at my car. He's carrying a handful of wildflowers in one hand, and there's no mistaking the appraising gleam in his eyes.

"Hi." He hands me the small grouping of flowers, a small smile crossing his full lips.

"Hi," I mimic. "Thank you."

"I just happened to be coming into town from a job site when I came upon these growing alongside the road. My truck stopped all on its own."

"All on its own, huh? And I suppose you had no control over yourself as you got out and picked them?" I ask, a playful twinkle in my eyes that matches his.

"No control whatsoever. But that's nothing new. I find I have absolutely no control over myself when it comes to you."

Ryan steps closer, invading my personal space. He smells like wood and fresh air mixed with a little sweat. Wearing a worn t-shirt and a dirty pair of jeans, he's almost edible in that 'I want to throw you down on the hood of my car and ravish your body' way.

Seriously? Clearly, I've been hanging around Grandma too much.

"Sounds like a personal problem. I hear they make little pills for problems like that," I retort, smiling sweetly.

Ryan's hearty laugh fills the air, his brown eyes twinkling with amusement. Zeroing in on my lips, he steps even closer. His body is almost touching mine, his breath fanning across my forehead.

"Oh no, sweetheart. That's not the problem I have. In fact, my problem is the complete opposite of that. I have positively no problem with not being able to *rise* for the occasion. In fact, the mere thought of you causes things to stand up and take notice. My body is humming and hard for you all the time. Every minute of every day. Hard. For. You."

Just like that, the air around us changes. It sizzles and crackles with a sexually-charged current. Want zips through my body and lands at the junction of my legs. I can feel my body responding, wetness soaking my panties.

"And I know you want me too. I see it in your eyes, Jaime. I feel it in the way your touch sears my skin. My question to you is are you willing to explore that feeling? I'm not talking about jumping into bed, though that thought sounds pretty damn good right now. I'm talking about dating. I'm talking about dinner and movies and the occasional family outing. We'll take this as slow as you need to, but I'm ready and I'm not going anywhere. I. Want. You."

Ryan punctuates those words with a kiss. A consuming, bruising kiss that leaves me weak in the knees and yearning for the privacy of a bedroom. Gripping the back of his shirt, I hold on for dear life as his tongue sweeps across the seam of my lips. I open my mouth moments before his tongue plunges inside. His lips devour me, his mouth commanda me. It's a delirious feeling to be so consumed that you have no control over your own actions.

A moan erupts from deep in his throat when I suck on his tongue. Ryan pulls me closer yet, his hands caressing my back, my neck.

Somewhere in the distance, a horn sounds, pulling me from the lust-induced spell he has me under. I startle, jumping back a fraction of an inch, unable to pull away since Ryan's hands are wrapped tightly around me.

"Tell me you feel it, Jaime." His words are husky, his eyes glazed with molten desire.

"I feel it." My words are breathless and trembling.

"Will you trust me? Will you give us a chance? You set the pace. You set the boundaries. You are in control here. Just promise me you'll try."

I want to hesitate. I want to argue with myself about why this is the worst idea in the history of all ideas, but I can't. Because at the end of the day, Ryan's right. This feels right. *He* feels right. He and I together. And sure that's scary as hell, and it'll probably result in me left heartbroken, but the alternative seems unimaginable. *Not* being with Ryan seems completely impossible.

So I don't hesitate. I nod my head, confirming what he already feels, what he hopes.

"I'll try."

And with those two words, I delve into my first relationship since my broken engagement. I willingly open myself up to the pain and suffering that is sure to come when this relationship ends. I'm risking it all.

And I'm terrified.

XX

"Can you get the door?" Payton hollers from the kitchen when a light knock sounds at her apartment door.

After glancing through the peephole, I throw the lock and grant entrance to Abby. Reaching out, I take the bag of chips teetering atop a bowl of something warm she's carrying with potholders.

"Thanks," she says quietly as she steps inside.

"What did you bring?" I ask, inhaling the aroma of melted cheese with a hint of pepper.

"Jalapeno popper dip. I found the recipe in one of Levi's magazines," she states casually as we slip into the kitchen to join Payton.

Levi is Abby's best friend, and, much like her twin sister, they're as different as night and day. Levi is funny, outgoing, and gorgeous, while Abby is quiet, shy, and conservative. They've always made the oddest pairing, but their friendship has withstood all other relationships to date. And when I say relationships, I mean his. I've never known Abby to really date. Probably because she's secretly in love with her best friend. Levi, on the other hand, seems to have a revolving front door with an endless stream of eager ladies willing to keep him company.

"Smells delicious," Payton says as she finishes blending mango margaritas.

"I've been told it's amazing. I left half a bowl with Levi, and I think he had most of it gone before I was out the door."

"Levi, huh?" Payton waggles her eyebrows at our littlest sister.

"Knock it off," she chastises with a fierce blush. "We're just friends and you know it."

"That's what you keep saying," Payton adds in a singsong voice.

Fortunately for Abby, she's saved from further scrutiny by the ringing of the doorbell. "Pizza's here!" Payton yells before taking off for the door.

Five minutes later, we're all sitting on the floor around the coffee table, stuffing our faces with cheese and sausage pizza, spicy jalapeno dip, and margaritas. Payton started *The Italian Job* when we sat down, but none of us pay Mark Wahlberg any attention.

"So I take it you and Ryan are an item now? For two days, you've had this dreamy look on your face every time your phone chimed with a text message. It's nauseatingly sweet," Payton says before taking a bite of her slice of pizza.

"I guess," I mumble, refusing to make eye contact. All day Thursday Payton teased me about the make-out session in the parking lot. Apparently, she walked by the back window when heading to her office and witnessed our little PDA episode.

"You guess?" Abby asks, her nose scrunching up in question.

"I mean, yes. We're dating, but we're taking it slow."

"Slow," Payton snorts. "If eating each other's faces off in public is taking it slow, I don't want to know what happens when you guys get serious."

"We won't get serious," I add, a little too quickly.

"It's okay if you do," Abby replies. "Not every relationship is going to end in failure, Jaime. Maybe Ryan is *the one*."

Air catches in my throat and refuses to dislodge as I think about *the one*. "Maybe," I say, appeasing my sister. Abby still believes in love at first sight, your forever love, and all that jazz. I believe that love hurts and is at the root of your worst pain. Clearly we're on opposite sides of the spectrum.

"What about you, Abs? Anyone special you're into?" Payton asks, but we already know the answer to her question.

"No."

"You know, Abs, the delivery driver for Wholesale Flowers just broke up with his girlfriend. He's cute and he's in town two days a week. I bet I could arrange for you to have coffee or lunch with him while he's here," Payton offers with a mouth full of pizza.

"No!" Abby's usually soft voice is loud and filled with urgency. Her eyes appear scared, as if she's afraid of being set up.

"Abby," I start, dropping my voice to a soothing, motherly tone. "I know you've been waiting around for Levi, but maybe it's time to move on. I mean, you guys have been friends for a decade and he hasn't shown you he's interested in anything more than your friendship, right? As much as you want it, he's just not on the same page as you."

Abby's eyes drop to her lap and refuse to look up. But if the glistening in them were any indication, I'd say she's on the verge of tears. She's still for several moments before glancing up at me, and that's when I see it. Confirmation of her tears. Slowly, she nods her head.

"Then, go have coffee with this guy. What could it hurt? If anything, maybe it'll make Levi jealous and give him the kick in the pants he needs," Payton adds.

Just when I think she's not going to acknowledge us, Abby says, "I'll think about it."

I finish off my plate before turning focus on the oldest Summer sister. "What about you, Pay? Why aren't you dating anyone?"

Payton squeaks out a noise while rolling her eyes. "Puh-lease. Who am I going to date in this town? All of the good ones are married, taken, gay, or there's a reason why they're still single. Besides, I'm not interested yet. I have Blossoms and Blooms, and that takes all of my free time."

"But even you need a night out every once in a while. Why don't you have coffee with the flower guy?" Abby asks.

"Besides the fact that he's probably six years my junior? I'm just not interested in him."

"Well, then who are you interested in? If not him, then who?"

"No one." Payton tries to act all casual, but I catch the way she fidgets with her hands. There's someone, she just won't say. I'll definitely have to keep my eyes open for signs of someone in her life.

When the closing credits start to roll, Abby and I each help Payton pick up her apartment and wash the dishes. We work in unison, as if we've each done this a thousand times before. And, truthfully, we have. We're a close bunch, spending a lot of our free time together.

I wonder how much free time I'll have now that I'm dating (albeit taking everything very slowly) Ryan?

That thought accompanies me on my drive home. It's what I think about as I get ready for bed. And it's definitely the first thing on my mind when I check my phone and find a text message from the man in question.

> **Ryan:** Hope you had fun with your sisters. Thinking about u. Call u tomorrow.

I smile at my phone, unable to stop it. He sent that message thirty minutes ago. Even though it's barely ten o'clock, I still type out a reply.

Me: It was fun. Thinking of you too. Night.

My phone isn't even down on my nightstand when it chimes.

Ryan: Thinking of me how? Am I naked in your thoughts?

Well he wasn't, but he is now. Before I can reply, my phone chimes again.

Ryan: 'Cause I'll b honest, you're naked in my thoughts right now.

I decide to take a walk on the flirty side.

Me: Naked in your thoughts AND naked in bed. Coincidence.

Ryan: You're naked? Now? Show me.

And because I can't help it, I snap a quick picture of my bare knee and hit send. Within ten seconds, I have a reply.

Ryan: Not funny. Though your knee is hot, I thought I'd get a glimpse at something a little higher up on your body.

Me: Like this? I ask as I attach a picture of my shoulder.

Ryan: Your shoulder is fucking hot. It makes me want to run my tongue along your collarbone and watch goosebumps appear on your delicious skin.

And just like that, the temperature rose about fifty degrees in the room.

Ryan: I think you should show me your shoulder tomorrow night. 6pm. I'll pick you up for dinner. Pack a bag but only for clothes the next day. And make sure you tell your fam where you're gonna b. Don't want National Guard showing up. ;)

My fingers tremble slightly as they hover over my phone. I'm a fraction of a second away from saying screw it and inviting him over now. Images of Ryan licking my shoulder, then blazing a trail southbound, flitter through my forethoughts. It's enough to make me wiggle a bit in bed, trying to relieve the sudden pressure between my legs.

Ryan: Is that a yes?

Me: That's a yes.

Ryan: See you tomorrow, beautiful. Night.

Me: Good night, Ryan.

I toss and turn for the better part of an hour, unable to find a comfortable position. Ryan's delicious mouth chases my thoughts and wreaks havoc on my lady parts. He's the ultimate temptation, and it's proving quickly that I'm unable to resist him. Finally, I relax enough to fall asleep.

And dream of Ryan.

Ryan

Occasionally, we have to work a Saturday. With Orlando out for the unforeseen future, I've been filling in more as needed at the job site. Sure, I could hire another guy to fill the vacancy, especially with the Hazelton job on the brink of breaking ground, but it doesn't feel right. Not to Orlando and not to the poor guy who'd probably be gone as soon as he returned.

The problem with filling in is that I'm left with barely any time for the office side of the business. I'd prefer swinging a hammer or running a table saw to signing papers and talking to suppliers on the phone all day, but if I neglect the office side, I find myself up shit creek without a paddle.

Mary helps. Mary helps a lot. Shit, there are days I wonder if I'd even have a business left if not for her. This week has been one of those times. Without Orlando, I'm onsite all day long, which is why I worked at the office until almost ten last night. Mary left me several piles of paperwork to sign. Contracts, bids, purchase orders, supplier and material lists, it was all waiting for me on my desk. Five hours it took me to comb through all the things I'd neglected during the week. Five hours of busy work that helped kill time until I could text Jaime.

She had a pizza night with a few of her sisters last night. That's one of the things I admire about her. She's super close to her family. Even though I have three siblings of my own, we've all drifted in our adult lives. I talk to my mom on the phone at least once a week, and receive texts or phone calls from my siblings when they can be squeezed in, but nowhere near the steady communication that the Summer family has.

I'm actually a bit envious. They're close. Sometimes, a little too close, but that's not always a bad thing. As long as they know where to draw the line between personal and complete invasion of privacy. So far I haven't seen anything to get worried about. Unless we're talking about Emma. Something tells me that woman doesn't know the meaning of *privacy*.

And what is up with Grandpa Orval? I haven't had someone offer me protection this much since I was sixteen and getting ready to take Kim Kohlson to the homecoming dance.

I can't help but chuckle as I load up the job trailer with the job tools. One of my first purchases for the business was a large enclosed trailer, which works perfectly to haul tools and equipment from one job site to another. It's a beautiful, sunny mid-June afternoon, and it looks like the rest of the weekend should be much of the same.

I've had little time to plan my date for tonight with Jaime. When she replied to my text last night accepting my invitation, I was giddy with excitement. I couldn't wipe the smile off my face if I tried, and it took me a while to fall asleep. I was excited to see her again, and even more excited at the prospect of her joining me in bed. It was a long, uncomfortable night to say the least.

After securing the trailer and waving goodbye to my guys, I jump in my truck and head for home. I've got just enough time to take a shower before I head over to her house. Plans for this evening will have to be made on the fly, but that's all right. As long as she's by my side, I don't give a shit what we do. Hell, maybe I'll take her to see the new chick flick at the cinema uptown. Women love that stuff, right?

First thing I notice when I pull into my half of the driveway is Mrs. Hanson out front, squatting on the ground and pulling weeds in the flower garden. How a woman who's eighty still gets up and down so agilely as she does is beyond me. There are days where my bones creak and pop just getting out of bed. My muscles scream in protest as I bend over to lace my boots. In my line of work, I'm hard on my body, and more often than not, I feel all of her eighty years opposed to my own thirty-two.

"I'm planning to mow tomorrow," I tell her as I slip out of my truck and walk around to where our dual doors meet at the garden she's pruning.

"That's fine, child. I'm just taking care of a few pesky weeds."

"I could get those for you, you know," I offer, watching her wrinkled hand wipe at her forehead, leaving behind a smudge of dirt.

"Tsk tsk, boy. This is my favorite part of the day. Besides, not only are you working more hours, but you have a lady friend to entertain." She tries to mask her smile, but she fails miserably.

Why am I not surprised that Mrs. Hanson would know about Jaime. "Dare I ask how you know about my lady friend?" I ask, setting my bag on the porch before dropping down to sit on the step beside her.

"Besides the fact that you haven't been very subtle when sniffing around for information about Miss Jaime Summer, I can't ignore the fact that her entire family showed up here bright and early, looking for her last weekend when she failed to come home Saturday night."

My eyebrow raises in question.

"What? I was on my way to church, and I ran into Orval in the driveway."

"Sure. You probably had a glass against the wall."

"No need for that, son. These walls aren't as thick as you'd probably hoped. I was well aware you were entertaining."

Flames shoot up my face and I look down. "Well, that's embarrassing."

"From what I heard, you have nothing to be embarrassed about," she says, laughter oozing from each word.

I shake my head and finally glance up, meeting her aged blue eyes. "I like her. A lot."

"I can tell. She's different than the other one."

I know exactly who Mrs. Hanson is talking about. When I moved to Jupiter Bay, Sara moved in with me for a short period of time. Of course, spending her entire life here, Mrs. H was well acquainted with the woman I dated. After the relationship ended for good, she finally told me exactly what she thought of Sara Sullivan. I believe her exact words were spoiled, selfish, and gold digging.

"She's very different than Sara. I never really saw myself settling down with Sara. I hate to admit, but she was convenient. But Jaime? I see forever, and I don't even know her. Isn't that crazy?"

"Love *is* crazy, child. The best kind of crazy. It makes you want to dance in the rain and scream from the mountaintops. Love makes you feel like flying, even when you have no wings. But, it's also terrifying. I promise you that when you find the right love–*your true love*–there's nothing else like it in the world. Love is the greatest feeling of all. It's the ultimate gift."

"Who said anything about love?" I ask, giving her a slight smile.

"I might be eighty, but my eyesight is twenty-twenty. I see it in your eyes when you speak of her. You might not be completely there yet, but it's coming. I feel it."

I find myself staring across the flower garden at my friend. She's right that I'm nowhere near ready to talk about those kinds of feelings, but I'm also not scared of them. For the first time in my life, I'm not scoffing at the prospect of falling in love the way Jaime is. I feel it deep in my soul. There's something there– something powerful and infinite. If or when it comes to that, I know I'll have to tread lightly or risk running her off for good.

"On that note," I say as I stand up and stretch. "I have a date with a beautiful woman this evening so I better hit the shower. And you should probably be warned, there could be entertaining later this evening."

"I'll leave my television on when I go to bed." Her soft chuckles follow me as I walk up the stairs and slip inside to get ready for the evening.

I'm probably more nervous tonight than I was two weeks ago when I pulled into this very same driveway. Last time, little did I know that I'd be introduced to some of the craziest grandparents known to man.

The breeze off the Bay is cool tonight, cloud coverage for as far as the eye can see. My plan is to take her to the small barbeque joint down by the docks, followed by that movie they've been promoting heavily on television. It's the latest Nicholas Sparks book to be turned into a big screen movie, and after my conversation with Jaime last weekend, I think she'd enjoy seeing it.

Wiping my clammy hands off on my dark jeans, I grab a lightweight jacket from the passenger seat and throw it on over my dark t-shirt. Fortunately, I found a few new shirts in the back of my closet that have never made it to work yet. Once they do, they're stained up or full of holes even after the first day of wearing them on the job.

Stepping up on the porch, I knock on the screen door. Orval comes to the door with a wide smile. "Heya, Ryan. Come on in," he says while holding open the door. "Your girl's just finishing up upstairs. She'll be along in a few minutes."

"Great." I shove my hands in my pockets and glance towards the stairwell. Just knowing that she's up there, getting ready, has my pants suddenly too small. I picture her naked except for some barely-there panties and maybe a lace bra.

"How ya been?" he asks, pulling my attention away from the walking wet dream upstairs.

"Good. Staying busy at work with more projects on the horizon. You?"

"Oh, I'm getting by. This arthritis is acting up in my wrist again," he says, flexing his wrist a few times. "Damn stuff makes it hard to make a fist." His demonstration is tight with jerky movements and causes him to grimace.

"I'm sorry to hear that. My grandma had arthritis in her knees. It made it difficult for her to walk at times."

"Can you imagine the wrist? It makes it hard to grip the tiger in your pants."

He says it so matter-of-factly that I almost miss his statement. Almost.

"Excuse me?" I ask, instantly regretting it as soon as the words spill from my lips.

"Oh yeah. It's hard to beat the bishop when it flares up. Emma loves to watch, you know." Then he elbows me in the chest.

"No. I...can't...just no," I stutter, wishing aliens would beam me up to their spaceship or a piece of the ceiling would fall on my head, causing temporary amnesia. Anything to get me out of my current situation.

"There she is," Orval sings.

My attention is pulled back to that staircase as Jaime makes her way towards me. She's wearing sexy jeans that hug her sweet curves, a pink loose top with see-through sleeves, and black ankle boots that I suddenly wish were wrapped around my neck. Her hair is swept to one side, exposing the long column of her neck. I want to lick every inch, every curve of that enticing section of skin.

And I won't stop there. I want to lick everywhere.

She's breathtaking every time I see her, and tonight is no exception. Blood zings, my body hums, and a desperate need to take her consumes me. Jaime has quickly become my obsession. She's my one desire, my greatest treasure.

Jaime must recognize the heat blazing in my eyes because hers suddenly widen, her breathing shallow. My pants are so damn tight that surely my legs will be numb any moment from lack of blood flow. Right now, every bit of blood my body possesses is in one concentrated location. It's horribly painful, but I'm unable to adjust myself because I'm trapped by the fierceness in her eyes. She looks like she wants to eat me for dinner and still come back for seconds.

I'd be all for that. In fact, I vow to make that happen.

As soon as possible.

"Looks like someone's a little excited," Emma whispers to Orval, yet she's loud enough that everyone within a two-mile radius probably heard.

"It's all right, boy. I still get wood every time my Emmy comes into the room."

Jaime makes a sound, which is a cross between a gasp and a choke. I, on the other hand, am stunned silent. The wood I was sporting a few moments ago is shriveling up so tightly that it might never reach its full potential again.

"Dear God, please make it stop," Jaime mumbles heavenward as she reaches me. "Ready?"

Taking her tight grimace as my cue, I reach for her hand and pull her towards the door. Before we breach the threshold, we throw quick goodbyes over our shoulders and escape into the night.

The tension and humiliation of the scene back at Jaime's place melts away as soon as I have her inside of my truck. Her scent permeates the cab, sending my blood flowing once more. The smile she offers me is small at first, hesitant almost.

"I'm sorry about them. God, they're so embarrassing."

"Serves me right for getting hard in their presence. I was pretty much asking to be ridiculed. But I can't help it. That's what happens every time I see you, every time I think about you."

"Yeah?" she asks, a small smile playing on her lips, a hint of bashfulness coloring her cheeks.

"Yeah."

And because she's so close, I pull her towards me and meet her in the middle of the truck cab. Her lips are warm and soft, perfect for kissing. My tongue teases the seam of her mouth, eager to slide inside and taste her. It's been one very long week, and I feel like an addict stealing his first taste of that succulent high his body craves.

"We should just skip dinner and go straight to desert," she suggests, nipping at my lips with her teeth.

In desperate need of applying the brakes before I throw down in the middle of her driveway, I pull back slightly so I can gaze into her lust-filled eyes. Honestly, that doesn't help. Her eyes are greedy and filled with dirty little promises. I almost give in to the desire to drive straight to my place and forego our dinner plans.

But I can't do it.

This is only our third date. I'm not the type of man who bypasses the date part of the evening and goes straight to the bedroom part. Though, if I were one of those guys, this would definitely be the time.

No, Jaime deserves to be treated fairly and like a lady. She deserves flowers and dinners and movies. She deserves romance, and I'll be damned if she isn't going to get it. The guy before me didn't appreciate her enough to give her those things, and that pains me.

Instead of ripping off her clothes, I opt to return to my half of the truck and adjust my very uncomfortable pants. When I glance back over, her face reads of shock and maybe a little disappointment.

Leaning back over and taking her hand, I say, "I would love nothing more than to take you home and ravish you for hours–days. But I won't do that yet. I promised you dinner and a movie, and I'm going to deliver. Even if I have to watch Chris Hemsworth on that screen while suffering from the biggest case of blue balls this side of the Atlantic. I'm determined to give you the date you deserve."

Her sweet laughter fills my truck. "I think if you manage to stay the course of this date the entire night, well, then you would earn yourself a reward." Her eyes are infused with mischief and excitement, which does nothing to defuse the situation in my pants.

"Reward?" I ask, playing along.

"Mmhmmmmmm," she says, which comes out more like a moan.

"I'm listening."

"Well, let's just say that I'm wearing something very special for you. If you're a good boy, I'll let you unwrap it. Like a present."

My eyes remain locked on hers, my body short-circuiting from the picture she painted in my mind. Red? Black? White? Lace? Satin? Silk? Thongs? Boy cut? Commando? The possibilities are endless, and I realize right then and there that I've officially met my match. I'm ready to wave the white flag, throw in the towel. I'm completely gone over a pair of gorgeous green eyes and pouty, pink lips.

"I'm afraid my blue balls situation has reached Defcon Five."

"That sounds bad," she says, rubbing my thigh. "We should just head back to your place so that you're not uncomfortable all. Night. Long."

Game.

Set.

Match.

Jaime

13

The way Ryan peels out of the driveway is reflective of that of a NASCAR driver making a pit stop. I sit over on my half of the truck trying not to distract him further, even though I'd love to reach over and run an appreciative hand up his rock hard thigh. The poor guy is already drunk on lust and quite possibly only thinking with the little head. The last thing I need to do is tease him further, distracting him from the main task at hand: Driving us back to his place, as quickly as possible, without causing an accident.

His jaw is tight, his lips thin. If I hadn't witnessed the transformation from polite Ryan to I want to rip your clothes off in less than one second Ryan, I wouldn't have believed I was capable of provoking a reaction in a man that quickly. He looks ticked off, but I know that's not the case. This man has the look of raw want and pure desire. Lord knows Gavin never responded to my mere presence like that, let alone made me feel like my kisses drove him wild.

Ryan reaches over and takes my hand. There's a slight tremble, but I can't tell if it's his or mine.

"I just need to touch you right now, and this is probably the safest way," he whispers, his voice hoarse and edgy.

"I can't wait for you to touch me," I state boldly.

He takes his eyes off the road for just a moment. They're wild and round, his jaw ticks with strain. I've never witnessed another human so close to out of control. He's teetering on a thin line, leaning heavily towards the side of rampant. Just one little nudge could cause this entire train to derail, our worlds to crash into one another, resulting in total annihilation.

It's a sight I can't wait to see, when Ryan loses all control.

I shouldn't push…but I will.

"You know," I start, loosening my seatbelt enough so that I can turn and face him. Leaning forward, I inhale the scent of his soap. He smells all clean and woodsy. Intoxicating. When my lips are just a breath away from his ear, I go for the kill. "I'm not wearing any panties."

And just like that, the levee breaks. The control he's been trying so hard to regain snaps like a toothpick. Ryan inhales deeply and swerves into the gravel alongside the road, but is easily able to regain control of the truck. He wasn't going fast enough to cause an accident, but the motion sends my body swaying towards the dash.

Quickly, Ryan pulls onto a gravel access road for a field. The path runs between Mr. Gerard's bean field and his timber, and seals us off from the main road. No one will be out on this path this evening, but by the look in Ryan's eyes, I don't think he cares much. His thoughts appear singular. Namely, me.

Before he even throws the truck into park, he's reaching for me. My seatbelt is removed and I'm hoisted from my own seat and pulled onto his lap. Hungry lips crash into mine in a frenzy of desire, a need to taste and savor. His tongue is urgent and sinful as it probes my mouth over and over again, mimicking the act that our bodies crave.

My hands are pulling at his shirt until I feel the warm, hard flesh of his abdomen beneath my fingertips. God, how I love the way this man feels. He's hard in all the right places, and right now, he's definitely hard in one specific place.

"I need to feel you. Right. Now." His words are urgent as he grips the bottom of my shirt and pulls it over my head in one swift motion.

We're each clutching at any clothes we can, a frenzy of grabby hands hell-bent on shedding the other of all offending clothing. I have no clue how it happened in the position we're in, but before I know it we're both naked. Ryan's erection is pressed firmly into my backside, my body wet and ready.

"Condom," he bites out, trying to grab his discarded jeans.

I reach his pants first and retrieve his wallet. Ryan doesn't say anything; just watches with hungry eyes as I find the packet inside and rip it open. Never having been brazen enough to do this, I maneuver myself so that I'm squatting beside him on the bench seat. Ryan's breathing comes in short little pants and his eyes roll back in his head as I grip the base of his cock and place the condom at the head. I've seen this done before, but am still a bit uncertain how it actually works.

"Pinch the head of the condom and slide it down gently," he instructs as if reading my thoughts.

I do as he instructs, loving the way his velvety steel length slides through my fingers. He's panting as I slide the condom all the way to the base of his cock. My hands glide easily up and down his erection. Ryan thrusts upward into the tightness I'm creating with my hand.

"Now," he growls, pulling me back towards him.

He manages to move his seat back, giving me as much room between him and the steering wheel as he can manage. My right leg is pinched between his outer thigh and the door, but the discomfort is the least of my concerns. Right now, I'm bracing myself with my hands against his shoulders, hovering over his cock.

"I'm sorry, baby. This is gonna be quick. I promise to do better next time," he grunts, gripping my hips.

"Please hurry," I plea, not caring about finesse or anything other than having him inside of me.

With one long thrust, Ryan pushes upward at the same time he brings me down on him. The impact steals my breath and causes the loudest moan to spill from my lips.

"Holy shit fuck damn," Ryan whispers before pushing me up and pulling me back down hard.

His pace is hard, but so is mine. I move up his shaft and slam back down, feeling myself stretch around him as he buries himself as deep as he possibly can. After each thrust, I grind myself against the base, each time pushing me closer to release. My clit throbs as I move my body in a way to maximize friction against it.

"You feel so fucking amazing," he groans as I continue to swirl my hips with him fully seated inside of me. "Shit, you keep doing that and I'm going to lose it."

"I like this out of control side of you," I confess.

Ignoring the burning in my legs, I lift myself up once more and slam down hard. Ryan grips my hips, trying to hang on to the last sliver of control he has. Unfortunately, now isn't the time for it. I continue to move, up and down, up and down, the tip of his cock nudging my cervix. I feel my insides tightening around him, gripping and pulling him in as far as I can get him. And yet it's not close enough.

My body is a live wire as my orgasm starts at my toes and rips through my entire body. I convulse around him, screaming his name over and over again, as I continue to move along with him. His cock thickens even more and he grips my hips painfully tight just before his own orgasm claims him.

"Jaime," he groans as he thrusts upward one final time before stilling and sagging in the seat.

I'm boneless, weightless, as I fall forward, my sweaty body molding to his. Our chests heave and our labored breathing mixes as we both sit still, neither of us able to move. Ryan is still fully seated inside of me, and it's the most comfortable and natural feeling in the world. It's also a thought I ignore as I place open-mouthed kisses along his smooth jaw and neck.

"Jeezus, are you trying to kill me?"

"Absolutely not. If I killed you, then we wouldn't be able to do that again in a bit."

Miraculously, I feel him thickening once more inside of me. Ryan's mouth claims me as his tongue dances with mine. I savor the taste of his mouth, the feel of his hot, damp skin beneath my fingers. Keeping our eyes open and locked on each other, I give in to an amazing, earth-shattering kiss. I don't care that my ass is wedged against the steering wheel, most likely leaving a permanent impression. I don't care that my leg is numb and that I can't feel my toes. I only care about this man.

It's a startling revelation, but one I'm not able to dwell upon at the moment.

See, I was so focused on the way Ryan's kisses leave me breathless and yearning for another round that I don't notice the headlights pull up behind us. I didn't see anything until the flashlight shines through the driver's window, straight into my eyes.

Even though the light temporarily blinds me, there's no mistaking the words he says as he bellows his order through the glass.

"Show me your hands and get out of the truck."

14

Ryan

In my thirty-two years on this earth, I've never purposefully broken the law in such a manner that would warrant a visit from the police. Sure, I accidentally threw a baseball through the church window when I was twelve. I paid it back with lawn mowing. Sure, I drove through downtown blasting Nine Inch Nails while my buddy Eric car surfed on the roof. We had just seen Teen Wolf on some classic movie channel. And sure, I helped graffiti the old train trestle bridge my senior year with profanity. I also helped repaint the inside of that entire bridge afterwards as part of a community outreach program with the baseball team.

Point is: I have never seen the backseat of a cop car.

And I don't want to start now.

"Show me your hands," we're instructed for a second time by a teenage Barney Fife who's barely old enough to shave.

Jaime gasps and plasters a hand on each breast. "Oh my God!"

"I said show me your hands!" Barney says with as much authority as he can muster, yet with a hint of nervousness.

"Okay, okay, hold your horses," I holler through the window.

I glance at the woman with my cock still buried deep inside her, as the light illuminates the fear in her eyes. Her legs try to close, though with her straddling me, that makes it impossible to conceal her nakedness.

"Would you mind lowering the light? There's a lady in here," I plea, using my own hands to help camouflage Jaime's body from the direct beam of the spotlight.

"I don't think so, buckaroo. Get out of the truck now before I call for backup," he states shakily.

"All right, all right. I'm going to slip out of the truck," I tell him.

Keeping my eyes locked on Jaime, I slowly start to move her towards the passenger seat. "I'm going to slip out and talk to him. You get dressed as quickly as possible."

"But…you're naked," she whispers, her eyes wide and focused on mine.

"It'll be okay, sweetheart."

Placing a kiss on the end of her nose, I slide her over to the passenger seat and open the door. Barney's standing there, one shaky hand holding the flashlight and the other on his holstered pistol. He looks like he's about to piss his pants, and if I jumped towards him and hollered BOO, I bet he would.

"Good evening, sir," I start as I move a single hand cover my junk. "I think we have a bit of a misunderstanding here. I was just talking to my girlfriend in there," pointing over the shoulder towards my truck, "and, well, there's nothing going on here to cause alarm."

"Nothing going on?" the officer asks, his voice raising an octave. "You're standing there naked as the day you were born, and you're telling me there's nothing going on here? I've got you on two counts of indecent exposure, not to mention trespassing on private land."

"Well, with all due respect, officer, I wasn't indecent until you asked me to step outside."

Wrong thing to say.

Barney's ears turn red, and a vein starts to pulse near his temple. Even in the low light reflecting off my own naked body, I can see it. Signs lead me to believe I just pissed the deputy off.

"Put your hands behind your head and face the truck," he says, pulling his cuffs from behind his back as he gives my shoulder a gentle shove.

My mouth drops open, and I'm at a loss for words as I turn and face my work truck. My hands weave into my hair just before Barney kicks my feet apart.

This can't be happening.

"Excuse me, officer?" I hear Jaime's sweet voice moments before she flies around the front of the truck. "You can't do that."

She's fully dressed now, though her hair is slightly disheveled, assuming from where I had my hands gripped in it just a short time ago. How the hell did we get so far off course?

"Ma'am, you need to step back and place your hands on the hood of the truck," Barney says, pointing towards the front end.

"Oh my God," she mumbles just before Rent-A-Cop throws the cold metal cuffs around my wrists. "At least let him get dressed," she pleads, tears filling those gorgeous green eyes.

"Yeah, yeah, you're probably right. I don't want things...exposed...in the car. Can you help him get dressed?" he asks Jaime.

She runs around and grabs my clothes from the floorboard of my truck. There's a smile playing on her lips as she steps in front of me, refusing to make eye contact.

"I actually prefer to help get him undressed," she mumbles to herself as she grabs my boxer briefs and drops to her knees in the dirt.

I'm unable to help it, but my cock starts to thicken at the sight before me. Jaime's eyes go wide as she takes in my half-hard erection. "God, do you have to do that now?" she mumbles, eyes dancing with delight. At least they're not filled with tears anymore.

"Can't help it, sweetheart." As she starts to slide my boxers up my legs, I remember I'm still wearing the condom. "Uh, Jaime? Do you think you could help with the…thing?"

Jaime closes her eyes briefly before reaching up and touching my dick. Sure, it's to remove the protection from earlier, but it's contact nonetheless.

As soon as my boxers are around my hips and my junk safely concealed within, she helps me slip into my jeans. There's no way I'm getting a shirt on while wearing the cuffs, and I don't foresee Barney removing the restraints so I can fully dress.

"That's good enough," he finally says and pulls me towards the squad car. "You, too, missy. Get in the car."

Locking eyes with Jaime, I'm lowered into the back of the car. Jaime runs over to my truck and grabs the keys from the ignition, my wallet that was discarded on the floor, and her purse. She's still gripping my shirt and boots when she walks around to the opposite side of the car. Barney helps Jaime get in, her sans cuffs.

"Next stop, central booking," he says as he throws the car in gear.

Jaime deposits my clothes, drops my keys and wallet into her purse, and slides over to the middle of the car. I feel her warm fingers link with mine behind my back just before her head rests on my shoulder.

As fucked up as this entire situation is, with her curled up against me, it doesn't quite seem so bad.

At least that's what I'm gonna keep telling myself.

It's official.

Sitting on the hard plastic bench in central booking, surrounded by a drunk who is passed out, a woman repeating 'I didn't do it' over and over again, and a ninety-year-old man known around town for continually being busted for stealing garden gnomes, I realized something big. I have fallen in love.

I'm talking paint it on the water tower, using cutesy nicknames like snookums and peaches, in it for the rest of your life kinda love. Forever.

Sure, I realized that this was probably heading in that direction, but sitting beside Jaime on this hard bench after both being processed by an old friend of hers from high school, I made the life-changing realization. Like a flashing neon arrow board, all signs have led me straight to her.

I'm in love with Jaime.

It's a realization I don't take lightly, yet am unable to react. Jaime will hightail it so fast in the other direction that I'd barely see her taillights through the cloud of dust. It's a risk I'm not willing to take. At least not yet. I need to gradually work towards confessions of the heart.

My arm is wrapped protectively around her, her head resting comfortably on my shoulder. Neither of us have said too much as we sit in a pee-scented cell with three other people. After being processed and all personal effects removed, I was allowed to put on my shirt, socks, and boots. Jaime had to turn over her purse and cell phone but was still able to call Payton to come and get us.

Charges are still pending, but I'm hopeful that this entire mess can be swept under the rug. No way do I want–or *need*–an indecent exposure and trespassing rap attached to my name. As a business owner in a small town, that could be a career killer. And I don't want that for Jaime either. I don't want people looking at her and whispering behind her back all because I couldn't control myself another five minutes until we could get to my condo.

I'm just about to apologize once more when a door is pulled open and closed somewhere in the distance. The echo drowns out the mumblings from the other woman in the cell, if only for a few short seconds.

"Indecent exposure *and* trespassing? You know we expected this kinda behavior from Lexi or maybe AJ, but never you, Jaime."

Emma and Orval are both standing on the other side of the bars, each one wearing their own brand of cat that ate the canary smile.

"Thanks, Payton," she mumbles under her breath as we both stand up and head towards them.

"It's not what it looks like," I start.

"No? So you weren't busted fornicating with our granddaughter on private property? 'Cause that's what it looks like to me," Orval says, trying hard to fight a smile.

"Okay, so maybe it is what it looks like, but this is entirely my fault."

"Oh, quit being so noble, Ryan. I remember those days when Orval and I would go parking around town and go at it like crazed felines. Of course, we didn't always have a car, but that's another story. Heck, one time when we were at a softball game for the twins, Grandpa and I..."

"Grandma, please don't finish that sentence," Jaime begs, her face as red as a cherry.

"Anyway," Emma starts, clearing her throat. "My point is that sometimes you just have urges. Impulses that need to be fulfilled right then and there or you risk permanent damage to your special parts."

"Oh, God," Jaime groans.

"It's okay, kids. All we're saying is that we get it. We understand," Orval adds before winking at me and leaning towards me. "I used to tell Emmy that my pecker would fall off if we didn't get it out and play with it at least twice a day."

"The good news, kids, is that Mr. Gerard isn't pressing charges on the trespassing, and I talked with that sweet Barney kid about letting the whole free-roaming willy thing slide. I might have mentioned that I would tell his grandma about seeing him come out of the Gas N Go with a Penthouse magazine and a bottle of vanilla scented lotion."

"Wait, the Gas N Go has Penthouse?" Jaime asks to no one in particular.

"Where do you think Grandpa gets his copy from? Anyway, the good news is that you're both free to go!" Emma adds, smiling wide and eyes brimming with excitement.

As we follow them down the corridor towards the outside, I look over at Orval. "The kid's name really is Barney?"

"Last name, son. First name George."

We're quiet as we head towards their Buick. Obviously, my truck is still out at the field, so I follow behind Jaime as she slips into the back seat. "Don't get any ideas back there," Orval hollers as he pulls out of the police station.

Emma talks from the passenger seat the entire trip out of town. Even if we wanted to join the conversation, she leaves no room for exchange. Instead of trying, I spy Jaime's hand sitting on the seat and link my fingers with hers. It's a subtle touch, but one I crave, like the desert craves the rain.

Her green eyes are warm, holding a hint of laughter. I'm damn thankful she isn't throwing me out on my ass right now, not that I'd blame her. I rejoice in the smile that plays on her lips. It makes my heartbeat kick up a notch, and a smile of my own graces my face.

Twenty years from now, this is a story I hope to share with our kids. Okay, maybe not the full story, but a PG, abbreviated version. And, yes, call me a pansy or a pussy or whatever you want. I can actually see my future with her in it. Jaime's the only one I see. The only one I want.

When we pull up to my truck, Jaime and I both jump out, eager to end the humiliation part of the night. I thank Orval and Emma for springing us from lock up, even though we would have been released on our own since no charges are being filed. But still, I appreciate them picking us up and delivering us back to my truck.

I open the passenger side door to help Jaime. The first thing I notice is the condom wrapper discarded on the floor, followed by my cell phone. Some of the content of Jaime's purse is there, lying on the floorboard beside a dropped water bottle. I can't help it, I start to laugh. Hard. Her eyes follow mine to the evidence of our tryst, and she too bursts out laughing.

Gently grabbing her upper arms, I pull her into my body, cradling her as if she were a priceless treasure. And she is. To me, she is.

When the laughter subsides, my lips find hers. They're warm and soft and cause my body to fire to life once more, even after the shame of being busted parking. Before I'm able to take control, Jaime's tongue pushes against the seam of my lips, begging for entrance. Passion surrounds me, engulfing me, from nothing more than just her clothed body and sweet tongue sliding against mine. She's my biggest high and my greatest weakness.

"Can I still go home with you?" she asks without breaking the kiss.

"I'd be disappointed if you didn't."

"Then let's go. I think we both need a shower to wash the criminal scent off. Together."

She doesn't have to tell me twice. I wrap my hands around her hips and lift her into the truck cab. Slamming to door, I run around to the driver's side and slide in without an ounce of couth or finesse. Jaime's pulling my keys from her purse and thrusting them at me before I even have my seatbelt fastened.

We keep our hands to ourselves the entire ride to town, both of us clearly not wanting a repeat ride in the back of a squad car. By the time I pull into my driveway, the truck is so sexually charged I'm sure the electricity flying around is visible.

Helping Jaime from the truck, we walk hand-in-hand up the sidewalk to my front door. Our gait is a bit hurried as we slip inside, and I fumble for the light switch. Before I can locate the one I'm after, she pulls on my hand, wraps her arms around my neck, and plasters her body against mine.

Forget about the light.

Forget about being arrested.

Forget about everything other than Jaime.

"Shower. Now." I don't need any further direction.

As I pick her up and her long legs wrap around my waist, I thank my lucky stars that I chose flowers as a gift for Mrs. H. If not, who knows if or when I would have met Jaime.

Pushing thoughts of Mrs. Hanson out of my head, I carry my woman towards the bedroom. Her lips caress my neck, sending goosebumps rippling across my arms. With my hands firmly gripping her ass, I walk straight into the bathroom and into the shower. Our clothes will need to be washed anyway, right?

When the cold spray hits our bodies, Jaime shrieks, wiggles in my arms, and laughs against my neck. My lips claim hers urgently as the water finally heats up, but neither of us notices.

We're too busy creating our own warmth.

Jaime

15

"The convict is up," AJ hollers over the 80's hairband music pumping through the overhead speakers at The Lanes, a local bowling alley.

It's sisters' night, and all six of us are competing for bragging rights as the top bowler. For as good as I am at putt putt golf, I'm a horrible bowler. Surprisingly, Abby is the star bowler of the family. For someone who hates all sorts of physical activities and keeps her nose firmly in the pages of a book, she's shockingly good at throwing a bowling ball.

It has been a week since my run-in with the local law. Between Grandma and Payton, who I have yet to forgive for sending the grandparents to bail us out, the entire family knew about our pending incarceration before they even pulled into the parking lot at the county jail.

Ryan and I have spent every waking hour together–and some not-so-waking hours. In fact, I spent three of the last seven nights at his house. And the ones that I wasn't there, I was up half the night with him on the phone. We are firmly lodged in coupledom, even if that was never my intention. So much for taking it slow and steady. Instead, we're officially dating and doing all things expected of us as a couple.

I don't find myself freaking out the way I would have expected when facing my first relationship since my broken engagement. My need to make major life lists has also seemed to decrease. It's like Ryan evens me out, neutralizes me in a way I never expected. Now, my lists are little things like what ingredients I need to make dinner and gift ideas for Ryan's birthday in a few months.

Every time I feel that hesitation creep up, I think about the way I feel when he kisses me, and that uncertainty seems to fade away. I'm nowhere near ready for marriage, but I realize I'm settling into the idea of a future with Ryan more comfortably than expected.

In fact, let's be honest: I feel a lot more than comfort when it comes to him.

The way my heart skips a beat and pounds recklessly in my chest when he's near is a sure sign of something more. Throw in the fact that I can literally picture him in every scenario I conjure up involving my future, and that's another indication. He's everywhere, surrounding me like a warm blanket. I feel him breaking down the final barriers, exposing my mangled heart. I just pray he's willing to mend the pieces and make me whole again instead of the alternative, which would destroy me.

Ryan's right, there's something special between us. I do feel it. I feel myself falling more and more for him every single day, yet I'm still scared. But it's his strength and determination that keeps me pushing forward, towards him instead of running away.

"Jaime, are you taking your turn or just going to continue daydreaming about lover boy?" Lexi asks, waggling her eyebrows.

I'm pulled from my thoughts and notice all of my sisters staring at me, most with knowing smiles on their faces. Of course, they think I'm lost in fantasies of Ryan, not that I'm trapped in my own mind again and trying to keep the panic at bay. I've let him in, plain and simple, and it scares the hell out of me.

Hell, I didn't *let* him in, the sneaky bastard weaseled his way in and burrowed in for the long haul.

"Yeah, I'm going," I declare, hopping up from the hard chair to retrieve my ball.

The Lanes does cosmic bowling every Saturday night, which features a big selection of neon balls that glow under the black lights and disco balls. I slide my fingers in the neon pink one and take my stance. Def Leppard wails overhead as I send my ball spiraling down the lane. At the last moment, it shoots towards the left gutter, barely clipping two pins.

"You suck," Meghan giggles, tossing back her third margarita of the night. Or was it her forth?

"I'm a horrible bowler," I confirm.

"I would suggest it has something to do with that tall drink of water staring at you from the bar, but I've seen you bowl before. You suck." This from AJ.

Her words finally permeate my mind, and I quickly glance behind me at the bar. Ryan is sitting there, right next to Josh. Meghan's boyfriend always shows up at some point during our sisters' nights, but I wasn't expecting to see him sitting with Ryan. Earlier in the day, when I told him I would be going out this evening with my sisters for our monthly get-together, we made plans to attend my family's July Fourth cookout tomorrow. Never did he mention that he planned to show up this evening.

I smile as realization sets in. I'm happy he's here–excited, even. Never had someone of the opposite sex shown up for *me* during one of our Saturday night outings. Always Meghan, sometimes AJ and Lexi, but never me.

"I can't believe he's here," I mumble absently as my ball reappears for my second throw.

Eyes that I didn't feel earlier are glued to my body as I take my position. Without even turning for confirmation, I can feel his gaze, heating my body clear down to my toes. Desire pools between my legs causing a break in concentration as I send it rolling. Halfway down the lane, my ball is in the gutter.

"I think he's distracting her," Payton says to Lexi.

"Hell, I'd be distracted too if someone looked at me like I was an ice cream sundae on a hot July day." Payton elbows AJ, who just laughs at her own comment.

"Twenty bucks says they're doing it in the parking lot before the night is over," Lexi adds.

"Once a criminal, always a criminal." The grin Meghan wears after her comment consumes her whole face. She gets that same look every time Josh is around.

"You should just stick to drinking tonight," Abby suggests with a hint of a smile.

"I think you're right," I reply as I glance down at my empty beer bottle. "Anyone ready for another?"

When I get orders for three of my five sisters, I head up the bar. Brown eyes the color of dark, rich chocolate track my progress every step of the way as he chats with Josh. Each of them enjoying a beer, their conversation halts the moment I step beside them.

"You are the worst bowler in the history of bowlers, Jaime. Even the blind girl I went to school with was better than you."

"Thanks, Joshy Washy," I say in a sing-song voice while ruffling his hair in a total juvenile move.

"You know I hate it when you call me that," Josh growls, rapidly smoothing down the wild locks.

"You started it by insulting my bowling skills. How do you know I'm not sandbagging so that the others don't feel so bad about their own lacking?"

"I'm going to tell them you said that," he retorts before taking another sip of his beer. "And unless you sandbag every time you play, which I'm pretty sure you don't, then I think I'll stick with my original claim. You suck."

Turning my attention to the bartender, I place my order before glancing at Ryan. "What are you snickering about?" I ask.

Leaning forward until he's a whisper away from my ear, Ryan says, "I was just thinking about how much I love it when you *suck.*"

Warmth spreads up my neck and burns my cheeks at his dirty little insinuation. It catches me so far off guard that I'm unable to come up with a single retort. My tongue is thick and my mind filled with naughty images featuring Ryan and myself. And if the wicked gleam in his eye is any indication, I think it's safe to say he's picturing the same things.

"Behave."

"You prefer when I'm being bad," he whispers as he slides a single finger down my forearm and wraps his arm proprietarily around my waist. It's a claim. A statement. He's letting everyone know that I'm his.

Before, I would have scoffed at the notion. Now? I want to wrap my arms around his shoulders and let his lips make a declaration of their own.

"Don't let the others see you do that," Josh says to Ryan. "It's a law that no boys are allowed on girls' night." Josh makes air quotes when he says the last two words.

"Yet you're always in attendance every month," I sass back.

"I'm watchin' my girl." His eyes seek out Meghan.

"No one's going to mess with her, Josh. We won't let them," I say.

"I know, Jaime. I just like to see her having a good time with you guys. She's been working crazy hours at the dental office and it makes me happy to see her enjoying herself."

"And you being here, ready to take her home at the end of the night has nothing to do with it?" My smile is wide and I feel Ryan's hand flex against my hip, as if confirming his intentions for later this evening as well.

"Well, that's an added perk," Josh confirms with a laugh.

"Jaime, quick fraternizing with the enemy! Get over here and play!" Payton hollers.

"Yeah, no boys, remember?" Abby adds.

As if on cue, the bartender places a tray with three beers and a margarita in front of me. I try to retrieve my wallet, but Ryan drops a twenty on the bar before I'm able to dig one out.

"I'll pay you back later," I tell him with a wink as I grab the tray.

"I look forward to it."

There's a little extra swing in my hips as I make my way towards my sisters to resume our game. But the entire time I'm playing, I'm watching the clock, waiting for the moment I can make my escape with Ryan.

16

Ryan

I'm pretty sure the little extra sway in her hips is for my benefit. My eyes are riveted to her ass as she sets each drink down on the table. When Jaime deposits the last one, she glances over her shoulder and gives me a little wink. My cock is so damn hard that I could use it as one of my tools on the job site.

"Have you told her yet?" Josh asks before taking another swig of his beer.

"Told her what?"

"That you love her."

I meet his pointed look head on. There's no denying it so I won't even try. "Not yet." I take a deep pull of my beer, trying to quash the tension that's suddenly coursing through my body.

"Why not?" he asks while turning to face me.

"It's kinda complicated. She's still freaked out from the douche who left her right before the wedding."

"Asshole. I never liked him. I met him a few times, and each time he just gave the same cocky asshole vibe."

"Yeah, well, he sure did a number on her."

Josh drops his head. "I know. I was there when it happened. We had all just arrived in Cleveland for the wedding. It was the weekend before and the girls were all going to do a bachelorette party. I was invited to go to the bachelor party, but I made some excuse about not feeling well. Truth is I didn't want to spend the evening with him and his friends. Chris had some meetings he couldn't get out of so he was coming in on the Friday before. It was just me, Brian, and Grandpa Orval. Sad that I was happier staying with them back at the hotel, isn't it?" Josh shakes his head before continuing.

"Anyway, middle of the week, things just changed. I could tell something was wrong. Meg got a call from Payton and she was hysterical. I drove them over to the house Gavin and Jaime shared. I'll never get over seeing her crumpled on the floor crying her eyes out. Fucking gutted me, you know?"

Yeah. I know.

"She's like my sister. Shit, all of them are. Anything happens to any of them and I'd be the same way. Took everything I had not to track down that son of a bitch and knock his teeth out. I wanted to, but Meg wouldn't let me."

I snort and think of how much satisfaction I'd have at seeing Josh deck Jaime's ex. Well, behind me, of course.

"She was a mess for a while after that," Josh confirms what I already know.

"She told me."

"You in it for the long haul?" he asks.

The seriousness of the moment causes my heart to race. Yet it's significantly important when realization sets in that there's only one answer to his question.

"Absolutely."

"Then don't be afraid to tell her. She might be a timid cat right now, but I know what she ultimately wants in life. Husband. Kids.

House. Deep down she still wants all of those things that douche promised to give her and didn't. Don't be like that douche," Josh says, extending his beer bottle out.

"Never. I only want to make her happy," I say as I tap my bottle against his.

"Good to know. Have I told you about the time I got caught sneaking out of Meghan's bedroom in the middle of the night?" he asks, an ornery gleam filling his blue eyes. Happily, I welcome the change of topic.

"Nope."

"Meghan and I had only been dating for a few months, and she was still living at home with Brian and the grandparents. I brought her home one night and she convinced me–it wasn't very difficult, mind you–that I should come upstairs to her room. I woke up in the middle of the night and tried sneaking out. Walked out in the damn hall and Orval is standing there in his tighty whities with a damn smirk on his face. I've never been so embarrassed before in my life!"

My laugh is instantaneous and hearty as I picture that scene. Knowing that Josh and Meghan had their own embarrassing rendezvous busted by Orval and Emma makes me feel a lot better about mine. Okay, both of mine.

"The next time I saw him, he slipped a box of condoms in my truck cab and told me to knock myself out. I thought I'd drop dead on the spot right then. Good thing I was already head over heels in love with her. Otherwise, I might have been tempted to run."

I can't stop laughing.

"Fortunately, it didn't take me long to realize that's just how they are all the time. They're completely nuts but I love them." Josh takes another drink, emptying his bottle.

"Yeah, they have a way of sticking with you," I confirm knowing that even after only a month of seeing Jaime, I'd do just about anything for her family as well.

An hour and two glasses of water later, the girls are finally wrapping up their game. I'd be surprised if Jaime actually broke eighty points. Watching her laugh and carry on though, that was the highlight of my night. The more alcohol they consumed, it appears the livelier they became. Bon Jovi, Poison, and even Joan Jett had them rockin' 80's hits like they were on stage, but let's not get into how bad they were off-key.

"Handsome, take me home," Meghan proclaims as she struts to the bar, if not slightly unsteady on her feet.

"I'd be honored, beautiful. Let's get you to bed," Josh replies. He practically jumps off his stool and throws money on the bar before turning and catching his girlfriend in his arms when she stumbles. Josh waves as he leads a tipsy Meghan towards the exit.

Turning my attention back towards the others, I find the five remaining sisters making their way towards me. Jaime's leading the pack and none of them appear to be any more stable on their feet than Meghan was.

"I need a favor," Jaime purrs in my ear, her warm breath tickling my ear and sending all blood rushing southbound towards my belt.

"Anything for you, gorgeous." Her eyes dance with excitement.

"Well, since you and Josh were both here, we decided that the designated driver for the night could have the night off. Since Josh and Meggy already left, that leaves you and your truck."

My cock doesn't mistake how she licks my earlobe as if to punctuate her statement. "So you need me to give everyone a ride home?"

"Yes, please. I promise to reward you handsomely." Again, that wicked tongue darts out and slides along my jawline.

"We stopped drinking an hour ago, and I only had a few beers, so I'm fine to drive," I tell her, wrapping my arms around her thin waist and pulling her in close.

"I figured. Josh always stops drinking early in the evening so he can drive us home. This may or may not be the first time our DD has ended up three sheets to the wind."

I open my mouth to respond, but she cuts me off. "But don't worry, if we didn't have a driver, we would call Grandma. It wouldn't be the first time she's come to collect us."

"Good to know you guys wouldn't drive intoxicated. I'd be happy to take them all home. Might be a tight fit though. I only have seating for five."

"That's okay, Ryan. We're used to piling in the back of a truck. At least your truck is a crew cab. Josh's is only a cab and a half. Try fitting four in the back and three in the front of that thing!" Lexi exclaims through laughter.

"That was the night I got my head stuck between the seat and door panel," AJ says somberly.

Jaime, Payton, Lexi, and Abby all burst out laughing, each one competing to be louder than the others.

"All right, ladies, let's head out before they kick us out."

With my hand resting comfortably at the base of her spine, I steer a weaving Jaime towards the truck. The giggles get louder the closer we get to my vehicle.

"Is this, like, the scene of the crime?" Payton giggles, her green eyes brimming with unshed tears.

"Oh God, it is! This is where they did it before the Po Po interrupted," AJ adds.

"Hey, Ryan? Is it true you went outside without your clothes on?" Lexi asks, her eyes bright with laughter.

"Wait. You were free-ballin' it?" AJ's mouth is wide open as she stops, awaiting my answer.

"Ladies, ladies, ladies. Let me just tell you, Ryan has nothing to be ashamed of in the package department. In fact, I think he got a lot more than his share, if you know what I mean," Jaime adds before being greeted by a chorus of hoots and hollers.

I shake my head and open the back door. Three slide in, while Jaime and Payton slide in the front. They're a mess of giggles and cackles as I pull out of the lot and head towards AJ's apartment.

"No wonder you couldn't wait to get back to his place. If he's packin' that kinda meat–and he wasn't already taken–I would have jumped him in the parking lot before he even had the truck in drive," Payton says.

"Jaime, are we talking bratwurst or summer sausage?" Lexi questions from the back seat.

"We're talkin' the biggest summer sausage I've ever seen." Jaime turns around as far as she can, considering the seatbelt to nod her head. "Like…big." She uses her two hands and moves them apart a good fourteen inches.

As good as she is for my ego, clearly she's exaggerating the size of my cock. If they weren't three sheets to the wind right now, I'd put a stop to her comparing my man-meat to a something you'd buy in the grocery store. But it's actually kinda hysterical–and flattering–so I let them go.

"It's been so long since I've seen a bratwurst, let alone enjoyed a summer sausage," Abby says absently. By the look on her face and the redness in her cheeks in the rearview mirror, I'm pretty sure she didn't intend to say that out loud.

"I'm going to have to break out BOB tonight," AJ mumbles to another chorus of laughter.

"Bob?" I ask.

"Battery operated boyfriend," Lexi replies before breaking out into more laughter. I'm pretty sure the burn in my cheek is a blush.

It's a long fifteen minutes as I deliver Jaime's sisters to their respective homes, especially when they're talking about sex the entire way. When the truck is finally quiet, I glance over and see startling green eyes focused entirely on me.

"Can I stay at your place tonight?" she asks. As if there was any other option.

Nodding my head, I reach over and link her fingers within mine as I make my way towards my condo. Jaime waits as I slip around to the passenger seat to help her out. Keeping one arm wrapped around her, I open my door, thankful to finally be inside the privacy of my own home.

The moment the door is secure, Jaime pounces. She leaps into my arms, causing me to stumble a few steps until I right myself. Her lips are urgent and filled with passion as she deepens the kiss. We go from zero to sixty in less than a second with no sign of slowing down. We're each grasping at clothes, yanking and pulling until there's nothing between us but air.

I lead us to my bedroom, savoring the taste of her beer-stained lips every step of the way. Still wrapped around me, I press her against the wall, my throbbing cock so very close to sliding into heaven.

"Can I tell you something?" she whispers against my ear.

"Sure."

Jaime pulls back slightly so that she can see my eyes. "I'm falling for you."

Her words are heavy as they settle right in the middle of my chest. I grip her ass and pull her as close as possible, her legs wrap tightly around my waist. "Is this the alcohol or Jaime speaking?"

"A little of both, I guess. If not for the alcohol, I'm not sure I would have the courage to tell you, but they're still my words."

Shaking my head, I keep my eyes locked on hers. "Well, then, it's only right to confess that I'm falling for you too."

The truth is that I've already fallen. I'm in love with her, but I still won't say it. I don't want the first time I proclaim my love for her to be while she's intoxicated and I'm about to thrust inside of her ready body. I want it to be perfectly timed where she's liable to receive my declaration better.

Instead of plunging forward against the wall the way I had planned only moments ago, I move us towards my bed. Laying her down atop the comforter, I cover her body with my own. Her skin is warm and her face flush, and the look in her eyes convey everything I need to know. Trust. Desire. Love.

"I need a condom," I state, caressing her lips with my own.

"Please hurry," she replies breathlessly. I make quick work at sheathing myself and slide back atop her waiting body. Our gaze is fire and locked on each other as I push forward, sending us both spiraling into a world of pure nirvana, like nothing I've ever known.

Jaime is quickly becoming my world, my everything. Life without her in it doesn't seem like much of a life at all. In fact, it would fucking suck sweaty, hairy balls.

So, I vow to make sure she's always a part of my life. I won't let her go. Hell, I won't be able to. Even if I wanted to, I need her like I need air. She's it for me.

The one.

Jaime

17

I crush the Doritos and stir them into the taco salad, while Grandma pulls her famous potato salad from the fridge. She's humming along to the new Justin Timberlake song on the radio, which instantly puts a smile on my face. Not that I'm lacking for smiles much lately anyway. Anytime I see, hear, or think about Ryan, a smile graces my lips.

"I'm glad to see your father has help at the grill today," Grandma says casually, but the meaning is clear. She's happy Ryan is here.

Glancing out the window in the kitchen of my childhood home, I take in the sight of Ryan helping my dad flip burgers and brats. It's a sight I all but gave up on seeing before he came along.

"Me too. They seem to get along well."

"Of course they do. Your dad sees Ryan for who he is: A sweet, caring man who's in love with his daughter."

Grandma's words startle me. In love with me? She thinks he's in love with me? Sure, Ryan confessed last night that he's falling for me, but full-blown love? It hasn't been long enough to fall in love, has it?

"You think so?" I ask, the words all but lodging in my dry throat.

"I don't think. I know. You can see it in his eyes when he looks at you. All day I've caught him staring at you when you're not looking. His eyes lighten and soften at the same time, and a little smile plays at the corner of his lips every time. He's in love with you."

Realization slams into me hard. Sure, I've fallen in love with him, but to know that the feeling could be reciprocated leaves me lightheaded and breathy. I never expected this. Hell, I never even wanted this, but here I am, in love with a wonderful man who makes me happy. Every second that I'm with him, memories of Gavin become cloudier and more distant. The hurt and pain that I experienced then is replaced with smiling brown eyes and tender touches.

"I take it you're in love with him, too, right?" Grandma says behind me, pulling my gaze from Ryan at the grill. "I mean, I've never seen you look at anyone the way you look at him. And that includes the douche bag who will not be named on this gloriously sunny day."

Chuckling at Grandma's bluntness, I confirm what she already knows. "Yes, I'm in love with him."

"Good. Now what are you going to do about it?" she asks, grabbing the basket filled with plastic silverware.

"I don't know," I confess. "I'm scared."

Turning to face me, Grandma looks me square in the eye. "Love is a scary thing, honey. When I realized I loved your grandpa, he was ready to head off to boot camp. I was terrified that I would never see him again, or worse, that he would forget all about me."

Realizing I'd never heard this story, I sit down on the stool, and encourage her to continue. "What happened?"

"He left for Texas and wrote me every day. Turns out, he was afraid I'd find someone else and forget about him, so he took a few minutes at the end of his day to write me. Those letters kept me going when I was sad. They brought me comfort when I was lonely. He told me he loved me every day, even when he wasn't here to do it face-to-face."

"I didn't know that. When did you see him again?"

"When he graduated boot camp, I rode with his parents to Texas in a station wagon with no air conditioning and windows that barely worked. It was a long, exhausting trip, but so worth it. I got to see him graduate with his peers and friends in the Army. As soon as the ceremony was over, he ran across the yard, threw his arms around me, and asked me to marry him as soon as possible."

"That's the sweetest." Tears fill my eyes as I picture my young grandfather proposing to my grandma.

"It really was. Then we snuck off to the car and did it until we were both so exhausted we couldn't move."

"Grandma," I chastise.

"Jaime, just know that it'll all work out if it is meant to be. I know this is scary for you, but don't be afraid of it. Embrace it. Love is a beautiful thing if you let it in your heart."

Pulling her into an impromptu hug, I let her words wash over me. I vow that as difficult as it's going to be, I won't run and hide from Ryan or the love he's offering. When the time comes to have the conversation, I'll tell him what's written in my heart. As difficult as it will be to say the words for the first time since Gavin broke my heart, I'll tell him exactly how I feel.

"Come on, sweetie. Let's get all this food out there before the natives start to get restless."

I follow Grandma outside, arms full of side dishes. When Ryan catches my eye, there's no mistaking the smile he gives me, or the look of love in his eyes.

It's time I embrace it.

Ryan slides in beside me at the picnic table. Both of our plates are loaded up with enough food to feed a small country. My eyes were definitely bigger than my stomach. I try to eat on the healthier side, but that still doesn't stop me from making a fully loaded cheeseburger and adding taco salad, Grandma's potato salad, strawberry Jell-O salad, baked beans, and a deviled egg to my plate.

"This looks amazing," Ryan says before taking a big bite of potato salad.

"She's famous for it. Anytime she goes anywhere, she's expected to bring it."

"I can see why," he adds before taking a bite of his burger.

"Thank you for helping my dad man the grill."

Wiping his mouth, he says, "It was no problem. I enjoyed it, and I got to talk to him for a bit."

"What did you talk about?" I ask casually, even though I feel anything but.

"Wouldn't you like to know?" he replies with a cocky smile and a wink before turning back to his burger.

I watch him for several moments before I realize I'm staring. Averting my eyes, I look across the table and straight into the smiling eyes of both Payton and AJ. Payton's eyebrows shoot upward, as if silently daring me to deny the fact that I was gawking. A blush sweeps across my cheeks, but I won't deny it. I can't.

"Ryan, how is the Hazelton place going? I heard you started it last week?" Chris asks from the other end of the table.

"Good. It's a big house, but we got all the floor beams and joists in place and started on the walls. The tresses were delivered Friday, and I don't think I've ever seen so many on a house," Ryan replies between bites.

"I saw the layout of the house when they came in to the bank a few weeks back. It's going to be a grand house," Josh adds. He works for his dad at a local bank that has been in their family for four generations.

"Maybe we should talk to Ryan about building a house for us. I'd love to have something that's completely ours, where no one lived before us," Chris says to Lexi.

There's something in her eyes that tells me whatever problems they were having before are still unresolved. "Maybe," she replies happily, but the smile she presents him is fake. I can tell.

Ryan must pick up on it as well. The look he gives me is questioning and filled with concern. Even after only a month of dating, he seems to already know and understand my sisters.

"Sorry I'm late," I hear over my shoulder and turn to see Levi strolling through the backyard.

"Hey, Levi," I add to the chorus of greetings for Abby's friend.

I watch out of the corner of my eye as Abby sits up a little straighter and flattens her skirt. She won't outright admit it, but I know she has feelings for her best friend. Even with his bed-hopping ways, I've always gotten the vibe that the feeling isn't entirely one-sided either.

Levi sets a platter of cookies down on the table of desserts and heads over to Abby. He's always been super protective of her, in that big brother sort of way, and it doesn't surprise me when he places a kiss on the top of her head.

"Glad you could make it, Levi. Did you just get off work?" Dad asks from the second table.

"Yeah, it was a long shift. There was a big accident out along Bay Road. Two cars, head-on."

Levi works as an EMT full-time, and still manages to squeeze in time as a volunteer firefighter. But what really draws the attention from the ladies is his time playing guitar for a local band, Crush. He wears a uniform *and* plays guitar. No wonder women throw their panties at him every time he's on stage.

"Are they okay?" Abby asks, tears prickling her green eyes. Abby and her tender heart. She's never met a stranger who she wouldn't give the shirt off her back or the food off her plate.

"Eventually. One was air lifted out early this morning, but he's expected to make it," he replies as he piles food on his plate.

When he's loaded, he slides onto the end of the bench beside Abby, completely ignoring the fact that there's room at the other table. She slides over as much as she can, but with Meghan on the other side, it's a tight fit. I watch as they attempt to make room for each other, yet neither of them appears as though sharing a single seat is a hardship. Levi might be hanging off the end of the bench, but he smiles a bit as he plasters himself against Abby.

"I'll add them to my prayers this evening," Grandma says.

"You don't say prayers, dear," Grandpa replies from her side.

"Sure I do. I believe I talk to God almost every night," she sasses with a wicked grin.

"Shouting his name over and over doesn't constitute prayers, my love." Grandpa leans over and places a tender kiss on her knuckles. Shades of pink tinge her cheeks.

"Please, for the love of all things holy, do *not* talk about sex at the dinner table. I haven't finished eating yet, and if you continue, I'll lose my appetite," Meghan whines.

Though Grandma and Grandpa giggle like school kids, each of us look like our lunches might make a reappearance.

Conversation is light throughout the rest of the meal. I glance around the patio and notice that only two of my sisters are without a companion. Sure, Abby's guest is a friend, but that doesn't mean it won't someday spark into something bigger. AJ has brought guests occasionally, and even Payton, though that's been several years. Chris has been a part of the family since he and Lexi were both in high school, and Meghan and Josh have been a couple for three years now.

For several years, I was absent from many family functions. After college, I stayed in Cleveland and eventually met Gavin. I came home at least four times a year to be with my family, but even after the engagement, I was generally on my own. He rarely made the trip with me.

"Come sit with me?" Ryan asks, extending his hand down to mine.

"Sure." Gathering up our empty plates, I follow behind as we dispose of our trash.

Ryan takes my empty hand in his and leads me towards the big Oak tree. He sits down, with his back against the wide trunk, and I slide between his spread legs. I snuggle in, my head resting against the planes of his hard chest.

"Having a good time?" he asks, running his big warm hand down my arm.

"Mmmmmm," I purr, sensations flooding my body and stirring to life a need that Ryan quenched twice last night.

"Behave. I can't be walking around your family gathering sporting wood in my shorts," Ryan says, his warm breath fanning against the shell of my ear.

After a few silent minutes watching my family, I turn a little and face him. "Do you get to see your family much?"

"Since I moved here, not as much as I'd like. I went home for Christmas this past year because it was my first one away. I'm thinking of flying home in August for a long weekend. It's my parent's thirty-fifth anniversary. I got an email from my sister and she wants us all to come home to celebrate."

"That's nice. You definitely need to go," I tell him, touching the coarse skin where his shorts reach his thigh.

"We'll be neck deep in the Hazelton job, but I'm preparing to go. As long as I plan ahead, it shouldn't be too much trouble to sneak away for a few days. In fact, I'd really like you to go with me."

Startled by his statement, I look over my shoulder, gauging his sincerity. "Really? You want me to go? Meet your family?"

"Yeah. I mean, you're going to meet them eventually, right? Might as well be next month."

"You're awfully confident that we'll still be together next month," I add.

"I'm very confident, sweetheart. Now that I have you, I'm not letting you go." He punctuates his words with a kiss.

His lips caress mine softly at first. But the longer there's contact, the needier we both start to feel. Slipping my tongue inside his mouth, I stroke and suck on his tongue. Fire burns in my veins, as warmth floods between my legs. From this position, I can feel the rock-hard ridge of his erection against my back. It takes every ounce of self-control that I possess to not turn around and wrap my legs around his waist.

"God, you're driving me crazy. Kissing you is the best thing ever," he confesses without breaking the kiss.

"Kissing's pretty great, but there's something else that I like a lot more," I purr against him, scooting back an inch and wiggling my backside against his length.

Pulling back, Ryan's eyes are ablaze with desire. They're dark and burning with his need for me. "Ready to go?"

Before I can answer, Meghan yells my name from the yard. "Jaime! Quit making babies in front of Dad and get out here and play!"

I startle back and turn to face my family. A dozen pairs of eyes are staring back at us, each set dancing with laughter. "God, that's embarrassing."

"Not as much as them all showing up while you're in your underwear," Ryan adds with a laugh.

"That may be true," I laugh.

"What's going on out there?" he asks, nodding towards the net.

"Volleyball. Three on three. It's a tradition."

"Jaime! We're waiting…" Payton hollers from across the net.

"You better get going," he says with a smile.

"Yeah. You wanna come play?" I get up and turn back towards him.

Ryan closes his legs and pulls his shirt down to conceal his erection. "Nope. I better just sit over here by myself for a bit and collect my thoughts."

Laughter spills from my lips as I look down at him.

"Jaime!" Another yell pierces my ears.

"I better go before they come over here and get me." Crouching down, I place a firm kiss on his lips before turning and running out to play volleyball with my sisters.

18

Ryan

"You any good at bags?" Orval asks, pulling my attention away from the gently seductive curve of Jaime's ass as she runs to play with her sisters.

"Not bad," I tell him moments before he tosses a red beanbag from their corn-hole game into my gut.

"You're lucky I missed. Now get rid of that hard-on. You're on Brian's team. Lord knows he could use all the help he can get." I glance over and see the small smile playing on Jaime's dad lips, even while his head is shaking.

Nothing kills an erection faster than your girlfriend's grandparent drawing attention to it in the presence of her father. In fact, since I met Orval and Emma, they've essentially squashed many hard-ons. He's like hard-on repellant.

Wait. That doesn't sound right.

Shaking my head, I jump up and head towards Brian. When I reach his side, he hands me a beer. "You get used to the constant state of embarrassment that seems to accompany their presence. Back when I started dating Trish, I wanted to crawl under a rock on more than one occasion."

I snort as I raise the bottle to my lips.

"Ryan, get over here. You're supposed to be across from your partner," Orval chastises as Chris, who is Orval's partner, takes his place next to Brian.

"We play the winners," Josh says as he and Levi pull up lawn chairs beside us.

We each take a few practice throws before we start keeping score. The first thing I realize is that there's a lot of trash-talk in this family. Not only is it spilling across the yard from the girls, but from the guys too. In fact, Orval seems to be leading the pack.

"Since you boys are all dating my granddaughters, I -" Orval starts, but is cut off.

"Wait. I'm not dating a granddaughter. We're just friends," Levi cuts in, sitting up straight in his chair.

"Potato, poe-tah-toe. Maybe you should get your keester off the sidelines and play ball before someone else benches you for good." The pointed look he gives Levi has him sliding back down in his seat and averting his gaze. Interesting.

"What I want to talk with you about today is sexting," Orval says as he throws his first bag.

Eyes as wide as dinner plates, I look over to Levi and Josh and see them both snickering uncontrollably.

"Don't laugh, don't laugh. Back in the day, we didn't have these fancy little devices that you could use to send dirty messages or pictures. We had to draw a picture and send it in the mail or use the telephone and call them. Now, with all this technology stuff, you guys can snap a dick pic or send a naughty message in seconds."

Josh spews the swig of beer he just took. "Did he just say dick pic?" he asks Levi.

"I'm serious, boys. Girls love getting naughty messages. It lets them know you're thinking about them."

"Or you could send a message that says thinking of you," I add through fits of laughter.

"Boring. Nothing says I miss you and am thinking of you like a picture of your dick." Orval says with a pointed look. "Emma loves it when I send her messages on her little phone-thingy. It makes her all sorts of crazy when I'm in the next room and she gets a picture of me holding my -" Orval says, but is cut off again.

"Dick pics. Got it. Thanks." Tears brim Levi's eyes as he tries to control his laughter.

"You boys will thank me one day," Orval adds with a firm head nod.

"Where would we be without you, Orval?" Josh asks, fighting to control his own laughter.

"Probably at home–alone–with your Penthouse magazine and a bottle of lotion," he says as he throws his bag, sinking it in the hole.

The rest of the afternoon progresses with more laughter and goodhearted teasing. I've never had such an enjoyable afternoon in all my life. Orval and Chris beat us the first game, but Brian and I took Levi and Josh the next time we were up.

Sitting in the shade, I'm enjoying a cold beer with Josh. "So, can you keep a secret?" he asks as we both watch the girls play volleyball.

"Sure."

"You can't even tell Jaime," he says under his breath.

"Okay," I tell him, concerned that something's wrong. I don't want to keep anything from Jaime, especially something that might involve her family.

"I'm going to ask Meghan to marry me." I'm surprised by his admission, but thrilled nonetheless.

"That's great news. When?"

"Later this year. Our anniversary is in December so I was thinking of doing it then."

"That sounds like a great plan. You got the ring?"

"Yeah," he says, taking his eyes off Meghan for a moment and looking at me. "I've had it for a few months now. I was waiting for the right time, and lately she's been talking about going somewhere for our anniversary, so the idea presented itself to do it then, you know?"

"That's awesome, man. Congrats," I tell my new friend. Josh and I hung out for quite a while last night while the girls were having girls' night, and with our conversations today, it only cemented the fact that I really like Josh Harrison.

"Thank you. I can't wait to make her my wife," he states while his eyes follow Meghan.

I get it. Even when things were good with Sara, I never pictured marriage and kids. But with Jaime, after only being with her for a month, I picture nothing but that scenario. I see her wearing white on the day she takes my last name. I see her belly round with my baby. I see her smiling face greeting me at the door every night when I come home from work. I know exactly how Josh feels right now, because I feel that too. We're just not quite in the same place, relationship wise.

Yet.

When the girls finish up their volleyball game, Jaime joins me in the lawn chair. She's a bit breathy and has a light sheen of sweat glistening on her forehead. Honestly, the way she looks reminds me a bit of sex, which I'm finding I think about all the time in her presence. But when she reaches over, grabs the beer bottle from my hand, and tips it back, her lips touching the same glass mine just were, I'm unable to fight the flash of desire. Her ass presses against my growing erection as she talks to one of her sisters. It's heaven and hell all at the same time.

"Ready to go?" she whispers against my ear.

"In a minute. I like holding you like this," I reply, wrapping my arms around her, loving the way her body fits against mine.

Jaime snuggles against my chest as we both watch her family talk and enjoy dessert. Still full from lunch, Jaime and I opt to skip the sweets and remain seated in the chair. When no one is paying us any attention, I take her chin between my thumb and pointer finger and turn her until she's facing me.

Her lips are plump and ripe, perfect for kissing. Ever since that first taste of her sweet lips, I've been unable to resist them. Leaning forward, I lightly graze my lips across hers. It's featherlight, but, like all kisses shared with Jaime, it packs a punch.

I continue to sweep my lips across hers, slowly and deliberately, each movement calculated and precise. Neither of us rushes it. Instead, we take our time, savoring and tasting. I'm consumed by only Jaime, lost in a world where only she and I exist.

It takes one swipe of a tongue before the kiss turns molten. Heat and desire pools in my stomach and spreads through my veins like wildfire. I'm gone, trapped in a world between reality and fantasy. Everything I have, everything I am, is right here, wrapped in my arms, and kissing me with those sweet, heavenly lips.

"Get a room," Lexi hollers from the picnic table.

Snickers are heard around me, but I keep my attention solely on the woman in my arms. Her lips are bee-stung swollen as I stare at her. Three little words are on the tip of my tongue, begging to spill from my lips. I hold her gaze, silently wondering if she is repeating those same three words over and over again in her head as I am in mine.

I'm rewarded with a smile so perfect it was surely created by the angels themselves. Without saying a word, I help her stand and extend my hand. We walk towards my truck, ignoring the catcalls and the whistles. There's only one thing on my mind–one person. She's standing beside me with the most beautiful smile and flawless lips; lips that I can't get enough of. I want more. I *need* more.

All of her kisses are this consuming. Every. Single. One.

These are my kinda kisses.

My phone rings for the second time since I climbed the ladder to set this roof tress. If I wasn't suspended two stories above the ground, I'd grab it, but seeing that my safety and that of three of my employees is at risk, I let it go to voicemail again.

We've had several consecutive days of beautiful July weather, which makes working outside a lot easier. The sun is shining brightly, high in the sky, but a light breeze blows from the water, which makes for comfortable afternoons in Jupiter Bay.

The tractor holds the tress steady while Danny and I work on this half to fasten it in place. My tool belt is loaded with nails as I drive one after another into the two-by-six, securing each piece of the roof onto the wall. We've been up here half the day, but should be finished by quitting time.

"You have a good holiday, boss?" Danny asks while we wait for the next tress to be brought up.

"Yeah, it was good. You?"

"Went to Sheila's parents by the Bay. They had a big cookout. Where'd you go?" he asks, a hint of a smile crossing his mouth.

In a small town like Jupiter Bay, I'm sure everyone already knows that I've been seeing Jaime. Hell, it's not like we were hiding it. If fact, if it were up to me, I'd be painting that shit on the water tower, or whatever it is people do nowadays to proclaim their relationship status. If I had Facebook, I'm make sure to mark 'In a relationship' and tag her.

"I went with Jaime to her family's cookout."

"Jaime Summer, right? I might have heard something about you and her."

"Yep," I reply, getting ready to grab the moving piece of roof as the operator shifts it up into place.

"Might have heard something else, too," he says, cockily, and pauses for dramatic effect. "Maybe something about a certain business owner naked along ol' man Gerard's bean field. You wouldn't know anything about that, would you?"

"No clue what you're talking about," I reply, straight-faced as can be.

"Huh. Musta been another six-foot two, two-hundred pound man with Elson Construction on the side of his truck."

"Musta." Poker face firmly in place, I fight to keep the corner of my mouth from turning upward.

Danny stares at me for several seconds, neither of us wanting to crack first. Finally, Danny starts to laugh. "Man, really? You aren't gonna give me anything?"

"Nope," I reply, smiling. "I'm not gonna give you anything."

"Whatever. I'm not gonna tell you what else I heard then," he sasses, turning and grabbing the tress to help guide it into place.

"What else did you hear?" I finally ask, unable to resist the temptation of knowing what is being said about me.

"Well, my sister's friend, Kami, works as receptionist at the jail, and she often helps log evidence. Apparently, you may not be aware of this, but the squad cars are equipped with dash cameras." He wiggles his eyebrows repeatedly as a big smile crests his face.

I think about the insinuation for several seconds while Danny starts to pound nails. Knowing that someone might have seen me naked doesn't both me, but the thought of someone seeing Jaime? Well, that makes my blood pressure spike to stroke level.

"Don't worry, man. She was in your truck the whole time until she came out to talk to Barney, and when she did, she was clothed. You, on the other hand, might want to remember to keep the family jewels covered as much as possible. Though, according to my sister, you're packin' enough heat to not have to be too embarrassed about everyone seeing you naked."

"Jesus," I reply, dropping my head a bit.

"Oh, and she says your ass is finer than anything she's ever seen. Her words, not mine. Definitely, not mine." Danny laughs again as he drives the final nail, and I move to unhook the chain that's connected to the tractor for transport and support.

"Have you heard from Orlando?" he asks while we wait for another tress.

"I talked to him a couple of days ago, and it wasn't looking too good," I confirm to my employee.

Paula has taken a turn for the worse, her cancer winning the long fought battle. Orlando was dismal when he called, having recently called in Hospice care, but still remains optimistic, as any husband would in this situation.

"It just sucks, you know? I mean, she's forty. She's still got a whole lotta life left to live. Not to mention Cassie is a senior in high school. She's gonna finish without her mom. Just blows."

Danny speaks the words we've all thought numerous times. Life isn't fair sometimes.

"Hey, did I hear your ex was caught screwing the mayor?" Realizing that Danny's pulled another one-eighty on me and spun the conversation in an entirely different direction–again–I turn towards him, unable to hide my surprise.

"*What?*"

"Yeah! Rumor is they were busted in his office. He had her bent over the desk when his wife walked in to take him to lunch," he chuckles.

"Sounds like the only place she's taking him is to court. Isn't the mayor, like, fifty?" I ask absently.

"Fifty-four with his first grandkid on the way in October."

"Huh, guess you never know what level Sara will stoop to."

I don't care so much about what Sara's up to in the present, but I do care that innocent people are being hurt by her selfish actions. The mayor has been married for thirty years and is the father of two. He and his wife are active in the community and push to promote and support their charities of choice. The fact that his wife is collateral damage in Sara's self-centered quest to find herself a sugar daddy turns my stomach. It also makes me damn glad I wised up and got away from her after I moved here. If I was still with her, I could be in the same boat as the wife.

My thoughts turn back to the only woman I can see myself settling down with. No way would Jaime screw around on anyone. Not only is she loyal, but she knows what it feels like to be discarded. She understands the heartache bestowed upon by your partner better than most, because she lived it. Jaime doesn't trust easily, I can tell. Not since her douche ex left her before the wedding. That's why I'll take extra care of the trust she's given me in the past month. That simple gesture is a true gift.

We just secure the final tress when my phone rings a third time. I watch as the guys all make it safely to the ground before I pull the phone from its holster on my tool belt.

"Hello?" I ask, recognizing the office number immediately.

"Ryan! I've been trying to call you! Where are you?" Mary asks, her voice hoarse and filled with emotion.

"I'm hanging tresses at the Hazelton place. I told you I'd be here all day. What's up?" I'm instantly filled with concern, and maybe a bit of dread.

"It's Paula," she cries into the phone. "She's gone."

My heart drops into my steel-toed boots and a ball of emotion lodges firmly in my throat. My soul aches for my friend and the wife he has lost. At such a young age, to be stripped of life by a horrible disease that shows no mercy, no prejudices, no discrimination.

Realizing I'm still on the roof, I say, "I'm on my way." I slip my phone back into the holster and climb down.

Back on ground, my guys are gathered around, snacking or drinking to rehydrate. When they see the stricken look on my face, they know. Each one stands up and faces me. Fighting the emotions threatening to choke me, I deliver the bad news. "She's gone." They know who I'm referring to. They've been fighting this battle alongside Orlando and his family since the beginning as well.

The mood is somber, all eyes dropping to the dirt as they process what I've said. Orlando has been a part of our team since day one for Elson Construction, but he and his family have been a part of this community their entire lives. Everyone knew and loved Paula and respects Orlando as a co-worker and friend.

"I'm running back to the office to help Mary. Why don't you guys pack everything up for the day and take off."

"Should we go over there, boss?" Tyson asks.

I contemplate what Orlando would want. Does he want a house full of sweaty construction workers? Would he lean upon us as friends, drawing strength from the group, or would he prefer to not be seen in this moment of weakness and loss?

"Why don't I stop by and see how he's doing? If he's up for a visit, I'll let you know."

"Sounds good. Maybe we can all meet up at The Beaver later. Have a beer and toast in her honor," Danny suggests.

A beer sounds great right about now. Hell, maybe even a shot of something strong, something that sets my stomach ablaze. Even though it's barely three o'clock, I could definitely use a stiff drink.

Waving goodbye to my guys, I slide into the truck and head towards the office. If I'm going to head over to Orlando's place, I'm sure Mary will want to go with me. Plus, she always has a way of saying the right thing, so it'll help to have her as a buffer between my fumbling mouth and the bereaved.

I hate this, but if I'm going to do it, might as well get it over with.

Jaime

19

"I'm going to need help with deliveries this afternoon. I called in Rachel, who fills in occasionally for me when I'm in a bind. She's coming in at two to watch the shop. I have to take all of the arrangements over there to Serenity Chapel and Jupiter Bay Hospital," she says, pointing to the workbench loaded up with dozens of plants and arrangements. "And I'd like you to take all of the smaller deliveries. There's three business stops in downtown, plus another six to go to other places. That okay with you?"

"Of course. Whatever I can do to help," I tell her. I'm a little nervous, though. It's my first official delivery run.

"Okay, well, why don't you get this place straightened up the best you can. I'm sure once we get all of these arrangements out of the way, Rachel will be able to clean up better while we're gone," Payton suggests.

I glance around at the mess we've created today, since just before lunch. In fact, lunch consisted of sharing a sleeve of Ritz crackers with Pay while we put the finishing touches on a dozen arrangements to go to a memorial service at one of the local chapels. Today was, by far, the busiest day I've had at Blossoms and Blooms, and it's barely after one.

"You take my car. I've got boxes in the back with holes cut out to help hold the arrangements. That'll keep them from falling over while you're driving. I'll take the van because there's no way we're getting that plant into my little Ford," she says, pointing to the three-foot tall potted Peace Lily plant that she's delivering to the hospital.

For the next thirty minutes, we work to strategically place all of the orders in either the shop delivery van or her car. It's like a giant jigsaw puzzle, each piece needing to go in just right to ensure easier transport.

A few minutes before two, Rachel comes flying through the door. She's in her early twenties, with shoulder length blond hair and sparkling blue eyes. She reminds me a lot of a young Reese Witherspoon, circa *Cruel Intentions*.

"I'm here! And I brought smoothies," she adds, setting a container with three strawberry smoothies on the counter.

"Oh my God, you're a lifesaver," Payton groans as she plucks one of the cups from the tray and takes a long pull. "Soooooo goooooooood."

"Clearly we didn't get much to eat for lunch," I chime in, reaching for the third remaining smoothie. "I'm Jaime, by the way."

"Rachel. Nice to meet you. When Payton mentioned you guys worked through lunch, I thought you could use a little pick me up. This smoothie is rich in...well, it's rich in sugar and carbs. But, hey, the strawberries they use are fresh, so that has to count for something, right?"

"Right!" I chime in at the same time Payton says, "Absolutely!"

"And besides, something had to offset the healthy, so I had them add extra whipped cream," Rachel says without pulling her mouth away from her straw.

"Genius." I'm practically chugging the fruity drink, anxious to get to some of that whipped cream that's layered on top.

"Anyway, we're going to go. You know what to do with the store, but call me on my cell if you have any questions," Payton says before grabbing her purse from behind the counter.

"Got it. Go make your deliveries, and I'll take care of everything here," Rachel says before turning and grabbing a broom. The floors are covered with remnants of leaves, flowers, and ribbon.

When I get out to Payton's loaded car, I'm instantly assaulted by twangy country music. I was always more into pop, but Payton always steered towards country. When we were growing up, sharing a room, our differences in music always caused petty arguments. It's not that I didn't like that style of music; it's just that I preferred Maroon 5 and Britney Spears over Jason Aldean and Luke Bryan.

My first delivery is to an insurance office only two blocks down from Blossoms and Blooms. The receptionist smiles when I deliver a beautiful arrangement of red roses from her husband. The next two stops are equally as excited to receive their flowers.

I head off the main drag and start to hit my other deliveries. There are four to houses, one to a hotel, and the final one to an agency that wasn't around when I lived in Jupiter Bay before.

Addie's Place is housed in a large home on the west edge of town, clear on the opposite side of the Bay. The house is familiar, of course. Back when I grew up here, and until the time I graduated high school, a local physician and his family lived in this home. It's a two-story, white home with pillars on the front porch that extends all the way up to the second story. Blue shutters frame each window, and the entrance is a beautifully carved oak door with ornately etched glass spanning both sides.

I step up to the door and ring the bell. A series of harp-like chimes can be heard echoing throughout the house. It only takes a moment before a woman wearing jeans and a fitted tee comes to the door. Her smile is friendly as she looks between me and the flowers I'm holding.

"Can I help you?" she asks.

"I'm from Blossoms and Blooms and I have a delivery for Jasmine Ferdinand."

"That's me," she replies, that smile widening, blue eyes twinkling.

"Then these are for you," I say, holding the bouquet towards her.

Behind her, a phone begins to ring, pulling her attention back into the house. "I'm sorry, could you step inside for a moment? I have to answer that," she says, holding the door open.

Stepping inside, I realize quickly that, while it's an older home, it's bright and cheerful and tastefully modern. The old woodwork remains the same, but it's painted a soft beige color. The walls are a darker taupe with brightly colored paintings adorning every wall. In fact, upon closer inspection, the paintings appear to be original pieces, possibly done by a child.

My attention is drawn to the fireplace where instead of logs and a fire, it's filled with tractors, cars, trucks, and airplanes of every shape and size. Instead of a couch, loveseat, and chair, as you might normally find in a large living room, the room is filled with smaller plastic chairs, bean bags, and a card table with a half-finished puzzle on the top. There's no television, but there's a mural depicting children playing at a playground.

I'm lost in the beauty of this place, still unsure exactly what *this place is,* when Jasmine returns from another room.

"I'm so sorry about that. I'm the only one inside right now, so I need to man the phones," she says with another friendly smile.

"Oh, it was no problem," I reply, stepping closer. "These are for you." Extending my hand, I finally hand over the desktop arrangement of white lilies and pink roses.

"These are splendid! And two of my favorite flowers combined. Thank you so much." Reaching for the envelope, she quickly removes it from the holder and rips it open.

This is the part where I would leave, but something is drawing me to this place. While Jasmine reads the card, I glance around at a grouping of four paintings. Each one depicts a different season along the coastal shores. Falling snow along the sandy dunes, spring flowers in full bloom, a blazing sun over sandcastles, and fall leaves blowing out to sea; each one drawn with great detail and love.

"Those were completed earlier this spring by four students in high school who come to our program after school each day."

"Program? What kind of program is this?" I ask, turning my full attention to the woman behind me.

"It's a safe haven for children who come from less than ideal circumstances. If a single mother is in need of someone to watch her young children after school, but she can't afford to pay a sitter, she can bring them here. If a child needs help with homework but isn't able to use a tutor for whatever reason, they can come here. We offer a place for children to come hang out in a safe social setting, completely supervised."

"So, you help kids who are less fortunate?" I ask, completely in awe with the idea of this place.

"Yes. We have a young man who is a freshman in high school whose father struggles to keep food on the table. He comes here after school, studies and completes his homework, and even helps the younger kids with their studies. We feed him a nutritious meal before sending him home for the night." I'm completely transfixed on her words.

"Another young girl's mother and father were killed in a boating accident last summer. She now lives with her grandparents. She's withdrawn and doesn't speak much. She's been seeing a therapist since it happened, and everyone thought that subjecting her to a social setting with other kids might help. The little girl has been smiling lately and even says a few words every now and again," she says.

"This place is amazing. You help children."

"We do. At least, we try our best. Addie's Place was named after a little girl I knew once. She was a beautiful child with long, raven black hair and dark brown eyes that looked almost midnight. Her mother was an amazing woman who helped me once upon a time. When I needed it, she was there, and her daughter was as well. Every step of the way, I could count on both Laurie and her daughter Addie to keep me safe and provide me with friendship and love. That's what this place represents."

I don't even realize that a tear slipped from my eye until I feel it hit my hand. "You were one of these kids," I state.

"Yes. And I grew and thrived because of their help. Now it's my turn to give back and help those kids who need a little extra guidance or those parents who need a bit of assistance."

"And they don't pay you? How do you keep this place going?"

"Well, the home was donated by Laurie and her husband, Dr. Keith Whitmore. They continue to pay the property taxes and the electric and gas bills each month. And we seek donations, which help cover two small salaries, as well as food and the remaining utilities. We've also secured several grants over the last few years, which aid in different areas such as supplies and building maintenance."

My mouth is hanging open as I gaze around once more. "You truly have a beautiful place, and your cause is amazing."

"Well, I think so too. My assistant's husband was relocated for his job and they are moving away next week. This beautiful arrangement is from them. I have yet to fill her position. I keep hoping that if I don't fill it, she won't leave," she adds with a laugh.

"You're looking for an assistant?" I ask, something that feels like hope mixed with excitement bubbling to the surface.

"Yes," she confirms and gives me a long look. Suddenly, her face lights up. "Wait. You're not looking for a new job, are you?"

"Maybe," I whisper.

"But you have a job at the flower shop."

"It's my sister's place," I inform her. "She just gave me a job until I found what I want to do with my life."

Lines form between her brows. "What is it you want to do with your life?"

"I don't know." That particular confession has always been difficult, at least it has in the last year. Before, I knew what I wanted. I had lists to prove it. Now? I'm still trying to figure that out.

"The pay is barely above minimum wage," she says, hope filling her eyes.

I glance around, taking in the handmade paintings and the toys and the life that's breathed into this place. Within these walls, I feel something bigger, something great. Something important. And I want to do my part, even if it's just a tiny piece of the monstrous puzzle of life.

"If you're offering, I'll take it."

After going back to the flower shop, I help Rachel, and eventually Payton, close up. It has been a long, stressful day, but excitement still courses through me. Of course, I have yet to talk to Pay about the things that transpired this afternoon while I was out on deliveries.

Once Rachel leaves, I turn my attention towards my oldest sister. She's closing down the register and pulling the receipts from the bin.

"I can feel you staring at me. What is it?" she asks without taking her eyes away from the task at hand.

"I, uh, have something I need to talk to you about," I tell her nervously.

Hearing the uncertainty in my voice, Payton turns her full attention on me. "What's wrong?" she asks, her face pinched with worry.

"I think I'm quitting," I whisper.

"You *think* you're quitting? Honey, you better be pretty darn sure," she says, grabbing her stack of paperwork.

"I made a delivery today to Addie's Place," I start.

"Yeah, I've heard about that place. Never been there, but I've heard great things."

"Well, the lady who runs it, Jasmine, we, umm, got to talking. Turns out, her assistant is leaving town, and she's going to need someone to help her with the center and some of the activities."

Payton smiles at me. My heartbeat instantly drops to a more normal rate as I take in her relaxed demeanor. "That's wonderful, Jay. You're going to work at Addie's Place?"

"Yeah," I tell her confidently, a wide smile cresting my face.

"That's awesome! And I can see it in your eyes that you're super excited about it."

"I am."

"Good. I've been waiting for this moment. I knew floral arrangements wasn't your thing," she says as she steps towards me.

"You're not mad?"

"Mad? Why would I be mad at you for finding what you want to do with your life?" she asks, those lines back between her manicured eyebrows.

"I don't know, I guess I just thought you'd be mad that I left you shorthanded."

"Oh, don't you worry about me," she says with the wave of her hand. "I have a stack of applications in the office that I can pull out. I'm just excited for you! When do you start?"

"A week from Monday." I pause before continuing. "I'm a little scared, Pay. I feel like I've been drifting for so long, not really knowing what I want to do, but finally I have purpose. I feel like, for the first time in my life, I have something new, something that's mine. Does that make sense?"

"Of course it does. For so many years, you were a Stepford Wife in training. It wasn't who you were deep down. This is your first major step at finding who the real Jaime Summer is."

"Yeah."

"And I bet Ryan is going to be excited for you," she adds, eyes sparkling.

"You think?"

"I know. Because if that boy has any feelings for you, it's love. He'll be excited because *you're* excited. Trust me."

My heart flutters as the word *love* radiates through the room like the first ray of sunlight after the darkest of nights. An uncontrollable smile spreads across my lips, and my heart rate kicks back up again. Love. Does Ryan really love me? I've been ignoring it, denying those feelings that keep warming my body, because I'm afraid that they might not be reciprocated.

Sure, Ryan has told me he cares about me, but caring and loving are two different things. I care about a lot of things, but I only love a select few.

But I'm also unable to deny it any longer. I can tell my head over and over again that I don't feel that way about him, but my heart won't let me deny it. I feel it settle in my soul, warming my entire being from the inside out, wrapping around me warmly and completely.

I'm in love with Ryan.

kXk

I can't fight the excitement I feel as I head towards Ryan's condo. We have plans for dinner at six, but I just can't wait to see him. Instead of being nervous and scared of my revelation, I'm embracing it. For the first time since my mess of a relationship with Gavin ended, I've allowed myself to feel something beautiful, something great.

Pulling into his half of the driveway at barely five-thirty, I get out and run to his door. After my insistent knocking goes unanswered, I finally stop and look around. Ryan's truck isn't in his driveway. Usually when he gets home, he leaves his garage door open while he helps Mrs. Hanson with any yard chores. Glancing back around front, I realize the door is still closed.

I am thirty minutes early, but I can't help but feel a bit disappointed that I won't be able to share my news with him right away. Making my way around back, I decide to sit at the patio and enjoy a little bit of the evening July warmth. When I step around the side of the house, I'm greeted by the smiling face of Mrs. Hanson.

"Good evening, child. I haven't seen Ryan yet today," she says as she walks towards me.

"I'm a bit early for dinner. I hope you don't mind me coming back here and hanging out," I tell her as I follow her towards Ryan's stairs.

"It's not entirely my backyard, sweetie. Ryan will be happy to see you here with he arrives home," she says. The warm smile she gives me causes my lips to mirror hers. "You don't mind if I keep you company for a bit, do you?"

"Of course not. Do you want something to drink? Lemonade?" I ask, then instantly realizing that I don't have access to Ryan's house. The doors are locked, and until he comes home, I don't have any of the lemonade I just offered.

"Actually, I have a pitcher of sweet tea that just finished brewing on the counter. Would you mind going over to my place and grabbing it for us?" Mrs. Hanson offers.

"Of course," I respond, standing up and walking towards her door.

"Grab the tray of cookies beside it, as well," she hollers just as I reach the back door.

Mrs. Hanson's condo is just as I'd picture it. Floral prints and decorative knick-knacks as far as the eye can see, and it smells like home. Warm cinnamon and baked bread fills the air. And right where she said it would be, a pitcher of cool tea sits beside a small tray of homemade oatmeal raisin cookies. Stuffing two glasses beneath my arm and grabbing the other items, I head back outside to where I left Ryan's neighbor.

"Oh, bless you, child," she says as I deposit the pitcher and tray on the tabletop. Mrs. Hanson holds the two glasses so that I can pour the fresh tea. "I hope you like a hint of raspberry. My grandma used to always add fresh mint leaves or raspberries to her tea when she brewed it."

"I've never had it this way," I say before taking a sip. The tartness of the tea, mixed with the sweet and fruitiness of the raspberries is delicious and incites my taste buds.

"Good, right?" she asks, her kind, warm eyes sparkling.

"I think your grandma was on to something," I confirm.

"This is her recipe, too," she says, offering me the tray of cookies.

It's still warm as I take a bite, the cinnamon and sugar dissolving on my tongue. "Oh my God," I groan moments before stuffing the rest of the cookie in my mouth in a very unladylike fashion. "It's a good thing I don't live next to you, Mrs. Hanson. I'd weigh over three hundred pounds."

Besides a brief chuckle, we're both quiet for several minutes. The breeze is starting to cool as the sun begins to descend. Birds chirp and the air is fragrant with the scent of Mrs. Hanson's flowers. It's a perfect little spot to enjoy the evening. Maybe when Ryan gets home from work we can sit outside for a bit.

I smile a bit to myself at the thought of Ryan and me enjoying this patio more often, maybe even every night. That one little thought sparks a thousand more just like it. The two of us sharing a place of our own. Us sitting on a deck similar to this one as we watch a child run and play in the yard. Those thoughts consume me, but don't scare me. Instead, they ground me.

"Have you told him?" Mrs. Hanson asks, pulling me away from my thoughts of Ryan.

"Told him what?" I ask curiously.

"That you're in love with him," she states matter-of-factly.

"Oh, I'm...well, it's not really..." I start, but then stop. "No."

Her smile is the same knowing smile my grandma gives me often. "You should. I bet he'd love to hear you say it."

"You think?" I ask both excited and inquisitively.

"I know, child. Tell him," she says, glancing down at the watch adorning her dainty wrist. "I'm sure Ryan will be along any moment. I'm going to slip inside. It's almost time for *Wheel of Fortune*," she says.

"Take the tea and cookies inside with you when he gets home," she adds while turning and walking to her door.

"Thank you," I holler before she slips inside.

Instead of a reply, she gives me a knowing nod and steps through the door.

I'm lost in thought, running through my afternoon one more time when I realize it's surely been a while and Ryan still isn't home. Grabbing my cell phone, I confirm my suspicions and realize it's already quarter til seven. No messages and no missed calls. A sliver of worry slips down my back, causing goose bumps to pepper my arms.

I quickly dial his number, but it goes straight to voice mail. "You've reached Ryan Elson. Please leave a message after the beep, and I'll call you back."

Beep.

"Hey, Ryan, it's me. I'm at your place, and I thought you'd be here by now. I was just checking to see how long you'd be. Let me know. 'Kay, Bye." I hang up and wonder how dumb that message is going to sound to his ears.

I sit another fifteen minutes, but don't get a return call. I pull up my messages, wondering if maybe my phone is acting up. But when I'm greeted with "No New Messages" on the screen, I start to get a little worried.

Standing up, I start to pace. I walk from one end of the deck to the other. It doesn't take long. When I finish what is probably lap number one thousand, I grab my phone again.

Nothing.

I pull up the text message screen again.

| **Me:** | Is everything ok? I thought you'd be home by now. |

Send.

Five minutes later, it goes unanswered.

Panic starts to set in. What if he had an accident at work? What if he had an accident while on his way home? Who would they call in case of an emergency? Ryan doesn't have any family around here. Would they call his family in? Or Sara?

That thought sends my stomach straight into my shoes.

I contemplate my next move. I can go over and get Mrs. Hanson, but I don't want to worry her if he's just working late. I could call all the hospitals, but I'm not family so they won't give me any information. I could drive around and look for him like some crazy, stalker ex-girlfriend, but that thought just makes me feel sad and depressed.

Surely this isn't Ryan's way of moving on, is it? He wouldn't drop me like this without so much as a word of goodbye, right? Everything I've discovered, everything I know of this man is that he is nothing–and I mean, *nothing*–like Gavin. Ryan has given me no reason to distrust him, so I'm not about to start now.

Pushing thoughts of Ryan leaving me high and dry as far out of my mind as possible, I focus on the theory that something is wrong. I spend another thirty minutes coming up with my game plan, which is essentially nothing. I don't know where to look for him, and I don't know what to do. I make several laps around the front of the house, just to check the driveway, and still come up empty.

When the clock hits eight, I'm beyond worried. I'm terrified.

Not even noticing that the sun has almost disappeared and that I'm cold in my fitted tee and capris, I grab my keys and purse. I have no idea where I'm going, I just know that I can't stay here. If something has happened, I need to find out what. Sitting here isn't doing anything but sending me into panic attacks.

As I slip into the driver's seat, my phone starts to ring. My hand shakes as I pull it up and see the name. Relief sweeps through me as I fight the onslaught of tears threatening to fall.

"Ryan!" I practically yell into the device.

"Is this Jaime?" I hear my name, but the voice doesn't register.

"Yes," I whisper, barely audible.

"This is Danny, and I work for Ryan. We've got a little problem."

20

Ryan

When I glance out the dusty window, it looks as if the sun was setting, but that can't be right. The guys and I just got here a bit ago, an hour maybe. Two tops.

"You all right, boss?" Danny asks, his eyes full of concern.

"Yep. Feelin' greaaaaaaaat," I slur, drawing out the vowels as if it were a thirty letter word.

"I can see that. Hey, I went ahead and called Jaime for you, okay?" he asks, setting a glass of clear liquid in front of me.

"I'm not mixing vodka with my tequila, Dan-Oooooooo. And why would you call Jaime? I'm supposed to meet her for dinner in a bit. Let me know when it's five so I can head home and clean up."

"Yeah, it was five about three hours ago," he says with a firm slap on my back.

"Bullshhhhhhhhit," I grumble and grab my phone. The numbers on the clock dance before my eyes as if they're suddenly on the move. As steady as I try to hold it, the damn numbers just keep shaking. "Why'd ya call my girl?"

"Because someone needs to come help you home. I'd do it, but I'm not as pretty as she is to wake up next to," he laughs. "Besides, you're not really my type," he adds.

"She's fuckinnnn' beautiful, isn't she? Like, I can't breathe whenever she's around. I want to fall to my knees and thank God every time she smiles at me," I mumble. "But then I think 'bout Orlandooooooo and he's at home crying 'cause he lost his wife, his whole world. I don't want to lose my wife, man."

"You gotta have a wife to lose one," he says matter-of-factly.

"I want one. I want her to be my wife. Will she be my wife?"

"You're asking the wrong person, man. If you want to marry her, you should ask her," he says, throwing a twenty down on the bar as a tip. "But you should probably wait and ask her when you're sober."

"I am so-burrrrrr," I tell him.

"As sober as a fish swimming in a barrel of Jim Beam," he smarts off. Mr. Smarty Pants can kiss my...

I remember telling the bartender that drinks were on me, but I have no clue if I've paid anything yet or not. The rest of the crew all left throughout the course of the evening, but I didn't feel like going home alone. Instead, I decided to drink my problems away, lost in the despair I witnessed first hand when we went to see Orlando. His eyes were bloodshot and he looked like he hadn't slept in days.

Thoughts of someday losing a spouse have sent me spiraling into a bottle of whiskey. In every scene, I picture a gorgeous woman with long brown hair and light green eyes. The idea of one day waking up and finding her gone has left me troubled and scared. Suddenly, the life I want so damn bad with Jaime is looking more like a death sentence. I mean, why the fuck would I want to dive headfirst into a long term relationship just to be left gutted and heartbroken in the end?

I don't want that.

But I want Jaime.

But I can't have her without one day losing her.

But if it happens now, maybe it won't hurt as bad as it will later.

My brain hurts as alcohol-induced thoughts bounce from one extreme to the other. Closing my eyes, I take several deep, calming breaths just to try to settle my stomach. The booze I consumed threatens to make a reappearance, and my head pounds as if a drummer took up residence between my ears.

"Look who's here," Danny says as he slaps a hand on my back and stands up.

My goddess walks in, her eyes filled with concern. I'm finally able to breathe again. For the first time since I walked into Orlando's house, my lungs fill with air.

"Hi," she says stepping up to me.

Her hair is pulled back in a loose knot behind her head. My fingers twitch to dive in, freeing those sexy-as-fuck locks from captivity.

"Come 'er," I mumble, extending my hand towards her.

"You got him?" Danny asks.

"Yeah, we're good," she says without taking her eyes off mine.

Jaime steps forward, and I pull her flush against me. Her lips are parted, her breath coming out in little pants against my face. I need a taste; one final taste before I cut the cord and let her go.

I press my lips against hers, my body filling with desire. Suddenly, the thought of never tasting these lips again, never kissing her goodnight or seeing her sleepy, morning smile, isn't an option. It's the worst possible scenario there is.

As my lips urge her mouth open, I slip my tongue inside of her sweet mouth. She tastes like whiskey and fire; or that could be me. Jaime moans, my dick responding the only way it knows how. I'm hard and hungry for her. Only her.

She grips the back of my t-shirt, and suddenly, I'm trapped between a drunk that is fueled by whiskey and an intoxication that is pure Jaime. Both leave my head swimming and warmth spreading through my blood stream.

There's something soothing about her kisses, like a salve for my soul. They're sensual. They're potent. They're invigorating. They're all I can think about. Her lips are magical.

My cock is trying to burst through my jeans to get to her. I need to be inside of her like I need air. She's my lifeline. Jaime rubs herself against the strain in my pants, and I'm lost. I'm adrift in a world where only she and I exist. Pulling her closer yet, I feel the swell of her tits smash against my chest, her nipples tight little pebbles within her bra. Even through layers of material, I can feel them. My mouth waters to lick and tease until she's withering and begging for mercy.

"I need you to go home with me," I tell her without removing my lips.

"I am going home with you. I'm your ride."

"No, I need to be inside of you so bad. I need to feel your tight body wrap around my cock. It's the best feeling in the whole world. I don't want to feel that with anyone else ever again. Only. You."

Jaime gasps before I can resume the kiss. Her eyes tear up, and I wonder how in the fuck I messed it up already. She's only been here for a few minutes, and I've already made her cry.

"I'm sorry, I didn't mean to hurt you. Don't cry, baby. It breaks my heart to see you about to cry. Ignore me. I've been drinking and I don't know what I'm saying, and I -" I start, but stop when a small smile plays on her lips.

"No, they're not bad tears. They're the good ones."

"Women are so damn confusing sometimes."

"I know. How about we head back to your place?"

Grabbing my wallet, I pull the first plastic card I can find and throw it on the bar. The man who has served my employees and me all evening grabs it and swipes it through his machine. Without even looking at the total, I sign something that resembles my name and grab the card, jamming it back in wherever it will fit.

If I'm honest with myself, I'm staggering on my feet. Jaime wraps her arm around me, and I like to think that she's trying to get close to me and not solely because she's offering me additional support. Outside, Jaime leads me towards her car, opening the passenger door and helping me slide–uncoordinatedly, I might add–inside.

Jaime slips in the driver's seat and starts the car. I watch, mesmerized by her beauty, as she drives towards my condo. The streetlights reflect off her hair, lighting up her eyes. "You're stunning," I tell her, praying that my words don't come out of my mouth as jumbled as they seem in my head.

She looks over at me and gives me a sexy little grin. "You're drunk."

"True, but that still doesn't mean what I said wasn't true. You're the most beautiful creature I've ever seen."

Her throat seems to work hard at swallowing and her hands grip the steering wheel. I'm distracting her, I know, so I choose to keep my mouth shut until we're back at my place. Then all bets are off.

When she pulls into my driveway and parks her car, I jump out. Well, it might have reflected a stumble. I'm around to her side of the car before she even has the door open. Jaime startles when I throw the door open. My eyes are wild as they consume her long, slender legs as she slides out of her car. Suddenly more sober than ever before, I grab her by the hips and lift. Automatically, Jaime wraps her legs around my waist.

"You shouldn't do this," she tells me breathlessly. But the look in her eyes confirms that she's more on board with this plan than she's letting on.

Without saying a word, I walk towards my front door. My strides are swift as I take the steps two at a time and stumble into the front door. Jaime gasps as her back hits the steel door, but then giggles uncontrollably.

"Are you alright?" I ask, concerned that in my haste to get her inside and naked that I'd hurt her.

"I'm fine. Are you alright?"

"I've never been better, baby," I tell her just before I claim those lips once again.

The kiss is feral, hungry, possessive. Mine. But she owns me, as well. Jaime has every piece of me. Body, mind, and soul.

Somehow, I get the door open. I hear my keys hit the floor just as the door slams behind me. I move hurriedly, each step I take bringing me closer to my bedroom. Jaime breaks the kiss, but only to slide her wet, swollen lips down the column of my neck. I shudder against her, my arms tightening around her.

We fall atop my bed a tangled mess of limbs and fumbling hands. My desire for her consumes me like a wildfire, ripping at and devouring me with every breath of air I take. Zeroing in on her neck, I lick a burning path along her tender skin. Gasps of pleasure erupt from her mouth, fueling my need even further.

"I need you so fucking much," I confess, running my large hand down the path I just licked, continuing down her side towards her hip.

"I need you, too." Her words stop my movements as I focus on those beautiful green eyes.

"I'm not talking about just tonight," I say, my heart rate spiking to a dangerous level.

"I'm not either."

I close my eyes, absorbing and savoring the meaning of those words. They may not be the three little words I long to hear spill from her lips, but they're equally as sweet. Equally as meaningful.

My fingers tremble as I rise up on my haunches and start to remove her clothes. Our eyes remain locked the entire time, unspoken words spilling forth between us. This is everything. *She's everything.*

Jaime lies naked before me and I want–no, *need*–nothing more than to be naked with her. With legs and hands that seem to only wanna work half the time, I strip myself of my boots, jeans, and t-shirt. The rest of my clothes are gone as quickly as possible too.

Her eyes drink their fill, starting at my chest and roaming down to my cock. He's jetting long and proudly outward, throbbing with need to be inside of this gorgeous woman.

"Baby, I need to be inside of you so bad. I can't wait another second."

"Don't wait," she pants, extending her arms out to me.

Sliding between her thighs, I rest my cock at her entrance. She glistens in the moonlight, wet and full of her own need and desire. Lining us up perfectly, I slide myself through her wetness. My blood ignites and my body shudders.

Deliberately, I slowly push the head inside. She's warm and hot and ready for me. Suddenly, I stop. Without moving, I look down and realize I'm not wearing a condom. "Shit."

"No," she says, grabbing my arm when I go to get up. "I'm on the pill. Please, Ryan. I want to feel you without it."

I hear her words, but it takes a moment for the meaning to register. No condom. No barrier between her body and mine.

Looking down at her, I see the conviction in her eyes. I don't need to ask if she's sure, because I'm witness to it. I feel it. So with a painstakingly slow stroke, I slide completely inside of her until I'm fully seated to the root. She's tight and hot and wet in a way that I've never experience before. Her eyes are wide with passion as she grips me from inside.

Leaning forward, I extend my body to completely cover her. Jaime wraps her legs around my waist and grips my back. With my eyes fully locked on hers, I pull out and slide back in. Warmth surrounds me, wrapping around me and pulling me forward. I'm trapped in a euphoric world that only Jaime creates, a place where only she and I exist. It's heaven, blissful and pure.

I keep a slow and tender rhythm as I make love to her. She never takes her eyes off mine as I convey everything I'm feeling, everything I want. Her. I want her.

Running my hands up her arms, I move them above her head. Entwining my fingers within hers, I slowly pull out and push back in, arching myself upward and grinding my hips. Jaime's eyes widen and her mouth falls open with each thrust of my hips. I place tender, open-mouthed kisses along her lips, jaw, cheeks, and forehead, only taking my eyes off hers for a few brief moments.

"Oh, God," she groans as I thrust upward with a little more force than before.

I continue to push her higher and higher until her eyes are glazed over with sweet surrender. Running my nose along her neck, I inhale deeply, committing the scent of her skin mixed with our arousal to memory.

"Jaime?" I ask, looking up at her lovely face. Her bottom lip trembles and her eyes fill with unshed tears. I get lost in the beauty of the moment, unable to control the words about to spill from my lips. "I love you."

A single tear leaks from the corner of her eye, getting lost in the sea of dark hair spilling over my pillow. Her jaw trembles as her intense gaze keeps hold of mine. "I love you, too."

Her words fall forth, lively and gripping. No words have ever meant more than those four little words coming from the woman I'm madly and truly in love with.

My lips devour hers in a bruising kiss that's filled with elation. My cock seems to recall exactly where it is and begins to move on its own. With each thrust, I drive us each closer to the edge of insanity. Mouths consume each other, swallowing each pant and groan of pleasure.

I feel her start to tighten around me, moments before she verbalizes her orgasm. Without the condom barrier, her body grips me so fucking tightly that I'm sure I'll never feel anything so wonderful in my life.

Against the pull, I pull out and push back in. Her arms squeeze around me as she quakes beneath me. I watch, mesmerized, as her orgasm sweeps blissfully through her body.

"Ryan," she moans loudly.

My name on her lips pushes me over the edge of white, blinding light. I'm consumed, but I keep my eyes on her, transfixed by her beauty and the power of our joint release.

"I love you," I groan. "I love you, I love you, I love you, Jaime." I can't stop saying it. Over and over until one orgasm turns into another for her. My hips continue to move, drawing out every ounce of pleasure I can lure from her body and my own.

When we're both finally boneless and spent, I fall, my body unable to hold up its own weight any longer. I slip to her side, worried that I'll crush her under my brutal weight. Jaime keeps her legs wrapped around me and moves in tandem with me. My cock is still fully embedded within her body.

Neither of us move. We're a mixture of sweaty limbs and panting mouths, as we lie perfectly still, wrapped in each other's arms.

Several minutes later, I start to feel her surrender to sleep. My arm begins to tingle beneath her, but there's no fucking way I'm moving. I have my arms wrapped around the woman I love, damp and spent from the most intense lovemaking I've ever experienced.

I've finally said it. I said the words I've wanted to say, but am now too terrified to speak. But she said them back. Jaime told me she loved me, without the look of fear or panic in her eyes. Tonight she gave me a gift. Not only her body without the barrier of protection, but her heart. Her broken heart that has been mended back together again, piece by piece.

And that might be the greatest gift of all.

As night consumes me, between the alcohol and the sex, I, too, finally surrender to the desire to sleep with a smile on my face.

kXk

Light pierces through my closed eyelids, penetrating my brain and causing the drummer inside of my head to breakout into an award winning solo. Whoever is jackhammering inside of my bedroom is about to find themselves on the receiving end of a right hook. I try to open my eyes, but the blinding light does nothing but cause a painful recoil in my stomach. Jeeezus!

I groan loudly, reaching blindly for a pillow to cover my head. When I'm encompassed in sweet darkness once again, I slowly try to reach for any fragment of memory as to what in the fuck happened to put me in this current state of pain.

"Ahhh, he lives." Her sugary voice permeates the horns and hammering pounding in my brain.

"The jury's still out on that," I mumble beneath the pillow.

I feel the bed dip beneath her body's weight and reach a hand towards her. "How's the head?" she asks as I feel the warm, smooth skin of her forearm.

"Shhhhhh. You're disrupting band practice. We must be quiet. Very, very quiet," I plead, my voice barely above a whisper.

"I brought you some Tylenol," she whispers, her fingers gliding across my chest.

Suddenly, my naked body stirs to life, pitching a tent with the sheet that would make the Boy Scouts proud. "I just want to lie here with you and sleep. Then we're going to put my hard cock to use because it seems to have missed the memo that I was hit by a bus last night."

Her chuckles fill the air as I throw back the sheet, the cooler air chilling my flush body. "Take these pain meds and I'll lie with you for a few minutes before I have to go to work."

Reaching blindly for the pills, I hold completely still until I feel the tablets dropping in my palm. Then she moves the pillow. "Fuck," I groan, pinching my eyelids closed as tightly as possible.

"It's not that bad, you big baby. Sit up and take a drink of water," she says sternly with an edge of authority in her voice. And holy hell if that tone doesn't turn me on even further.

I sit up but keep my eyes closed as I bring the bottle of water up to my lips. I chug greedily until half of it is empty, pop the pills in my mouth, and finish off the rest of the bottle. When I'm done, Jaime takes the empty bottle from my hands.

"Get in here," I tell her, yet to see her beautiful face.

"I have to go to work," she says, yet I still feel the bed dip as she inches closer to me.

Jaime lies against me and lets me spoon her body, her back to my front. She smells like strawberries mixed with my body wash, and I can't help but run my nose along the column of her neck. She's a combination of her scent and my own, and fuck if that doesn't turn me on even further. Right now, I've got a hard-on that'll last for days unless I do something about it quickly.

"Don't even think about it," she says, but it lacks the conviction she had earlier. She's all breathy and wiggles in my arms.

I pull her as close as humanly possible, ticked off that she's wearing clothes, so I slide my hand beneath her shirt and find the soft skin of her stomach. "What the hell happened last night? I don't remember being hit by a truck."

"What do you remember?" she asks as she gently runs her hand up and down my arm.

"I remember getting a call from Mary that Paula died. She's the wife of one of my employees," I tell her. "She had been battling breast cancer for a while now."

"I heard. I knew of them. It's a horrible tragedy, and I'm sorry for your friend's loss," she replies, pulling my arm tightly around her as if giving me a one-armed hug.

"Thank you. After I got the call, I went to see him. He was okay with all the guys coming over for a bit and we ended up hanging out, helping do a few things around the house. When his parents arrived, we all went up to The Beaver and decided to have a drink. Apparently, a drink meant half of the liquor they had stocked," I tell her, finally able to blink a bit in an effort to open my eyes.

"You appeared to be having a good time. Or a bad time, in this case."

"I was supposed to meet you for dinner," I say, pieces of last night starting to fall into place.

"Yeah, I tried calling you a few times. I was getting worried."

I squeeze tightly. "I'm sorry, baby. I didn't mean to scare you or miss our date. I don't know what happened really, but one minute we're all toasting her memory, and then the next minute sunlight is burning my eyes like I'm a vampire."

"You don't remember anything about last night?" she asks. There's no missing the disappointment in her voice. I've missed something or messed something up terribly, this I can tell. I just need to search my memory to figure out what so I can make it right.

"Not much. How did you get here?" I ask, praying that I haven't done something so bad I can't fix it.

"Danny called me before eight. He asked me to come up to The Beaver and help get you home."

"You helped me out to your car," I reply after the pieces of the puzzle in my mind start to fall into place.

"Yeah, you were able to walk well enough to my car, but I had to steer you a bit. I brought you back here," she starts, but stops talking. I can tell there's more to the story she's not saying.

I close my eyes again, letting the delicate contours of her body and the steady beat of her heart ground me as I search in my database for the memory.

And then it hits me.

Pulling her out of her car. Carrying her inside the house. Taking her to my bedroom. Stripping her naked. Not using a condom. Professing my love. It all comes back in a rapid-fire replay of lost time. I suck in a huge breath. I was going to end it with her because I was afraid. I was terrified knowing that, eventually, I would lose her, so the brilliant person that I am thought it was wise to let her go now so it would hurt less.

What a dumbass.

I move, letting her fall flat on the bed. She's resting on my arm as I hover over her. "We made love without a condom," I say, gazing down into her hypnotic green eyes, gently running my free hand along her side of her face. She gives me the faintest head nod. I know that it wasn't sex that we had last night, but something deeper, something truer. "And I told you that I loved you."

Jaime's eyes widen and her breath catches in her throat, but still she doesn't speak.

"I remember," I confirm. "I told you that I was in love with you, and you said it back."

"I did," she finally whispers, all hoarse and breathy.

"Did you mean it?" I ask, my lips hovering above hers.

Her only response is another head nod and eyes that fill with unshed tears. "Did you?" When the words leave her lips, she seems to hold on to her breath, waiting for my answer.

"I meant every word. I'm in love with you, Jaime. I'm an ass for finally saying it when I was three sheets to the wind. Believe me, it was never my intention to tell you like that, but I'm not sorry that I did. I'll never be sorry for telling you how I feel about you. And how I feel is that I'm so madly, completely in love with you, that the thought of not having you beside me, in my life, makes me feel crazy and out of control. I need you like air. I need your smile and your laugh and your goodness and your beauty surrounding me, because without it, I'm nothing. *You* make me whole."

A single tear spills from her eye, disappearing into her hair, and is quickly followed by a second and then a third.

"That might be the best thing anyone has ever said to me," she admits.

Just the thought of Jaime travelling through life without being worshipped for the magnificent creature that she is, is truly disturbing. It makes me want to find that Gavin guy and beat the crap out of him that much more. Every protective, not to mention jealous, inclination I have flairs to life with a vengeance.

I'd give anything to claim those soft, lush lips once more, prove to her how much she deserves to be adored and savored, but a cold bucket of reality splashes across my face. I haven't brushed my teeth. Fuck, I smell a nauseating mixture of two-day-old sweat and alcohol. Not to mention the fur that's growing on my tongue at the moment.

"I really want to kiss you, but I should probably clean up."

"I hope you don't mind but I used your cell phone to call that Danny guy who called me last night. I told him you weren't feeling well and that you'd be a little late."

"You did that for me?"

"Yeah, but I'm pretty sure he knows it's the brown bottle flu that's keeping you in bed this morning."

"I'm sure he does. And thank you," I say before brushing a closed mouth kiss across her sweet lips. God, what I wouldn't give to deepen that kiss.

"You're welcome," she purrs beneath me, her body arching upward as if seeking out the friction it craves.

"Stop that, temptress, or you'll never make it to work." To show her how serious I am, I rub the entire hard length of my cock against the junction of her thighs. My balls are painfully tight and swelling as we speak. At the rate I'm going, I'll need to spend a few extra minutes in the shower.

"I have an idea," I tell her, once again running my lips across hers and down her cheek to her chin, where I nip at the tender flesh on the underside. "Come away with me this weekend."

"What?" she gasps as I nibble down and along her collar bone.

"We'll go somewhere down the coast. Maybe a hotel in a small tourist town or a bed and breakfast out of the way where we can just be alone. What do you think?"

She mewls and pretends to be thinking about it, but I can tell by the way her eyes flutter and roll around that her mind is already set. "I think I get off work at two on Friday."

"I'll leave as soon as I get paychecks from the office. I can be ready to go by three. Come here when you're ready and we'll take off."

"Where are we going?" she asks, her warm hand sliding down and grabbing my ass.

"Don't know, don't care. As long as there's a bed and two uninterrupted days that I get to spend with you, then I just don't give a shit."

My eyes are met with sparkling green ones. "I'm in," she says, smiling an ornery little grin that's filled with dirty thoughts. "But first? I think you need a shower." Jaime reaches between us and cups my erection. The groan that erupts from my throat is loud and foreign, even to my own ears.

"Don't start something you can't finish," I threaten, thrusting my cock upward, loving the way it feels with her tight grip wrapped around it.

"Who said anything about not being able to finish?" she adds, the temptress.

My jaw is locked, my body rigid and tight with need. "Work. You. Leaving."

Jaime leans up and licks the shell of my ear. "I already called Payton and told her I was going to be late."

Jaime

21

Last night was the memorial service for Paula. Not only did Payton's shop make numerous deliveries of flower arrangements and plants, but Ryan asked me to go with him. It was our first big public display of togetherness, even if we've gone to dinner a few times. It felt like some sort of official proclamation to be at something so personal together, as if I was telling the world–or at least the town–that we were dating.

Not only did Ryan's company purchase the biggest display of flowers that we delivered, but he also made both a business and personal contribution to their daughter's schooling fund. As if I needed any more proof as to what type of man Ryan truly is, he goes and does something so selfless and caring that it brings tears to my eyes. "It's only money," he said after Orlando told me about the dual donations. "Your daughter's future is more important than it sitting in some bank account somewhere," Ryan had said before he hugged his friend.

I have yet to tell Ryan about my new job offer. I know, I know what you're going to say, but things have been a little hectic with his job and the memorial service. My plan is to tell him this weekend when we get to wherever it is we're going.

My bags are packed and in the trunk of my car, just waiting for the clock to strike two o'clock. Ryan isn't giving any inclination as to our destination, either. All he will say is that it's somewhere down the coast.

I'm giddy with excitement as I check the clock for the ten thousandth time since arriving at Blossoms and Blooms at nine this morning. Rachel has been working more hours lately, and has expressed interest in filling my vacancy when I leave for Addie's Place. She's more of the 'as needed' part timer with just a handful of hours each pay period. With her schooling schedule, she was always content with that. However, school dismissed at the end of May, and she's looking to fill more hours between the flower shop and Aces and Jacks, another local bar and grill that's a frequent hangout for the twenties crowd.

Next week is my last week with Payton, and even though arranging flowers into beautiful creations isn't my forte, I'm going to miss seeing and working with her. Payton and I, as the two oldest, have always been close. She supported me when the whole WeddingGate disaster went down, and helped scoop me up off the floor more times than I care to admit. I'm going to miss seeing her nearly every day, that's for sure.

"Earth to Jaime," Payton says just over my left shoulder, startling me.

"What?"

"Jeez, what is with you this week? You've been lost in your own little world with this lovesick little smile on your lips. It's nauseating," she adds goodheartedly.

"Whatever," I mumble. "I'm not lovesick."

"Oh, come on. Even a blind man can see how much you care for him. Maybe it's time you should tell him," she advises while gathering up fresh daisies for a bouquet.

I don't respond, but avert my gaze. That was a mistake. Eagle eye Payton zeros in on the change in my body language immediately. "What?" she asks.

"Nothing. Is Rachel coming in at two or are you going to cover the front counter?" I ask, deflecting.

"Jaime Marie Summer, look at me." Her tone is direct and full of authority. It reminds me of our mother's. Slowly, I turn around. Even slower, I draw my eyes upward until they're looking into the green eyes of my sister. "Say it."

"The other night, he told me he loved me," I say in one hurried rush of words and air.

Payton's jaw falls to the floor moments before she shrieks loud enough to wake half the dead at the cemetery. "OH MY GAWDDDDD! He said that he loved you? When? Where were you? Was it romantic? What did you say? Tell me, tell me! I need to know everything!"

"Calm down, Jessie Spano. Lay off the caffeine pills, will ya?" I ask, referring to a scene from my favorite childhood television show, *Saved By The Bell*.

She ignores my smart-alecky quip and stares me down until I produce the goods.

"Remember when I had to go pick him up at The Beaver?"

"Yeah?"

"Well, when we got back to his place, things started to get...hot, and he told me that he loved me."

"Wait." She gives me a pointed look. "So, he told you that he loved you...while you were having sex...while he was drunk?"

Well, when she says it like that it doesn't sound as beautiful as it was. "It wasn't like that. That night, things were different. It was slow and tender, and I could tell he was cherishing me. When he said it, there was conviction in his eyes. He meant every word. Plus, we talked about it the next morning."

"So, what did you say?" she asks, anxiously waiting for my response.

"I might have said that I loved him too."

"Might have said it? Honey, if you're going to say it, you best be sure."

"I am sure, Pay. I've known it for a bit now, but I was too afraid to put myself out there and say it first."

"I'm so glad you finally jumped. I have a feeling that Ryan is different. Hell, I've seen how he's different. When you're in the room, it's like no one else is around or matters. It's sickening, actually," she adds goodheartedly.

Without responding, I throw my arms around my sister and squeeze. "Thank you for all of the support and encouragement you've given me. I don't think I'd be ready to take this step if it weren't for you."

"Of course you would have, but if you want to give your beautiful older sister all the credit for the matchmaking, I'll take it!" Payton pulls back and smiles at me.

"Maybe I can return the favor sometime," I add, my mind flashing through mental pictures of local guys who would be perfect for her.

"Oh, no. No you don't! I don't need a man. I'm completely content being single and running my shop." I watch as she quickly keeps her hands busy by rearranging the daisies that are already displayed beautifully in the engraved vase.

"If you say so," I reply in a singsong voice.

I can't fight the smile that spreads across my lips as I sweep up the mess on the floor. Payton isn't destined to be alone any more than any of my other sisters. She's funny, driven, and beautiful, and she just needs a little nudge in the right direction.

I just moved Payton's love life up to the top of my to-do list!

We've been on the road for an hour, but it feels like we just started the journey. Conversation flows so easily with Ryan. We've each shared details of our day, and I've taken several guesses about our destination. I'm rewarded with a smile with each guess, but he doesn't give any hint as to whether I'm right or not.

"I have some big news to share with you," I start as we draw closer to the southeastern tip of Virginia.

"I'm all ears," he says, steering his big truck through countryside towns and small touristy destinations along the coast.

"I quit my job," I tell him confidently and with a huge smile, loving what those words mean.

Ryan's surprised, but I can see the excitement in his eyes. He's excited simply because I'm excited. "Tell me more. You're not moving two thousand miles away, are you?" He shoots me a look, and even through his sunglasses, I can see his concern. He's fearful that I'm about to up and leave.

"No, no," I reply quickly, grabbing his hand and linking our fingers. "I made a delivery earlier in the week to Addie's Place."

"Yeah, I know the place. We did some roof repairs there this past spring."

"Well, the assistant to the director quit and she was going to start looking for someone to replace her. Before I realized what was happening, I offered myself to fill her vacancy."

"That's awesome, babe," Ryan says, bringing my hand towards his mouth and brushing a kiss across my knuckles. "I'm not too familiar with what they do there, so fill me in."

"It's sort of a refuge for kids of all ages to go to play and learn after school or during the day if the parents need help. It's completely run by donations and grants, and does great things for kids who are less fortunate."

"That sounds like an amazing place, and I'm sure you'll be a real asset to the kids. I've never really heard what they do there, but I might just have to check into it further. If they survive on donations, maybe it's time I add them to my list of business contributions."

And there I go again, falling deeper in love with this amazingly supportive man.

"You're amazing," I tell him, unable to control myself as I lean over and place kisses all up and down his arm.

"Well, if that's all it takes to get you all worked up, I'll make donations more often," he quips.

"All you need to do is look at me and I get worked up. Thank you, though, for considering a donation. I'm sure they'll gladly accept any that they can get."

"What are you going to be doing?" he asks as we pull into a small town called Travelers End. Ryan turns off the main highway and winds us through a local route along the water.

"I'm not sure. When I was there, Amber, that's the assistant who's leaving, was outside reading stories to a small group of preschoolers. They said the after-school kids would be arriving soon, so they were trying to have a little quiet time before the chaos of a dozen older kids descended upon the house."

"I don't think it matters what you'll be doing, babe. It sounds like a great place," he adds while pulling off the road and heading down a short, gravel drive.

"I've done a little research since I accepted. I can't wait to start and do my part for these kids."

Ryan stops the truck beside an older Buick parked beside a garage and shuts off the engine. My attention is pulled towards a massive white house with lush, bright flowers hanging from baskets along a sprawling wraparound porch. Rich, brown shutters line each window, and lace curtains appear to be blowing in the open windows.

"What is this place?" I ask, following suit as Ryan unbuckles his seat belt.

"This, sweetheart, is where we're staying for the next two nights. It's a little Bed and Breakfast owned by Danny's grandparents. He said they're generally booked up months in advance, but when he called, they just happened to have a cancellation for this weekend."

"Wow, it's beautiful," I say, taking in the breathtaking view of the coastline in the background. The clear, blue water sweeps across the sandy shore, disappearing again in the vast Atlantic Ocean.

"Yes it is," Ryan confirms before opening his door. "Come on. The only thing standing between you and me getting naked is the elderly couple who will check us in." With that, he jumps out of the truck, comes around to help me out, and grabs our luggage.

The inside of the Bed and Breakfast is even better than the outside. The entire place has a Victorian feel to it, with floral prints and dark woodwork that looks original. The furniture looks antique, but comfortable at the same time. It doesn't have a 'look but don't touch' feel to it at all.

Off to the left is a large sitting room with wingback chairs and a deep burgundy settee. To the right, a dining room big enough to seat twenty comfortably. A buffet stands along the back wall with what appears to be fresh fruit, homemade muffins, and lemonade. There's also no mistaking the aroma coming from the kitchen. My stomach growls happily as the scent of Italian food fills the entire house.

"Ahh, you must be guests for this weekend," I hear.

Standing before us is a plump older gentleman with a friendly smile and a mischievous hint in his blue eyes.

"Yes, sir. I'm Ryan Elson. Your grandson, Danny, helped secure our reservation," Ryan says, stepping forward to shake the older man's hand.

"Of course, of course. You're Danny's boss. We're so happy to have you with us this weekend. I'm Martin, and my wife, Phyllis, is in the kitchen preparing dinner. I hope you both brought your appetites. My Phyllis knows how to cook homemade lasagna like no other. Her mother was Italian, and it's a specialty of hers. You're in for a real treat tonight," Martin says as he steps towards a small counter situated towards the back of the foyer.

"It smells wonderful. I can't wait," I add to the conversation.

"All of your reservation information was prepared over the phone, so we're all set on our end. Here's a pamphlet with tourist information around the area. You're free to come and go as you wish, and don't feel obligated to dine here every day," he says while handing Ryan a packet of information.

"Thank you," Ryan replies.

"If you'll follow me, I'll show you to your room."

We follow behind as Martin leads us towards a wide staircase. He's slow to ascend, but it gives me a moment to observe the artwork on the walls and the decorum filling every nook and cranny of the magnificent house.

At the top of the stairs, we're greeted with a large, bright hallway with four doors. "We have four guest rooms upstairs. Each is equipped with their own bathroom for privacy. Your room also locks, and we encourage you to lock your door whether you're in there or not. Though we've never had any problems of any sort here, you can never be too careful, you know?"

Ryan and I both nod our heads in agreement.

Martin opens one of the doors on the right, which happens to be at the back of the house, and steps aside. The view is breathtaking. The large, four-poster bed in dark, walnut wood is centered in the room. The duvet is white and plush, and is a strong contrast to the rich colors around it.

A small sitting area is situated in front of three large windows, all open to allow the ocean breeze inside. The dresser matches the woodwork of the bed, and has a massive brass mirror above it. Martin shows us two doors, one a nice-sized closet, and the other a bathroom. Inside, my attention is instantly pulled to the large, claw foot tub. While I've seen a few tubs like this before, this one seems larger than most.

Large enough for two people.

"Do you have any questions at this time?" Martin asks when we step back into the bedroom.

"I don't believe so," Ryan responds.

"Meal times are listed on the sheet with the pamphlet, as well as some amenities we offer. Dinner will be served in about forty-five minutes. We hope to see you there," Martin says as he walks towards the door.

"Thank you very much," I add, my eyes locking on Ryan's brown ones.

"You're welcome. Enjoy your stay."

I don't hear the door close, or the shuffle of Martin's feet as he walks away. I only hear my heart beating erratically in my chest and the heaviness of my breath. Oxygen is sucked from the room as I'm pulled into Ryan's ravenous gaze. He stalks towards me, hungrily, like I'm his prey, a small animal about to be devoured by the king of the jungle in one gulp.

"We don't have much time," I remind him as he reaches out and wraps his hand around my waist, pulling me into his broad chest.

"We have *just* enough time," he counters moments before he claims my lips with his.

The kiss isn't soft; it's fierce. Uncontainable. Driven. Like he has one job to do and that is to evoke the most pleasure as he can from this one act; a kiss to set the standard for any and all future kisses.

Well, Mr. Ryan Elson… Job. Well. Done.

kΧk

When dinner is finished, I'm so stuffed I can barely move. We're talking slip on your yoga pants and pass out on the couch after Thanksgiving dinner kinda stuffed. And Ryan didn't fare much better. He appeared to be groaning a little bit out of discomfort with that final helping of Phyllis' famous lasagna. Throw in a massive side salad–which we both skipped–and enough freshly baked Italian garlic bread to feed half of Virginia, and you have the makings of a hearty food coma.

Overeating isn't sexy.

But it couldn't be helped. Grandma is an excellent cook and spent my teenage years, like those of my sisters, teaching me to cook decent meals, but this meal? It puts all meals before it to shame. I may just decide to stay at this Bed and Breakfast forever.

The environment at this place is relaxed. Even though we're sharing a table with two other couples, it still feels intimate and personal. The other couples chitchatted with us through parts of the meal, but then it was easy to slip into cozy conversation with Ryan between.

One couple is from Illinois and is celebrating their third wedding anniversary. They, too, are staying the weekend. The second pair is a middle aged, married couple that have already been here for five days and is staying through Sunday. The final duo arrived shortly after us, but chose to dine in their bedroom this evening. Martin and Phyllis popped in and out throughout dinner to make sure there was always plenty of food available, to refill our drinks, and to visit with us all.

"Dessert will be ready in about thirty minutes," Phyllis says as she retrieves some of the dirty plates from the table.

"Uhhhhh," I groan. "It was so amazing, but I seriously don't think I could eat another bite."

"I have homemade apple pie with French vanilla ice cream and caramel sauce."

"I'll take her share," Ryan chimes in causing our tablemates to laugh. "I'm just fueling up for later," he whispers in my ear, hot breath fanning across my face.

"You're gonna be in a sugar coma and probably need insulin."

"I could never be too tired or too full to make love to you," he adds. Then, as if to seal his sentiment, he leans forward and kisses my lips.

"You two are so adorable. Ollie, remember when we used to make out like teenagers when we first met?" the middle-aged wife, Donna, asks her husband, Oliver.

"Oh, I remember. I believe that was back when kids had nothing to do but go parking on a deserted gravel road in the evenings," he says with a chuckle. Instantly, my cheeks burn with embarrassment.

"Uh oh, she's blushing," the female newlywed, Aimee, says with a big grin. "There's a story there," she adds with encouragement.

"No," I say at the same time Ryan snorts. "No, no story." I divert my eyes, dropping them to watch my finger slide nervously along my cloth napkin, all while reliving the entire embarrassing night we were arrested in my mind. Ryan remains quiet at my side and gives my knee a gentle squeeze.

So glad embarrassment could tail me all the way to the southern part of the state.

Ryan

There was a time in my life where being in Sara's company, even after a short period of time, was enough to drive me to drink. I know that's horrible to say, but it's true. The writing was on the damn wall in black paint well before the relationship officially ended.

She used to do this thing where she'd finger comb her hair with one hand and scroll through her social media feed with the other, paying absolutely zero attention to me or anyone else in the vicinity. I could have told her dancing elephants were in the room or that I wasn't wearing pants while dining at whatever fancy restaurant in the art district of Manhattan she begged me to take her to. Sara never paid attention to me unless it could directly boost her social status, and at times it was enough just to stick out the three-hour date.

Now Jaime? I want to be with her for hours, days, a lifetime. I don't ever want my time with her to end. I need her in my bed, in my home, and in my life. Period. In just the short time that I've known her, she has become my everything. When she's not with me, I'm lonely. When she's with me, I'm more content than ever before. I'm rushing headlong towards the cliff of Happily Ever After, at the corner of Matrimony Way and Forever Drive.

And you know what?

I'm ready.

If I could ask Jaime to spend the rest of her life with me right now, I would. But I don't think she's ready. Hell, deep down, I'm probably not quite ready. Not only have we not known each other for very long, we're both coming out of serious relationships, which come with scars. For me, they're surface scars, but that doesn't make them any less visible. Jaime's scars, on the other hand, aren't skin deep. She's still healing, whether she wants to admit it or not, and the last thing I need to do is push her away by talking about china patterns and reception venues.

No, instead, I'll take my time, savoring each moment I get with her. We'll create new memories that will smother the ones that fuckstick left her with. I'll work on replacing everything bad with new, beautiful things, because that's what she deserves, and I'll be damned if I'm not going to give her everything.

"Want to go for a walk?" I ask Jaime after we gorge on lasagna and garlic bread. Between the mouthwatering Italian food and the gorgeous woman beside me, this meal ranks in the top five meals ever consumed, that's for sure.

"Sure," she replies, offering me her hand.

Together, we walk hand-in-hand out the back door. The younger couple is sitting on the back deck, watching the waves crash along the shore. After a friendly wave to the others, I lead Jaime towards the gray sandy beach forty yards out.

For a bit, we walk quietly along the wet sand. I have her flip-flops and my own dangling from one hand, her soft hand in my other. Every so often, she bends down to pick up a seashell, and before too long, she has her hand full of iridescent shells of every shape and size. I could probably release her hand so she can collect more, but she's not volunteering to let go either, so I'll hold on a little longer.

"I can't believe how beautiful it is here," she says, watching the whitecaps crash on the beach, while we stroll leisurely along.

"I agree," I say as we head into the ocean. We don't walk out far—only ankle deep. It's just enough to feel the wet sand beneath our toes and the cool water wash over our skin.

"Tell me about the Hazelton place. I hear they've been considering putting in their own bowling alley."

Before I answer, I glance over. Her brown hair is blowing in the breeze, and she looks about as carefree as you can possibly be. The image causes a smile to slide up the corner of my lips. "Well, there isn't a bowling alley in the plans as of right now. Though, I guess it wouldn't surprise me since he was a champion bowler back in the 80's.

"They've been super easy to work with since they had an idea of what they wanted from the start. I was able to take their specifications and help them find a layout. They didn't make too many changes to the original plan, just a few tweaks here and there."

"I bet it's going to be amazing when you're finished."

"It will be. This is, by far, the biggest job I've ever completed. I'm eager to see what the finished product is going to look like."

"I'm sure they're going to love it," she adds with an encouraging smile.

And because I can't help it, I stop her and steal a kiss. It's a slow, tease of a kiss that leaves my pants tight and my blood pumping. That's exactly what happens every time my lips lock with hers. I want more, and if the way she slides against my chest and purrs is any indication, she's ready for more too.

But not yet, pushing aside my growing lust, I start to walk again. Jaime follows suit, grinning and gazing up at me from beneath those long, dark lashes. The smile I give her in return lets her know I'm thinking the exact same thing she is: I can't wait for later.

"So you're building a huge masterpiece for someone else, but have you ever thought of building your own place? Or are you going to rent from Mrs. Hanson for the rest of your life?" she asks, humor laces with each word.

"Oh, I've thought of it. When I was in New York, I knew I wasn't going to stay forever, so I didn't put much stock into the idea. But as soon as I set foot in Jupiter Bay, I started giving it a little more consideration."

"You should do it. There's plenty of land around to develop. Unless you're wanting directly along the Bay. Those parcels of land are going for a pretty penny." Jaime stops in her tracks, our hands pulled until they're almost apart.

"What?"

"Unless you're not staying around here. I mean, you might plan to head back to New York someday," she says, her words trailing off until the last is barely audible.

My eyes widen as I take in her stricken face. "No," I say loud and forcefully. "I'm not leaving. I'm not going back to New York. Not now, not ever."

"You can't be sure of that though, right?" Again, her words are a hush.

"I am sure. Even if this didn't work out between us, Jupiter Bay is my home. Honestly, Jaime, I'm not leaving," I reassure her, dropping our shoes in the sand and pulling her flush against me. "Why would I want to leave when my home is right here, in my arms?"

And then I kiss her. I kiss her with every ounce of passion, every piece of my heart I possess. I always wondered about my friends who would talk about their wives as if they hung the moon and the fucking stars. I never understood it. I never got the power that that sort of love possessed on your soul. But I get it now. I understand because Jaime owns my heart completely. There's no way I could ever love another woman the way I love her.

I lock eyes with hers because I want her to know that the words I speak are one hundred percent the truth. I want her to feel the words I say, not just hear them. "I'm not going anywhere because I love you. You, Jaime Summer."

Through hazy eyes, she gazes up at me, the sweetest smile gracing her lips. "I love you too."

"Come on," I say, pulling her back the way we came. "I want to make love to the woman I love."

×✕×

I'd fly up the stairs two at a time, the way we used to when we ran bleachers during hockey training, but Jaime's slightly shorter legs keep me from making a complete ass of myself. I'm tempted to throw her over my shoulder, but Phyllis appears at the top of the staircase with a knowing smile on her face.

"Good evening," she says sweetly as we approach.

"Good evening," Jaime replies.

"You look like you're retiring to your room this evening. You two skipped out on dessert earlier, so I saved you some. There is a container on the counter, the ice cream is in the freezer, and the caramel sauce is by the warmer. Heat it up for fifteen seconds and that should be perfect to drizzle over the ice cream. Help yourselves when you're ready." Phyllis gives us a wink and starts to head down the stairs.

"Oh, before I forget, the final guests have arrived. They're in the room directly behind yours."

"Thanks," I say as she descends the stairs. Before she reaches the halfway point, I pull Jaime towards our room.

Once inside, I slam my lips against hers in a hungry, needy kiss. Jaime locks the door behind her before winding her arms around my neck. Reaching around and grabbing her ass, I hoist her up and press her back against the door. Her legs wrap around my waist, lining us up perfectly as she starts to grind against my cock. I'm so fucking hard right now, I'm afraid it might do some sort of permanent damage from the pressure.

Jaime latches onto my bottom lip, each suckle rippling through my body like a lightning strike straight to my dick. Using the wall as leverage, I'm able to slide my hands up her body. Her soft skin is peppered with goosebumps and her nipples are hard little peaks against my chest. My mouth waters for just a little taste, knowing that I won't be able to stop at just one.

"Damn, I want to take you right against this door," I ground out, refusing to break the connection of our mouths.

"Yes, yes, I want that," she pants breathlessly. I can feel the heat of her pussy through two layers of clothes.

Tearing my lips away from hers, I set her on her feet and quickly start to rid her of it all. First her shirt is thrown somewhere in the room, followed very quickly by her white lace bra with red trim. Then I set my sights on her shorts. After unbuttoning them, I give them a hard tug. My eyes never leave the white lace with red trimmed thong she had hidden beneath. She must have brought them with her because she wasn't wearing them when I devoured her before.

"I've died and gone to heaven," I whisper, transfixed by that tiny scrap of lace.

"Please," she begs. She wiggles slightly, her legs trembling from need.

"Is this what you want, sweetheart?" I ask, leaning forward and swiping my tongue along the lace-covered seam of her lips. I'm rewarded with a deep moan.

"Do you want more?" I ask, glancing up and locking eyes with her cloudy green ones.

"More," she demands, her body craving another touch.

Sliding the thong aside, I part her folds with my fingers and run my tongue between them. Again, her moan is pure music and fuels the already raging inferno inside of me. I savor the taste of her arousal, loving the way it coats my tongue. Licking and sucking on her clit, I run a single finger through her wetness.

When I push gently inside her ready body, Jaime starts to buck against me. She's wild as she grinds down on my hand, chasing the orgasm she craves, the one I promised. Before I slide a second finger inside of her, I use my other hand to lift her left leg up and over my shoulder. She's open wide, a buffet for only me to enjoy. And I'm fucking famished.

I push two fingers inside of her and latch on to her clit with my mouth, sucking on her swollen flesh. Jaime's hands dive into my hair, gripping at my scalp and tugging on handfuls of hair. I ignore the sting. Instead, it drives me further. The desire to make her come is overwhelming as I work my fingers in and out of her sweet pussy.

"God, Ryan, that feels so good. Your mouth feels so fucking good."

Her muscles start to tighten against my fingers. They're pulling against me, drawing me in deeper, as her legs start to quiver. She's close now; I can feel the orgasm cresting.

"Let go, baby. I want to feel you come on my fingers and tongue."

My words are the spark she needs because she ignites right before my eyes. Her orgasm sweeps through her, powerful and all-consuming, as I work my fingers inside of her and alternate between licking and sucking on that magic button. I watch, hypnotized as her body rides out wave after wave of orgasmic bliss. It's fucking beautiful to watch, and even more magnificent to feel against my fingers and tongue.

When the last wave sweeps through her, Jaime sags against the door, spent and sated. But I'm not done with her yet. Not even close.

Standing up, I rid myself of clothes, all while keeping a close eye on her to make sure she doesn't fall. When I'm naked, I gather her in my arms once more. Jaime wraps those long legs around my waist; only this time, there's no barrier between my throbbing dick and what it craves.

I spin around, sitting down on the edge of the bed. I slide back enough so that my feet still reach the floor, and gently lift Jaime until I feel the head of my cock nudging at her entrance.

"I want you to ride me," I tell her.

Those hazy eyes start to brighten as she gives me a little smile. "I'm not sure I'll have the energy."

"Oh, don't worry, sweetheart. I'll gladly assist," I say as I lower her down and slide inside.

She's unbelievably tight from her previous orgasm that she clutches my cock in a death grip. "You're so wet. You feel abso-fucking-lutely amazing," I groan as she slides all the way to the base of my dick.

"God, I love it when you talk to me," she whispers, her cheeks pinking with her confession.

"Yeah? You like dirty talk?" I ask, moving her up again until I'm almost out.

"I didn't know I did until I heard it coming from you."

"Then prepare to come harder than you ever have, Jaime. I want to feel you come all over my cock." Then I slam her hips down on me. She grips me internally, and I swear I hit something deep inside of her that pushes me towards my own release. It's barreling down on me, getting closer with each second I'm inside her.

"Oh God," she whimpers.

I grasp her hips and slam them down again and again. Jaime uses her legs to help move and adds a little hip thrust each time she reaches the root of me. My balls are already tingling, but I refuse to let this end too soon.

I lean down and suck her nipple inside my mouth. It's hard and begs for me to bite down just a bit. I know instantly when she feels the bite. Not only does a gasp erupt from her mouth, but her body clamps down on my cock in the best way possible.

"Do that again," I instruct. "Your body fucking grips my dick so tight, I almost lose it. But I won't. Not yet. Not until you come again," I say just before I bite down on the other nipple.

Her body convulses above me. Just as I go to do it again, I hear a loud thud against the wall. It's loud enough that both of us stop in our tracks and stare at each other. Quietness surrounds us for a few seconds and I start to wonder if we imagined the entire thing.

Just as I get ready to plunge into her once more, a deep muffled moan pierces through the wall. Jaime tenses above me, eyes as wide as hubcaps, which I'm sure mirror my own. The moaning on the other side of the wall intensifies, followed by a whole lot of begging and pleading to the big man upstairs.

Jaime and I both burst out laughing at the same time. "We weren't that loud, were we?" she asks, her cheeks flushing darker than they already were.

"Not yet we weren't. Come on, babe. Let's see who can make the walls shake more," I say just before pulling out and slamming back up into her ready body. It's a challenge I'll gladly accept.

She's still clamped down on me, but her face says she's not quite on board with the idea. "Ignore them," I recommend just as a shout echoes through the wall.

I'll be damned if I'm going to let our neighbors kill the mood. We were both so fucking close to getting off before the amateurs auditioning for the lead in the next porn flick interrupted us. There's no way in hell I'm not getting her off right now; not until fireworks are erupting in her mind and she blacks out from her orgasm.

Working her nipples between my thumb and forefinger, I start to see the change. She's starting to come around, pushing the action next door out of her mind, so I start to pick up speed again.

Jaime moans. I can tell she's trying to muffle the noise. Fuck that. I want her screams echoing off the rafters. I want the police in the next damned county to get calls. "Don't hold back," I demand again.

Lying back on the top of bed, I watch as she rides me like a prized stallion at the rodeo. She's bucking and gyrating, a naked vision of beauty. If I only get to sleep with one woman for the rest of my life, I'd sell my soul for it to be Jaime.

She starts to come, gripping my dick tighter than ever before. Even if I wanted to, there's no holding back my own release. Keeping a tight grip on her hips, we move in unison until we're left with nothing but aftershocks and harsh breathing. Blood is rushing through my ears and my heart is going to rip through my chest. Jaime's sated body slumps forward, her sweat-slicked skin molding to my own.

Best. Sex. Ever.

"I'm afraid everyone in the house heard that," she whispers.

"Good. I want everyone to know what you do to me."

"I can't believe we just had a moaning competition with our neighbors," she says while running her nose along my neck and nuzzling against my throat.

"One we clearly won," I pant.

"Of course," she says, the smile evident in her voice.

Hating to break our connection, I slowly move us towards the pillows. Jaime's practically boneless as I pull her beneath the sheet, moving in close. I slip out from within her body, come spilling down both of our legs.

"Let me grab a towel," I say, trying to sit up.

"Nuhuh," she mumbles, latching on to my arms and legs with her own.

"We're a mess," I add while placing a kiss on her damp forehead.

"So. I like it."

"That's not all you like," I remind her. "I believe I have a dirty girl." Moving my hands downward, I grip her ass and pull her closer yet.

"I've never had anyone…talk to me like that." I can practically feel the heat of her blush against my chest.

"Well, as long as I'm the one doing all the talking, you can hear it anytime you want, sweetheart."

We're silent for a few minutes; each of us lulled closer to sleep by the steady beat of our hearts and the mix of our even breaths. Before I can fully fall into slumber, I make sure to say the words that I plan to say every day for the rest of my life.

"I love you."

Jaime

23

The sun is high in the sky, reflecting brightly off the blue ocean water.

We slept in, both of us apparently in desperate need of a little extra sleep. With no work obligations or other responsibilities to tend to, it was easy to forget everything for a little while and just relax. When I felt Ryan stir beside me, the clock on the nightstand read almost eleven.

We're both standing at our room door, ready to spend the day visiting all of the tourist places and specialty shops. I'm wearing my favorite blue summer dress with little white flowers, and cute white sandals. Coincidentally, Ryan is wearing khaki shorts and a blue polo shirt that looks as if it were cut from the same cloth as my dress. We're matchies in that super cute, bordering on annoying way that I never thought I'd find charming. But I do.

"Before we go, I want to tell Phyllis that we'll be missing dinner tonight. I have other plans," he says, wagging his eyebrows suggestively.

"Do these other plans involve food of any kind?" I ask, giving him my best flirty smile over my shoulder as I open the door.

"Oh, don't worry, babe," he says, leaning in as we stop to secure the door behind us. "There will be eating."

The provocative tone and naughty smile he gives me causes warmth to flood between my legs all over again. It's a natural and common occurrence whenever Ryan Elson is present. He bends down and places a tender kiss on my lips. It's completely PG, but the gleam in his eyes isn't.

"Let's go before I decide to forget the entire day and just keep you tied to the bed." Ryan grabs my hand and starts to lead me towards the staircase.

"That doesn't sound too bad, actually," I reply, tugging against his hand to try to slow his progress.

Before he can say anything further, the door before us opens. Instantly, I'm reminded of the competition we engaged in with the couple occupying the front bedroom. I feel the color burning my cheeks as we approach the open doorway. Ryan and I both avert our eyes, watching very closely each step we make towards the staircase that represents our freedom.

"Jaime, sweetheart, is that you?" I hear in an all too familiar voice.

No. Can't be. God isn't that cruel.

Looking up, my green eyes slam into the sparkling ones of my grandma.

Oh. My. God!

My mouth hangs open, my brain refuses to process thoughts and make words. I'm standing there, traumatized to the point of being speechless, while Grandma smiles sweetly and innocently.

Oh. My. God! I heard my grandparents having sex. Loudly!

"What are you doing here?" I ask hoarsely after Ryan squeezes my hand.

"Grandpa and I decided yesterday that since you and Ryan were going away for the weekend, maybe we would enjoy some time away as well. The Fellers were supposed to come here this weekend, but were unable to make it since Mabel fell and sprained her knee. They offered us their reservations to this cute little place they come to every summer."

Grandpa steps out into the hallway, a surprised look on his face when he sees Ryan and me standing in the hallway. "Jaime? What are you doing here?"

"This is where Ryan brought Jaime for their little weekend away," she says with a sassy grin. "Can you believe it? Out of all the bed and breakfasts in Virginia, we booked the same one!" Grandma adds enthusiastically.

"I can't believe it," Ryan adds, the corner of his mouth twitching just enough to give away the fact that he's fighting a smile.

Grandpa walks over to Ryan and shakes his hand. "So, you guys were here last night, huh?" he asks, bumping Ryan's shoulder with his, not the least embarrassed by the fact that they had a screaming orgasm match with their own granddaughter.

I see Ryan blush a little and give grandpa a small smile.

"You guys look like you're going out. I know! Why don't we go do something together?" Grandma asks, looking over at Grandpa.

Before Ryan or I am able to politely decline, Grandpa steps in. "Oh, Emmy, you know these kids want to be alone. Do you remember our first weekend away from our parents? We went to that little theatre to see that variety show a few towns over and slipped away to the men's restroom before intermission?"

A choking sound files the hallway, and I'm surprised to realize it came from me.

"Of course I remember. We stayed at that charming little hotel above the theatre that didn't have locks on the doors."

"Come on, love. Let's leave these kids to their own devices. We're going to picnic on the patio out back for lunch," he says, heading towards the stairs. Together, we all descend in silence.

We reach the bottom and Ryan places his warm hand on my lower back, steering me towards the front door. I suddenly feel like I'm sixteen again instead of in the final year of my twenties. Glancing back over my shoulder, I see that Grandma and Grandpa aren't even paying us any more attention. Grandpa has his hand possessively on Grandma's arm as he walks beside her down the hallway towards the patio. They're chatting animatedly about something, each laughing as he opens the door for her and they disappear out of sight.

Longing stirs my stomach, spreading warmth through my veins and to my heart. Will I have that kind of love when I'm their age? Is Ryan that love?

I always wanted happily ever after, but I never really pictured it until right now. Sure, I thought Gavin would be in that picture someday, but now? Gavin was never meant to be the man standing beside me, guiding me and laughing with me.

But Ryan? The slightest touch of his fingertips sends shivers up and down my spine as we step outside and he leads me towards his truck. The possessive gesture mimics that of the one I saw only moments ago with my grandparents. Is this what they saw in each other when they first met? When they realized they were destined to be together, even after only knowing each other a short period of time?

Looking up at the sexy man escorting me to his ride, I smile because I already know the answer. I feel it deep in my bones, down in the depths of my soul. Ryan is my other half, my soul mate.

My forever.

⁕⁂⁕

We dine on fresh crab cakes and shrimp scampi at a little seaside diner with plastic, red and white, checkered tablecloths. It was the first restaurant we came to when strolling along the causeway by the ocean. I've already scoped out several shops that I want to hit on our way back to the truck.

"I can't believe how good this is," I mumble before stuffing more food in my mouth. "I'm going to gain ten pounds just from this weekend alone."

"Wouldn't matter. You'd still be the most gorgeous woman in the world," Ryan replies while holding a piece of shrimp skewed on his fork across the table.

Leaning forward, I take a slow bite of the cheesy, garlicy sauce. "You're too sweet."

"I speak the truth. Gorgeous. Intelligent. Caring. Sweet. Sexy as hell. All things I see when I look at you. Your weight has nothing to do with who you are."

Blushing slightly, I give him a small grin. His words warm my heart like melted butter in a frying pan. I'm a goner.

"Ready?" he asks when there's nothing left but empty plates.

"Yes."

After paying the tab, Ryan and I step out onto the walkway and slowly make our way back to where we parked his truck. "There are a few places I thought we could stop on our way back. Is that okay?"

"Whatever you want, sweetheart."

Hand in hand, we walk half a block to the shirt shop I saw earlier. The ones in the windows have funny sayings on them, and I thought it'd be cute to commemorate our trip with cheesy tourist shirts.

A bored looking teenager mans the counter, and barely looks up from her phone as we step inside. Light reflects off of the ring in her nose, and her purple hair is spiked straight up. Clearly her conversation via text is more important than helping us, so I lead us towards the first row of t-shirts.

The first one I pick up is a black tee with F.B.I. printed boldly across the chest. I hold it up and show it to Ryan. His eyes light up and he chuckles as he reads the rest of it aloud. "Female Body Inspector. Now I know what F.B.I. really stands for."

Folding the shirt, I return it to the stack with the others. Ryan grabs a light blue one with a large crab on the front. Opening the shirt, it displays a smiling, cartoon crab with the phrase 'I'm too cute to be crabby.'

"This is the one we should get you," he says.

"You clearly haven't spent enough mornings with me before I've had my coffee," I retort as I reach for another shirt.

"Here's yours," I say as I hold open the white shirt. It's of a man from the thighs up wearing the smallest Speedo I've ever seen. His body is hard with ripped abs, a chest etched from stone, and arms that make ovaries weep. Across the back it reads 'This is my beach body.'

"Are you saying I should cover up my body with a better one?"

"Absolutely not. I just think it's a funny concept, you know? A middle aged, balding man walking around wearing this shirt to give the impression that he just left the gym after a long workout. All while he's covering up his beer belly and moobs."

"Moobs?"

"Man boobs."

Ryan laughs and grabs the white shirt beside the one I have in my hand. "Then this one must be yours."

It's similar to the one I hold in my hand, but this one is of a woman. She's wearing the skimpiest string bikini, with perfect double D's spilling from the top, and has a hard, flat stomach. She's curvy and voluptuous and flawless, really. She's nothing like me.

"Perfect. We can wear them to the next family dinner," I suggest, teasing.

"You don't think it'd be cute?"

"I think they're hideous," I confess. "There's no way I'm wearing that ugly shirt."

"Then we're getting them," Ryan says while digging though the pile until he finds the sizes he's looking for.

"I'm not wearing it," I throw over my shoulder as he heads towards the bored girl to pay for the gaudy shirts, his laughter following him the entire way.

There's also no hiding the smile on my face either.

Ryan takes my hand as we head towards another small waterfront shop in downtown Travelers End. This one houses small trinkets and souvenirs. Shark tooth necklaces, dolphin key chains, glass bottles with colorful sand; it's all here.

Together, we make our way down the aisles of goodies, checking out a few knick-knacks along the way. Ryan is checking out brightly painted glass coasters, hoping to find a set he likes for Mrs. Hanson. I grab an intricately decorated seashell covered photo frame without Ryan noticing and slip up to the counter to pay for the souvenir.

"What did you get?" he asks as he slides against my back. His breath fans across the shell of my ear, his lips trailing a warm blaze of heat against the column of my neck. An instant shiver rakes through my body.

"I'm not telling," I whisper as the cashier hands me my change.

"Is it a fish shaped spoon rest for the stove? I've always wanted one of those."

"I'll keep that in mind for Christmas," I snort.

"I have ways of getting it out of you," he mumbles as his lips caress the sensitive skin behind my ear. Suddenly, my breathing is shallow and my body on high alert.

"Your tactics hardly seem fair," I respond as I slowly turn to face him.

His eyes are bright with lust and gleam with playfulness. "All's fair in love and war, baby," he replies, the corner of his mouth slightly curled upward.

Ryan keeps his eyes trained on mine as he slowly leans forward. I know what he's thinking because I'm thinking it too. The moment our lips touch, it's like the Fourth of July. Sparks fly as I wrap my hands around his neck and hold on. His kiss instantly turns possessive, consuming, with vehemence. Will kissing him always be this way? God, I sure hope so.

A loud throat clears behind me as we quickly pull apart. Red faced, I turn to face the man, who only moments ago, sold me the goods in my bag. Now, however, his eyes are diverted and refuse to make eye contact. I'm sure my cheeks are the same color of fuchsia as his.

Ryan chuckles behind me and places his purchases on the counter. Besides the floral painted coasters, he tosses a beach scene key chain on the counter. The name scrolled across the front in big gold letter catches my attention right away. Laughter bursts from my throat as I take in that single word.

"Um, Ryan?" I ask sweetly.

"Yes?" Ryan stuffs cash back into his money clip and places it in the front pocket of his shorts.

"That's not how my name is spelled."

Ryan leads me towards the front entrance. "I know that, but apparently these key chains only come in Jaime with an M-I-E, and since they don't have one spelled with an I-M-E, I decided to go ahead and buy you the misspelled one. Jamie is still Jaime, right?"

"Except that it's not spelled right," I reply, fighting the smile threating to take over my face.

"Details. It still says Jaime, even if it's spelled Jamie. And since it's my favorite name in the whole world, I wanted to buy it."

We step outside into the warmer sea air. "That's a pretty big deal, favorite name in the whole world."

He stops and turns to face me. "It's a huge deal. It's not every day that I make a statement like this one," he chimes in, dangling the misspelled key chain from between his fingers.

"Then I should fall at your feet in appreciation, shouldn't I?" I step closer and grab ahold of the key chain.

"Dropping to your knees is unnecessary in public, sweetheart. Now, if we were...say, in private, I wouldn't be opposed to seeing you do a little worshipping." Ryan's eyebrow arches suggestively and his grin is pure wicked intent. And, honestly, if the way my body is humming is any indication, I don't think I'd mind showing Ryan a little appreciation for his two dollar misspelled key chain purchase.

Smiling sweetly, I snatch the key chain from his fingers and say, "I guess we'll just have to wait until later and see." He laughs as we turn, together, and head down the block.

Window shopping is exhausting when Ryan insists on stopping at most of the shops along the street. As we enter a store filled with handspun glass, my stomach growls. It's loud enough that Ryan hears causing my cheeks to tint a flattering shade of pink.

"Last store and then we'll head to our dinner reservation," he says, checking the time on his watch.

I'll admit, the glass and pottery in this place is beautiful. As we browse delicate vases, intricate glassware, and beautifully sculpted statues, we come upon a woman at the back sitting behind a pottery wheel.

"Good afternoon," she says while running her wet hands along a clump of dark clay. Instantly, the glob of material starts to take shape. She continues to work her wet hands upward, forming a long cylinder.

Ryan and I stop and watch as she hums along to the tune in her head while sculpting what I realize is a candlestick. Her delicate little fingers mold the clay, cutting grooves and decorative cords within the wet material. When the stick takes shape, she places her finger in the top and works in a groove to hold the candle. After the candlestick is complete, she turns off the machine and admires her handiwork.

"That's beautiful," I say absently, smiling at the finished product.

"Thank you. These are some of my best sellers. I go through probably ten pairs of candlesticks a week, and upwards of twenty a week during busy holiday weekends." The little pixie woman walks over and places the completed piece on a shelf with six others beside the kiln to dry.

"You have a beautiful place," Ryan adds, turning and looking at a glass place setting next to where we stand.

"I appreciate that. It's a lot of work, but it's my true passion. My glass shop is in a small building out back, and I work with pottery and ceramic back here. Feel free to browse around. If you need help with anything, just holler. I'm going to get the matching candlestick completed so they can dry together."

Ryan and I watch her start the next candlestick before turning and perusing at several pieces on glass display shelves around the room. A gorgeous ocean blue glass bowl catches my attention. As I approach, I see etched seashells around the rim. It's a stunning piece, one that would look amazing displayed in the center of a dining room table. Specifically, *my* dining room table.

The only problem is that I don't *have* a dining room table. Yet. Not one of my own.

But this piece is too stunning to pass up. With steady hands, I gently pick up the glass object. In direct light, the blue is more vibrant and sparkles like sapphires. The etchings are subtle, each shell different from the one beside it. Flipping it over, I see $74.99. Ordinarily, it's a little steep for my blood, especially for a piece of décor, but I have to have it. It's exquisite.

"I like that," Ryan says over my shoulder.

When I turn to face him, he's holding a large bag with something wrapped in tissue paper. "What's that?"

"Nothing for you to worry about right now," he replies, that cocky smirk playing on the corners of his mouth.

Taking my purchase up to the counter, I retrieve my debit card from my purse. "This is a gorgeous bowl," the woman who was making candlesticks says. "I love working with this blue glass. The outcome is always splendid, the colors rich and bold."

"My eyes were drawn to this piece, and I couldn't pass it up," I state as I sign my name to the little slip of paper.

"Since you and your husband both made a purchase today," she starts as she turns and grabs a small pottery vase off the display shelf closest to her. It's a lighter shade of clay with vibrant flowers complexly weaved around the base of the vase. "I'm throwing in this piece. It will complement the bowl beautifully."

As flattered as I am about the gift, I'm still trying to process her comment about my husband. "Oh, we're not… I mean, I'm not married."

"Oh." She gazes deeply at me, her deep brown eyes piercing me straight to my soul. "My mistake. When I see a couple so clearly in love, I guess I just assume they're married."

I blush a dark shade of red. "It's okay," I whisper. Glancing over my shoulder, I watch Ryan as he checks out some pieces by the front door. "Thank you for the vase. It's beautiful," I add as I take the proffered bag with the wrapped vase and bowl.

"Thank you. Enjoy your stay at Travelers End. If you're back in the area soon, stop by and say hello," she offers with a smile.

Offering a nod, I turn and head towards Ryan. We're both silent as we head towards where we parked his truck. My thoughts are stuck on that one word: Husband. A single word that causes my breath to falter and my underarms to perspire.

But now, it doesn't seem quite so scary. Now, the idea of a husband seems logical and pleasant. As Ryan and I walk together, I'm breathing harshly for another reason. I realize that the idea of Ryan as my husband isn't terrifying. In fact, it's completely the opposite. I feel at ease, peaceful.

It feels right.

24

Ryan

Jaime is curled up against me, sleeping peacefully. She's gloriously naked beneath the sheet, her soft skin pressed firmly against my body. It's a sensation I'll never get enough of.

The alarm clock beside me reads two a.m. I've been unable to sleep since we came back to our room at the end of the evening. My mind kept replaying the conversation between Jaime and the shop owner where she purchased the blue bowl and I bought the matching candlesticks that are still safely tucked away in the bag. The woman thought we were married, and even though I couldn't see Jaime's face, I could hear the surprise in her response.

All evening–as we walked hand-in-hand back to my truck, as we drove to the seaside restaurant Martin helped me make reservations at, and as we dined on fresh seafood–I was haunted by that one word: Marriage. I want to get married, someday, but now the idea has been planted in my mind and is blossoming into a full-blown tree of hope. I want to marry Jaime. I know it. I feel it in my heart and deep in my soul. I'd propose tomorrow if I thought she'd say yes. But I know she won't. She's not ready.

And that's okay–for now.

Maybe I'm not quite ready. We've hardly known each other two months. In all honesty, our instant connection and my resulting love for her seem too good to be true. I mean, we hardly know each other, right? I don't know what kind of toothpaste she prefers or whether she buys white or wheat bread. But for as hasty as our relationship appears, it also feels like I've known her forever. She completes my thoughts and grounds me. She wormed her way under my skin so damn quickly, it's as if she's always been there.

While we made love after returning from dinner, I showered her with as much adoration as I could give. I showed her, repeatedly, that I was here to stay, never once saying one of the millions of things I longed to say to her for fear of freaking her out. Instead I told her the one thing she has accepted: that I love her.

Everything else will come in time.

Yet that doesn't quiet my mind or slow the steady beat of my heart. Sleep has yet to find me because I've contemplated every scenario I can conjure up in my mind from begging her to move in to asking her to marry me. I've also come up with every excuse she could give me to say no. It's terrifying, putting your heart out there and risking someone trampling it into the dirt as if it meant nothing.

Not that I think Jaime would do that, intentionally. Jaime's still skittish when it comes to relationships, and while ours has been working out well in the time we've known each other, I won't risk that happiness to move this on into the next level.

But I want to.

Sliding carefully, I gently move Jaime until she's no longer wrapped around me. My body longs for her touch once more, but I push the feeling aside and get out of bed. Grabbing my shorts off the floor, I slip them on, followed by a t-shirt. As I carefully open our bedroom door, I glance back at the beauty sleeping peacefully in bed. A smarter man would rid himself of all of the clothes he just put on and climb back inside the warm covers, but I'm in desperate need of a little air, so I push aside the longing for her touch, and slip out of the room.

The house is silent as I move down the stairs and head towards the back door. I'm surprised to find it not only unlocked, but also ajar. Outside, the July night is calm. The salty air carries a hint of crispness and the fragrance of lavender.

"I'm a little surprised to see you out here," a familiar voice says from the shadows.

"Likewise," I reply, turning to face Jaime's grandpa.

"Can't sleep?" he asks while I pull up a chair.

"No."

"Me neither. This hard-on won't go down," he says casually as if he wasn't just referring to the junk in his pants.

Reflexively, I glance down and instantly wish I hadn't. Averting my eyes as quickly as possible, I clear my throat.

"It's okay, son. It'll go down eventually. The doc always says not to worry unless it's been four hours."

"How long have you…uh, *had* your problem?" I ask, wishing I could retract my question as soon as it flies from my lips.

Orval glances at his watch. "Only an hour since the missus and I finished up another round of making music on the flesh flute. I've still got another bit before it subsides. No amount of orgasms helps me when Viagra's in my system. I could go for hours with this little blue pill," he says, pulling a bottle from the chest pocket of his shirt. "Want one?" he offers.

"Uh, no. Thanks, but I'm good."

"Don't need 'em, huh? Yeah, it wasn't that long ago that I didn't need 'em. Unfortunately, old age can take a toll on the male body, son. You'll learn eventually. When your woman has a sex drive like a chimpanzee, you'll do whatever it takes to give her what she wants."

"Wow, that's a lot of information."

We both stare out over the blackened beach, hypnotized by the sound of the waves crashing on the shore. "So, you've never said what you were doing out here." Orval states.

"Couldn't sleep," I mumble, recalling the dilemma that has my mind bouncing all over the place.

"Female troubles?" he asks.

"Is there any other kind?" I ask, humorously.

"Nope. Most troubles seem to be centered around females. But in my experience, those troubles are the best kinds." His soft laughter fills the air.

Silence surrounds us once more as he waits me out. "I want something from your granddaughter that I'm afraid she's not ready for."

"Ahhh. I think I understand a little. You're ready for something more than you think my granddaughter can give."

I nod my head in confirmation.

"Son, let me tell you something about our Jaime. She loves fiercely, which I'm sure you've discovered. But she also loves completely. There's no doubt that she loved that jackass she was going to marry before." I bristle at the thought.

"But she didn't love him completely. She didn't look at him the way I've seen her look at you. She didn't smile or laugh as much either. Do you know why that is?" Words lodge painfully in my throat, refusing to escape.

"Because she loves you completely. Believe it, Ryan. She's timid and scared because of her previous mistakes, but don't let that fear detour you from seeing the big picture here. She's in love with you, completely, with her whole heart. There's not a doubt in my mind. It's the same way I look at my Emmy. It's the same way Trisha used to look at Brian before the cancer took her from us. It's everlasting and whole. Believe that."

Orval's gaze is fierce. "So whatever it is you're going to ask her, just do it. She might not answer you right away, but that's because she's going to give it her complete thought and attention. She won't make a big decision without considering it from all angles. She'll probably need to make a list like she used to when she was younger. Give her time and space, but don't give up on her. Time together means nothing, Ryan. I knew the moment I met my Emma that she was the one. The same way I'm sure you know it with Jaime. When she's ready, she'll make you the happiest man on the face of the earth."

I consider his words, mulling them over again and again while we listen to the night. His words confirm my suspicions that Jaime will pull back until she's had time to process her feelings. Asking her to move in with me will surely rock her foundation, but it's a risk I'm willing to take. Being without her isn't an option anymore. I'm ready to take that leap, ensuring more time with her.

"My little problem seems to have subsided," Orval says as he stands. I catch myself before I'm able to glance down at his shorts. That's an image I don't need repeated in my mind. "Think it over, Ryan, and when you're ready, know that she'll give your question complete consideration."

With that he turns and heads towards the back door. "And for the record, I'm certain she'll happily agree to whatever it is you want to ask her." Orval grins a broad smile and heads inside.

His words only seal the deal where she's concerned. It's settled. When we get home tomorrow afternoon, I'm going to take her to my place and ask her to move in with me. I'm ready, and I'm sure she's ready as well. She's already said she loved me, and that was a hurdle I was afraid she'd never jump over. But she did.

And now it's time to take the next step towards my future with Jaime.

I only hope she doesn't push me away for too long while she decides.

※※※

Jaime chats animatedly during our drive back to Jupiter Bay. The sun is high in the sky as we cruise along the highway, only a few miles an hour over the speed limit. Though I'm anxious to get home, traffic is a little on the heavy side on this Sunday afternoon and is slowing down the trip. Unable to pass, I tap my foot nervously on the floorboard as the sign for the city limits of home finally comes into sight.

"Are you all right?" Jaime asks, her hand on my leg pulling me from my thoughts.

"Yeah, sure. Why?" I ask, glancing over to see the sunlight reflecting off her hair.

"You just seem distracted, that's all." She shrugs and gives me a timid smile.

"Yeah, sorry. I guess I was. I have something I want to talk to you about when we get back to my place."

I notice her brow wrinkle as I return my eyes to the road, slowing down to abide by the city speed limits. My heart is racing and my right foot twitches to apply a little more pressure to the pedal. "It's nothing bad, sweetheart. In fact, I think it's great. Don't worry," I reassure her as I grab her hand and kiss her knuckles.

After pulling into my driveway, Jaime's car is still parked in the street where we left it, I hop out of the truck and run to retrieve our bags as if my ass were on fire. The keys are in my hand and the front door is open only a few seconds later.

Dropping our bags on the floor, I practically drag her into the kitchen. Placing my hands on her shoulders, I gently push her into the first seat. Then I pace. I move from the table to the kitchen sink and back again. Suddenly, the words I've been anxious to say won't come. My mind blanks and I have no clue how to start this conversation.

"Ryan?" she whispers behind me.

Turning and facing her, I stall. "Do you want a drink?" I grab two bottles of water from the fridge and place one in front of her. Then I proceed to practically drain my entire bottle in one long gulp. Even after the water is gone, my throat still feels parched, my tongue thick.

"So...Jaime, I was thinking..." Again, I start to pace.

"Ryan!" Jaime proclaims, breaking through and grabbing my attention. "Will you please sit down? You're starting to scare me," she says, her voice dropping to just above a whisper.

Quickly, I move to the table. Grabbing the chair across from her, I position it so that I'm sitting beside the table, directly in front of her. I reach for her hand and cradle it in my own. Running my thumb along the soft flesh over her hand, my heart starts to calm, nerves fade away.

"Hi," I say with a smile, her gorgeous green eyes directly in front of me.

"Hi," she replies with her own timid grin.

"I had an idea I wanted to run by you. I'll be honest, I'm not sure how you're going to take what I have to say, so promise me you'll listen until I'm finished and with an open mind."

"Okay."

I take a deep breath and begin my pitch. "I've had the time of my life in the last several weeks, and it's all because of you. Every moment I spend with you is greater than the last, and I look forward to the end of my workday because there's a chance I get to see you. Jaime, I know we've only been seeing each other for a little more than a month, but it feels like a lot longer, doesn't it?" I ask.

She seems unable to say words, but I'm awarded with a quick nod.

Getting up, I head over and grab the white bag from the glass shop we visited yesterday. Retrieving the goods inside, I slide back down into my chair and hand her the bag.

"I saw you yesterday admiring that blue bowl. Your face lit up, eyes sparkling like emeralds. I knew you had to have it. In fact, if you wouldn't have purchased it, I was going to get it for you. Open it," I say, nodding towards the bag in her hands.

Jaime takes her time, her hands slightly trembling as she carefully unwraps the first of two wrapped items. When she finally reveals what's inside, her mouth drops open and her eyes shine with unshed tears.

"I knew you had to have that bowl and I thought those would look great with it."

Cradled gingerly within her left hand is one of the blue glass candlesticks with edged seashells around the base. "It matches my bowl. It's gorgeous," she says, those tear filled eyes focused solely on me.

"I thought they'd be perfect on your table." Jaime swallows audibly. "I know you don't have a table right now, since you're temporarily living with your dad. And that got me thinking. I have a table here. I'd love to come home every night from work and see that bowl and those candlesticks on this table...because you're here. With me. Every night."

Jaime's eyes widen and her mouth hinges open. "Are you...saying..."

"I want you to move in with me."

She gasps loudly and looks away. I can practically see the wheels in her head spinning a hundred miles per hour.

"But we haven't known each other very long," she whispers, still not looking up at me.

"I understand that, but it doesn't bother me. I knew the moment I met you, the moment I first laid eyes on you, that I wanted you. I felt it in my heart that we would have something amazing, and you know I was right."

Jaime starts to speak, but I place my finger across her lips. "You said I could finish before you said anything." I take another deep breath. "Jaime, I love you. I knew weeks ago that I was in love with you; hell, I practically fell in love with you the moment I laid eyes on you. I was just too afraid to say the words then for fear that I'd scare you off or something. I know this is scary, sweetheart. I see it in your eyes that you're ready to run screaming from this room. Well, I'm not going to let you. We're good together, I know you feel it too. I don't want an answer right now. I want you to think about it, really consider it.

"Don't be scared, baby. I won't ever hurt you the way Gavin did. I only want to love you and spend as much time with you as

I possibly can. And when you're ready, I want to live with you. I want to wake up beside you every morning, and fall asleep with my arms around you every night. That's what I want, and I'm hoping you want that too."

I pull back, her eyes are wide with something that resembles fear. She's quiet for several moments, the only sound her shallow inhales.

"I need to go," she whispers, looking at me for the first time since I dropped my bomb in her lap.

I jump to my feet moments after she does. She starts to move towards the front door, retrieving her bag that I deposited on the floor earlier.

"Jaime, I know you have some things to process. Make a checklist," I add with a smile. But her eyes don't display a hint of humor. "Take your time and think about it. But know this: I'm not going anywhere. If you're not ready, that's fine. I still want to date you, get to know you, love you. But if you do want to move in with me, I promise to make you happy and smile and laugh, and maybe even scream my name at the top of your lungs every night." That got a crack of a smile.

"You're welcome to stay here tonight, but something tells me you need some time alone to think. So know that I'll be here, waiting for you, whenever you're ready."

With that, I place a hard kiss on her lips. It's a proclamation. The kiss says she's mine and I'm not letting go. I don't let the kiss deepen the way my body craves. Instead, I grab the bag from her hand and follow her to her car. She doesn't speak as she slides into her warm car, shaky hands trying to start the engine.

When the car finally starts, I crouch down beside her open door. "I love you. I'll talk to you soon," I reiterate. Leaning forward, I give her another kiss, this time in the middle of her forehead.

Jaime still doesn't say anything, and I try not to let it get to me. I know she's trying to process what I've said. Instead of trying to force her to talk to me, I stand up, leaning down with one arm on the roof of the car, the other on the door. "I love you," I repeat with conviction and meaning.

She glances up and gives me the slightest smile. Her eyes soften, my words seeming to push away the worry and fear that was so dominant only moments ago.

Without waiting to hear if she returns my sentiment, I shut her car door. I tap on the roof twice before stepping back, allowing her to pull away. She sits there for several tense moments, but eventually puts her car in drive and heads down the road.

I ignore the pang of dread that threatens to overtake me. I refuse to believe that this is it, that she'll run away from the happiness I'm offering. Instead, I focus on that tiny smile and the love in her eyes. She loves me, I know it. She believes we can have a future together, I see it. I just need to step back until she allows herself to believe it.

This might be my greatest challenge, yet, but one I'm committed to.

I will make her see how fucking amazing we are together.

There's no other option.

Jaime

25

Me: Code Red! Emergency gathering at Beaver in 20 minutes!

The group text message, which includes all of my sisters, is sent before I'm even out of Ryan's neighborhood. My hands are shaky as I grab the steering wheel and head towards one of our favorite hangouts.

My phone pings with responses, but I don't look at them. I don't have to. I know they'll be there if they can. There's something to be said for when a sister sends a code red message. Each one drops what they're doing and comes running, if at all possible.

It doesn't surprise me that I'm the first one to arrive. Snagging the round booth in back, I order a pitcher of strawberry margaritas and wait for my sisters to arrive. My leg taps nervously on the old, worn hardwood floor, anxiety has me wringing my hands together.

Abby is the first to arrive, which is no shocker since she lives only a few blocks away. She rushes in, hair wild in a high ponytail, and heads towards my reserved table. "Is everything okay?" she asks in a hurry, green eyes scanning me from head to toe as if checking for injuries or something.

"Can we wait until the others get here? I don't want to go through this four more times," I comment while pouring a strawberry margarita into one of the glasses left on the table.

Abby takes a tentative sip while we wait for the others. She's never been a big drinker. In fact, Abby's probably the most straight-laced, docile out of all of the Summer sisters.

Before I can make small talk with my youngest sister, Lexi and Meghan fly through the door at the same time. They're both attempting to talk over the other as they head towards our table. "What did he do? I'll kill him," Lexi proclaims while dropping on the booth and sliding around to my other side.

"Can we wait until the others arrive?" I ask, her eyes narrowing into little slits.

Just as I complete the question, Payton and AJ hurry inside. Lexi takes it upon herself to pour the rest of the margaritas into the empty glasses, and as soon as the others are in the booth, everyone has a drink in hand.

"Okay, spill," Payton instructs before she takes a sip.

"You all know that Ryan and I went away for the weekend," I start, which results in collective acknowledgements from the table. "We had an amazing time, even though Grandma and Grandpa showed up at the Bed and Breakfast we were staying at."

"Wait, what?!" AJ exclaims, wide eyed and mouth agape.

"Oh yeah, totally embarrassing, but I'll get to that in a minute." I take a hearty drink from my glass, the cold tequila burning my throat as it slides down. "Anyway, it was an amazing weekend, and when we got back, he asked me to move in with him." The words fly from my lips in a huge rush of air and excitement.

"What?" is hollered across the table at the same time as "Are you kidding me?"

"Oh my God, Jaims! What did you do?" Meghan asks with a straw in her mouth.

"I, uh, freaked out," I confess.

"I bet," Payton snorts before guzzling her drink.

"Did you breakup with him?" Abby asks beside me, her mostly untouched drink still sitting on the tabletop.

"Breakup with him? Why would I break up with him?" I ask, abandoning my own glass.

"Why? Maybe because you've made it very clear that you'd never put yourself in a position to be hurt again. You've been adamant for the last six months that you're going to be single until the day you die," Meghan adds.

I recall saying each of those things, mostly while I was consuming alcoholic beverages. And I feel that way, at least I did. Before Ryan came along to prove to me why I wasn't destined to live out my days lonely and afraid.

"I know I said those things," I confess. "I also know I didn't mean them, not really."

"So you're not freaking out right now?" AJ reiterates.

"No. Actually, it's completely the opposite. I want to move in with him." As soon as the words leave my lips, I feel the weight of the world lift off my shoulders.

"You do?" Lexi asks with a broad smile across her face.

"Yeah. I do."

"But you've only known him a few weeks." This from Abby, the ever-present voice of reason. She's like the angel conscience sitting on your shoulder.

"It's been almost two months, and you know what? I'm happy. Happier than I've ever been in my life, and I'm not scared to move in with him. I'm excited, and even more so to see what's in store for us next."

Realization dawns on me while my sisters all give me goofy grins. I'm in love with Ryan and want to spend the rest of my life with him. So what if it's fast? So what if it's scary? Love is scary.

Giving your heart to someone is the greatest risk, but if you can overcome that fear, it's the most rewarding thing ever.

And Ryan is offering me what I've always wanted. A life filled with love.

Will it work out? Maybe not. But I'm pushing all of my reservations aside to find out if a life spent with Ryan is as wonderful as I anticipate.

I smile as I glance around at my sisters. Each of them wear their own grins, drinking and laughing at something another one says. These are the moments I'll always cherish, moments filled with shared laughter and tears. These are my sisters, my best friends.

"So tell us about the bed and breakfast," Lexi encourages.

"Well, Ryan and I were kinda in bed together when we could hear this other couple going at it hot and heavy on the other side of the wall, and it turns out…"

Later that night, after we drank two pitchers of margaritas and consumed a few sample platters of appetizers, Josh arrives to take us all home. It takes two trips to get us all safely to our destinations, but he manages. He even arranges for a friend to help drive our cars.

Lying on my side in bed, the clock on the nightstand reads ten-thirty. As it has all night, my mind continually wanders to a certain tall construction worker with dark brown eyes and a sexy smile. As if he knew I was thinking about him, my cell phone chimes with an incoming text.

> **Ryan:** I know how much you like lists, so here's my top reasons why you should move in with me.
>
> 1. I think U R the most incredible woman I've ever known.
>
> 2. I want to spend the rest of my life proving to u how grateful I am that u chose me.

3. Because u make me smile & hearing ur laughter is sweet music.

4. And the most important reason of all...because I love u.

As I finish reading, I see the bubbles appear and know that he's typing.

Ryan: I see that u've read the message. Don't reply. I want you to wait until you're ready & the answer is YES.

I smile at his words and picture him lying in bed as he types them.

While I'm on the verge of typing that one word back to him, I know that he's right and I need to make sure this is what I want beforehand. So instead of replying, I reread his list a few dozen times before setting my phone down on my nightstand and curling up against my pillow. Ryan wants me to move in with him. He has asked, and I will accept. I feel it in my bones, there's no other option for me.

However, I might just sit on it for a few days and make him squirm.

kXXk

It's Friday. My last day at Blossoms and Blooms. I'm beyond excited to start my new job on Monday at Addie's Place, though a twinge of sorrow creeps in every once in a while when I think about not working with Payton every day. I've become accustomed to working beside her and now depend on her daily dose of dry humor to get me through. I'm going to miss her face.

I've also received nightly text messages from Ryan. He has continued with the same pattern and given me a few more reasons why I should move in with him. Out of all of them, the one that made me laugh the hardest was 'endless supply of orgasms.' What girl would turn that down? And, of course, he always ends his messages with 'Because I love u.'

I've kept my word not to reply until I was ready to say yes. Every night, I would actually type that one word–three little letters–but then I would delete them. I didn't want to tell him via text message. I refuse to be *that* person like my ex, even if it was good news. Instead, I plan to tell him this weekend. In person.

As I tidy up the workbench for what could be my last time, I feel my cell phone vibrate in my pocket. When I pull it out, I see a certain someone's name printed boldly across the screen and a smile instantly spreads across my face. His messages have been arriving later in the evening all week, so this mid-afternoon text is a welcome and pleasant surprise.

I slide my finger across the screen until his words are displayed.

> **Ryan:** I need to see you. Can't wait. Dinner tonight. My place. 7pm. Say u'll come.

My fingers fly over the keys as fast as they can to type out those three little letters.

> **Me:** Yes

> **Ryan:** That's my new fave word. See u tonight, gorgeous.

My heart sings in my chest at the thought of finally seeing Ryan again. It has been the longest and loneliest week of my life without him, especially when he's just a text away. I'm still smiling when Payton comes back from her afternoon deliveries.

"Anything happen while I was gone?" she asks, dropping down onto the wooden stool behind the counter.

"Nope. Nothing."

"Damn. I was hoping you'd have some massive floral rush that required half the town to stop in and purchase flowers."

"Well, I did sell something to the pharmacist who stops by to get something for his '*friend*'." His friend is his mistress.

"God, what a tool. I hate making money off a jerkwad like that," she says before looking me over with a critical eye. "What's going on? Why are you so happy?"

"Oh, nothing, except that Ryan just sent me a message asking me to dinner tonight," I say in a singsong voice.

"And you're going, right?"

"Of course I'm going. I miss him like crazy," I reply, turning my attention away from the already clean bench.

"Are you going to answer him tonight?"

"Yep. Definitely going to give him an answer. I can't wait to see the look on his face," I add, recalling how happy he was the moment I told him that I loved him too. I imagine the moment is going to rank right up there with that one.

"I would ask you to call me with all the details, but I imagine the two of you are going to be pretty busy most of the night," she sasses. "Especially when you haven't seen each other all week."

We're laughing together as the bell over the front door announces a customer. Payton looks up first, her face instantly full of surprise. Her statuesque posture causes a tingle of unease to slip down my spine. I'm almost afraid to turn around and see who just walked in. Whoever it is has left my sister speechless.

Finally giving in to the temptation, I turn towards the door and come face to face with Gavin.

My ex.

26

Ryan

Tonight. She's coming for dinner tonight. I'm not sure if she's any closer to giving me an answer to my question or not, but at this moment, that doesn't fucking matter. Seeing her, kissing her, and hopefully making love to her is what matters right now. My body craves her like never before. Five days is too long to be without her, and tonight I'm going to have her.

I pull in front of her sister's flower shop, a handful of wild flowers resting on the passenger seat, anxious to go inside and see her. I know she just replied to my text thirty minutes ago and I'll be seeing her in about four hours, but I'm driving by, heading to the office to collect paychecks, so it's only logical that I stop in and say hello. And maybe steal a kiss. Every day for the last four days, I've contemplated stopping by, but always talked myself out of it.

Not today.

Flowers in hand, I pull open the front door, the familiar bell announcing my arrival. When I step inside, I'm disappointed to find only Payton standing at the counter. As I step closer, her face registers shock and something else. Maybe worry?

"Hey, Payton, is Jaime here?"

She glances nervously over her shoulder and averts her eyes. "Um, yeah, she stepped out back for a minute. I'll go get her," she says quickly turning towards the back entrance where she parks her delivery van.

"No, you stay. I'll go," I tell her, walking around the counter like I own the place.

"No!" she exclaims with a squeak in her face. Her eyes are wide, her entire face clearly betraying the composure she's desperately trying to hang on to.

"Why are you acting weird? Am I not allowed to go out and see her?" I ask, curiously.

"No, it's not that. Of course you're welcome," she starts.

"Great. Then I'll just head out this way," I reply, indicating the back door.

As I approach the back door, I see Jaime standing out back talking to a man. They're smiling at each other, standing about a foot a part. The man reaches forward and pinches the tip of her nose, making her laugh. My gut tightens painfully as I watch their exchange, unable to push the door open. They look comfortable. Familiar.

I'm rooted in place, watching as the man steps forward and hugs my girl. *Fucking hugs her* and I see red. Jaime smiles as she wraps her arms around his chest and squeezes. That single act mimics what's happening to my heart right now. It feels like someone is squeezing my chest, stripping me of the ability to breathe.

Hell no. You don't touch her.

Before I can even give an ounce of consideration to my actions, I push open the door and step outside.

"Ryan, it's not what you think," Payton says behind me, but I'm already gone, heading towards *my* girl and her douche of an ex. I know it's him. I can feel it.

The caveman in me wants to race up to them, throw her over my shoulder, and stomp away. Maybe even throw a right hook in the middle of the smug bastard's face on my way by. But that won't get me anywhere, especially where Jaime's concerned.

I keep my steps deliberate and steady and do my best to keep my breathing the same. There's no time to take any deep, calming breaths as I reach them too quickly. When my movement registers to Jaime, she turns towards me, shock mixed with something lighter spreading across her gorgeous face.

She takes my breath away, every damn time.

"Ryan," she whispers, a soft smile spreading widely across her face.

The man beside her turns full on and faces me. Gavin Morris is just as Jaime had described him, lean and tall and wearing crisp Dockers with a wrinkle-free polo. His blue eyes are wary and take me in from head to toe, as if sizing up the competition.

Game fucking on, asshole.

"What are you doing here?" she asks, eyes shining brightly which honestly shocks me. I expected her to be a bit more, I don't know, scared? Worried? Guilty?

"I was just on my way back to the office and saw these. I knew you had to have them," I say, extending the wildflowers towards her. Her hands are steady as she takes the small bundle of blooms.

Before she has a chance to say anything, I lean forward, claiming her lips in hard, possessive kiss for Gavin, God, and everyone else on the east coast to see. I don't open my mouth, just keep my lips plastered to hers as if making a claim, pronouncing our status as an unbreakable couple.

I don't let the kiss deepen, even though I'd love nothing more than to ravish her lips and her body with my own. Instead, I pull back and gaze into her semi-foggy green eyes. "I'll see you in a bit."

As if she's unable to speak, she gives me a small head nod. Satisfied that I've rendered her speechless, I turn and head back the way I came. I don't turn around, even though I'm dying to. I keep walking, tossing a smiling Payton a wave as I amble by.

Jumping back in my truck, I pull away from the flower shop and head towards my office. Mary should be getting ready to leave for the day, and I'll need to tie up loose ends before she goes. I'm surprisingly lighter as I pull into the first available parking spot behind my building. Even though I found Jaime with the douche, something in her eyes and the way she smiled left me feeling happier, brighter.

Full of hope.

Now, even more than before, I can't wait to see her tonight.

I'm spreading sauce along the pizza crust when I hear her car pull into the driveway. My heart rate kicks up with elation in a way that only Jaime can incite. It takes every ounce of self-control I can muster to keep from running to the front door and throwing my arms around her. But for as much as I long to hold her and kiss her, I know that there are things we're going to need to discuss first.

She knocks on the door and pushes it open when I holler. Her scent precedes her. She's all flowery from spending her day at the shop, but also has a distinctive scent that is seared into my brain. She's fucking heaven.

"Hey."

Damn, that one word spoken from her lush lips renders me completely speechless. She's standing there wearing a tight cotton tee in a deep red, sexy as fuck cut-off shorts, and a pair of black flip-flops. My pants are suddenly so tight, I'm afraid circulation is going to be cut off to my favorite appendage.

But what really catches my attention is the duffle bag thrown casually over her shoulder. I zero in on it, my mind filling with all the possibilities that could be in there. First and foremost: something to wear tomorrow.

"Hi," I finally reply after the silence gets too heavy.

Jaime gives me a knowing smile, yet neither of us moves. She's even more gorgeous than she was last Sunday when she left here.

I take in every detail of her appearance, committing it to memory, so fucking excited that she's here, yet fearful that she'll leave at the same time.

"Pizza, huh?" she asks, her eyes zero in on the covered dough before me.

"Yeah, I thought we'd throw it on the grill," I start, turning my attention back to the bowl of mozzarella cheese. "Throw your bag anywhere. There's beer and a bottle of Merlot still in the cabinet that you left here a week or so ago."

Out of the corner of my eye, I watch her drop the bag on one of the kitchen chairs, and head over to the fridge. I expect her to pour herself a glass of wine, but instead she surprises me and grabs a beer from the fridge. Twisting the cap off, she moves until she's standing directly beside me. My pants tighten even further as she brushes against me. The hairs on my arm stand up, my body like a live wire ready to zap anything and everything that gets in its way.

Reaching for my bottle, Jaime removes it from the koozie and throws it in the trash, replacing my empty drink with a full one. Before she places it back on the counter though, she takes a long pull. Her lips are plump and wet as they wrap around the lip of the luckiest beer bottle in the world. Our eyes remain locked as she slowly removes the bottle from her lips and hands it towards me. A drop of brew glistens on her plump lip, drawing my attention like a strobe light. Without even wiping my hands, I take the bottle and put it to my own lips, loving the fact that they're touching the exact same place as Jaime's just a few seconds ago.

My cock is so hard it could break the concrete sidewalk outside. Jaime's breathing hitches and her eyes dilate to little black orbs of desire as she watches me drink. Who ever knew drinking could be so damn erotic, but hell if I'm not turned on more than ever before. I'm sure it has nothing to do with the fact that I haven't seen her in a week or the fact that her scent is permeating through the lusty fog suddenly consuming my brain.

As I'm setting the bottle down on the counter, Jaime gently pushes aside the ingredients for the pizza. "So, I was thinking," she starts before hoisting herself up on the countertop before me.

My eyes devour her movements. My body moves to fill the void between her legs. "What were you thinking about?" I ask huskily.

"About your question," she states matter-of-factly as she takes hold of my hips and moves them until I'm snuggly against the apex of her legs. Best place in the world.

"Which question was that?" I ask, toying with her just a bit. I know exactly which damn question she's referring to. It takes every ounce of self-control I can muster to keep my hands planted firmly on the countertop. My palms twitch to touch the line of smooth skin that runs up the insides of her thighs.

As if losing her own battle with self-control, Jaime runs her fingers from my hips up my torso and around to graze against my chest. My body is so tight with desire that I'm sure she can feel the tension in every muscle she touches.

"The one that references our pending living arrangements," she replies quietly, her eyes following the path she makes with her fingers.

"Ahh. I *do* recall that particular question." Vividly. I've thought of nothing since.

Jaime dances her fingers up my chest and around my shoulders. She wraps her arms around my neck and pulls until I'm heavenly plastered against her body. Her luscious tits are flattened against my chest, the hard length of my cock nestled against her stomach.

"And I have an answer for you," she whispers breathlessly.

"You do?"

"Yes, but first I want to tell you about my visitor today."

I feel my body tense, but not in the way it was earlier. "Tell me."

"Gavin drove to town to apologize. He wanted to do it face-to-face instead of over the phone the way he did when he broke off the engagement."

Jaime takes a deep breath, but keeps her arms locked around my neck, as if anchoring her body to mine somehow makes it easier to talk about the past. But I can still see the pain in her eyes. The difference is, now, I see something that looks like acceptance and forgiveness.

"He said he felt horrible for treating me the way he did, ending it the way he did, but he was so confused. He knew in his heart he couldn't go through with the wedding and said he actually realized it before that week, he was just too afraid to acknowledge it. I suppose I can completely understand that, you know? I guess now it felt like we were better friends than we were lovers."

Just hearing that word *lovers* coming out of her mouth makes my jaw tick. Call me possessive, I don't care. Being reminded that Jaime has had other lovers before me causes every jealous bone I have in my body to rev to life. It's stupid, I know. There were women before her, but none since. There will never be another. She's it. I feel it.

"Anyway, he started to have feelings for someone else. He said he tried to deny it, but couldn't. The night before he broke it off with me, he worked late. I was fine since my family was in town and us girls all went and got pedicures. Apparently, there was a coworker that was there with him and the next thing he knew, they were kissing."

Wait. I search her face, looking for any sign of distress or anguish, but I still see nothing. "He cheated on you?" I ask, dumbfounded.

"Not really. I mean, it was a kiss, but that was as far as it went. At least, that's what he said, and I believe him."

"So he kissed some office skank and then broke off the engagement?"

"No."

"No? He didn't break up with you?"

"No. It wasn't an office skank." Jaime takes a deep breath before continuing. "It was a man."

"He kissed a man?"

"Yeah. He realized that he was gay."

"Gavin is gay?"

"Apparently after we broke up, he spent some time soul-searching and realized that he loved me as a friend, but not as a man loves the woman he's pledging to spend the rest of his life with. He was fighting his attraction and feelings for the same sex, probably always had been."

"Wow," I reply, taking it all in.

"Yeah. I guess he and Chad started seeing each other recently. He says they've really hit it off and he's happy."

"And Chad is?"

"The coworker."

"And you are?"

"I'm okay. I feel like I'm finally able to put this all to rest. I know there was nothing more I could do to make him happy or make him love me more. It wasn't me, and I'll be honest, ever since it happened, I always thought it was my fault, that I did something wrong."

"You did nothing wrong, sweetheart. I'm sorry he hurt you, that you had to endure that heartache."

"I'm finally able to see that now. I mean, I was there, I knew it, but he gave me the closure I think I desperately needed. Being with you, well that was when I knew what happened with Gavin was supposed to occur, because *we* were supposed to happen."

Instead of confirming what I already know, I choose to kiss her lips instead. It's an affirmation that yes, we were supposed to happen. When I pull back, her eyes are dancing with exhilaration.

"So, back to that question you asked me," she says, pulling me in close once more. Her lips dance along the shell of my ear, her tongue darts out as if stealing a taste.

"I'm all ears." My voice sounds foreign, even to myself.

She turns and looks me straight in the eye. Green eyes dance with excitement as I wait to hear that single word that will set me on the path I'm ready to travel. A path that I'll travel with Jaime, maybe even for the rest of my life.

Her lips graze across mine, her breath rushing out in quick pants. "Yes."

Gazes locked, I slam my lips into hers fiercely. There's no teasing or tenderness in this kiss. It's full of want and passion. It's full of love. My love.

Suddenly, I'm removing her shirt, exposing a soft pink bra made of lace. Her nipples are already erect and straining through the delicate material, beckoning for my touch and calling for my mouth.

I run my tongue along the lace-covered peaks. Blood swooshes through my ears, drowning out the sound of her joyous moans. Tugging the material, I reveal two perfect tits, the nipples wet from my mouth. "Say it again."

"Yes," she whispers once more.

Hearing that word sparks another onslaught of red-hot lust. I need nothing more than to rid her of every piece of clothing she's wearing and bury myself to the hilt inside her body. Claim her. Possess her. It's all I can think about, everything I want. Her. I fucking need her.

"You know what that means, right?" I ask, unbuttoning and removing her shorts.

"An endless supply of orgasms?" she quips, the sexiest smile spread across her bee-stung lips, as she references one of the items from the list I texted her.

"You fucking know it," I laugh.

Things turn serious quickly as she tugs on my shirt and throws it somewhere in the kitchen behind me. My lips descend to hers once more as her hands work vigorously at removing my shorts. She pushes until she can't reach any further, so I help her rid me of everything below the waist.

Standing naked in my kitchen, I feast my eyes on the glorious woman sprawled before me on my counter like some all-you-can-eat buffet. She's still wearing her bra and the matching lace panties, though not for very long.

Sliding my hands up the silkiness of her thigh, I take the delicate lace between my fingers. "Are these expensive?" I ask huskily.

"Yes." She's every bit as breathless as I am.

"I'll buy you another pair," I state as my hands rip the undergarment to shreds.

Jaime's gasp echoes through the kitchen, but my eyes zero in on the Promise Land between her legs. Wet and slick, she's beckoning me like a lighthouse on the coast. With her legs wrapped around my waist, I lean forward and run my tongue along her seam. She tastes better than anything in this world, all musky and sweet.

I place my hands across her waist and devour her with my tongue. Jaime grinds against my face, her body seeking out every ounce of pleasure I offer. Parting her folds, I stroke her pulsing clit with my tongue, sucking it gently into the warmth of my mouth. She convulses beneath me, so very close to the edge of rapture.

With my free hand, I slide a single finger along her entrance, teasing and drawing out a bit more pleasure. "Ryan, please." Her words are panting pleas, a prayer of need and desire.

"Do you want to come?" I ask, her internal muscles tightening around my finger as I slowly push inside.

"Please," she begs.

I slide a second finger inside as far as they'll go, curling them upward as I gently suck on her clit. The action sends her soaring above the clouds, screaming her release for everyone to hear. Continuing to gently stroke her, I release her clit and kiss my way up her abdomen. Jaime flops back on the counter, boneless and spent.

"Still with me?" I ask, showering her chest with a little more attention. Her only response is a grumbled groan of satisfaction.

"I'm not done with you yet," I warn her before standing up. My height and the position of the counter lines me up perfectly for my next move.

With my hands gripping her hips, I gently move her towards the edge of the countertop and right onto my hard cock. She's still tight and pulsing as I slowly push inside of her warm, wet body. I move until I can't go any farther, and then I revel in how amazing it is between us. Every. Damn. Time.

"God, you feel so fucking perfect."

Jaime seems to awaken beneath me as she arches her back and pushes down with her ass, ensuring I'm completely seated within her. My body is burning with the need to move, but I force myself to remain perfectly still for just a few more minutes. I'm captivated with how right she feels, how we feel together.

"You've gotta move," she pleads. Her words pull me from my own trance, and I'm pulled into the depths of her deep green eyes. They're so alive and full of love right now in this moment.

"I love you." Bending down, I claim her lips with mine before she can respond.

Then, I move.

I stand up, grab her hips, and steadily pump into her with long, fluid strokes. Jaime grips the edge of the bar behind her and holds on tight as I guide us towards release. Her body moves with mine, gripping and milking my cock from within. I reach with my left hand and pinch a perky nipple between my fingers. Jaime's internal muscles grip me tighter. She's close.

Swirling my hips around, I slam into her. The angle hits that sweet spot within her body, and after a few more pumps, Jaime's tumbling over the edge in orgasm. She cries out my name, her nails biting into my forearms, as I lose myself in my own release. White light fills my vision, and the air in the room evaporates making it difficult to breathe. All I can do is feel. Feel how tight and wet she is while she's coming on my cock. Feel how amazingly perfect her body feels wrapped around mine. Feel how fucking much love I have for this one woman.

My woman.

Stretching over the top of her, I find her sweet lips. Her mouth is open with little pants of warm breath peppering my face. Slowly, I steal kiss after kiss, savoring and tasting her. I know right then that I'll never get enough of her kisses. I crave them as much as I crave her.

"Come with me, beautiful," I say.

"Where are we going?"

"To shower. Together."

"What about supper?" she asks while I help her sit up and slowly pull myself from her body. Right now we're a sticky mess, and all I can think about is getting my hands on her while I help clean her up.

"It will keep," I reply, throwing the bowl of cheese and other pizza toppings in the refrigerator.

Then with her cradled in my arms, I carry her back to my bedroom, finally absorbing her decision to move in with me. Just the idea of waking up beside her every morning and falling sleep with her leg draped over my own every night is enough to put a huge smile on my face. We're definitely going to need a bigger place. STAT.

But first things first: I'm going to devour the woman I love in the shower.

27

Jaime

THREE MONTHS LATER

It's funny how quickly the weather turns from warm and comfortable to brisk and cool. The mid-October air is chillier than normal, but that hasn't stopped us from sitting on the deck of the new home Ryan and I purchased together. He insisted that both of our names be on everything from the mortgage to the utilities. We're a team, he says repeatedly.

Tonight will be our first official night under our new roof. It didn't take too long to find a house that we both agreed on, and our offer wasn't countered by the Morgensons. Thirty days later, we were signing on the dotted lines (so many dotted lines), becoming homeowners for the first time.

We spent the last month fixing it up. Ryan put his master carpentry skills to work, designing and completing a beautiful new kitchen and bathrooms. The rest of the rooms in our two-story home just needed a little paint and TLC. We discovered beautiful hardwood floors beneath the brown shag carpet, and on his days off, my dad helped Ryan sand and refinish them. Josh has even been over here almost nightly to help in any way he can. They've become good friends through the whole home remodeling project.

The only thing this place is missing is a garage. Back up, it *has* a garage, but it's a little one-car detached thing that you can barely manage to maneuver yourself around when the car is inside, it's so tiny. But there's enough yard space for a larger garage, so Ryan has ordered the lumber to erect a two and a half car garage with a workshop in back, plus a breezeway that'll connect the garage to the side door.

The location is perfect for us, too. It's closer to the edge of town, about two blocks off the Bay. It's a double, corner lot with young families as neighbors. In fact, watching the three-year-old little boy throw a ball around in his backyard today has gotten my biological clock not only ticking, but thumping and bumping.

My entire family, as well as Mary and Mrs. Hanson, all helped pitch in to combine my belongings with Ryan's household into our new home. We had sorted through most of the big things, tossing or donating what we didn't want to keep, so the process of moving today was smooth and seamless.

To thank them all for their time and help, Ryan and I prepared burgers and brats on the grill, and picked up a few sides from the deli uptown. When the last box was unloaded and the final piece of furniture arranged, my grandma, Mary, and Mrs. Hanson set out to organize the kitchen and find what we needed for dinner. Dad and Ryan manned the grill, while Josh and my sisters brought around lawn chairs and the patio furniture, all with Grandpa supervising from the sidelines.

The sun set hours ago, but we're still sitting on the small deck behind our house. Everyone but Mary and Mrs. Hanson are still here, huddled around the fire pit my dad gave us as a housewarming gift. Ryan stoked the fire warm and large, the yellow and orange glow lighting up a portion of the expansive backyard.

I'm huddled against Ryan, partly because I'm cold and the other part because it feels good to be snuggled up to him. He's drinking a beer, but I stopped an hour ago. Exhaustion is starting to creep in, and I plan to be fully awake to enjoy our first official night together in our new house.

"Did you hear that Donny Casem and Shelisa Franklin broke up?" Meghan asks from her position atop Josh's lap.

"Really? He was in your class, right, Payton?" AJ asks, sipping from her glass of wine.

"Yeah," Payton replies nonchalantly.

"You should ask him out," Lexi insists, her side empty since Chris had to work all day. Again.

"I don't think so," Payton mumbles.

"Why not?" Abby asks.

"Because he's a goofball," Grandma hollers from the opposite side of the fire. Grandpa chuckles and wraps his arm tightly around her slender shoulder.

"Truth," I add.

"He's not a goofball, Grandma. Why would you say that?" Abby asks.

"Any man who sits around playing video games all day long instead of working a job is a goofball. There are so many other more productive things he could be doing with his time like golf or having the sex."

Collective groans erupt around us, but Ryan laughs. "I kinda like all the sex, too," he whispers in my ear.

"Let's not talk about sex right now, Grandma," AJ pleads after guzzling the rest of her drink.

"Fine. I know! Why don't we give Jaime and Ryan their housewarming gift?" Grandma turns to Grandpa with a big smile on her face. Without even being asked, Grandpa gets up, shuffles to the doorway, and retrieves a bag.

The bag isn't too heavy, but makes a noise as it's moved. Grandpa gently sets the bag in my lap before returning to his seat beside Grandma. Ryan's brown eyes sparkle in the night as he nudges me to open it.

The first thing I pull out of the gift bag is a small crystal bottle with a clear liquid inside. There's no markings or label indicating the contents. I glance over at Ryan as I hand him the bottle, then glance up at my grandparents with a questioning look.

"It's something special just for you two. I picked it up at that herbal place by the Bay. Try it," Grandma encourages with a smile.

"What is it?" I ask after Ryan pulls out the cork and takes a whiff, resulting in his nose wrinkling.

"Don't do it," Lexi mumbles, causing all of my sisters to giggle.

"I'll tell you what it is after you each try it." Grandma gives me that look that always made me step in line as a child.

Without giving it further thought, I grab the bottle and take a shot. It burns as it slides down my throat like scotch or cheap whiskey. My eyes water and I can't help the sputter and cough that follows.

"You're next, son," Grandma says, eyes twinkling like stars in the sky.

Ryan gives me a curious look before taking the bottle in his hand and tossing back a drink. He instantly coughs and turns his watery eyes back to me. "Did she just poison us?"

"It's not poison, silly. It's a fertility potion."

The only sound is the crackle of the fire. Everyone is stone silent as we absorb her words. "A fertility potion?" I croak.

"Hey! Guaranteed to help with the baby making process," Grandma coos.

"Uhhh, I don't want to sound ungrateful, Emma, but we haven't been trying to have a baby, so I'd appreciate it if you wouldn't wound my manhood before it's had a chance to prove itself."

"Oh, fooey! I'm sure there's nothing wrong with your manhood, Ryan. In fact, it looked rather impressive that day at your condo. Not to mention the sounds coming from my granddaughter that night at the Bed and Breakfast."

"Nope, not happening. Change the subject," my dad begs.

"Oh, Brian, it's a natural part of life. Everyone has the sex, some just better than others." With that, Grandma winks at me.

"Let's see what else is in here," I say, digging into the bag.

I pull out a beautiful pillow in hues of white. An intricate design of different types of white fabric is weaved throughout. It's delicate, yet resilient. "Oh, Grandma, this is beautiful."

I show the pillow to Ryan before passing it to AJ beside me.

"Isn't it? When I saw it, I knew it was perfect for you and Ryan. I could just picture it gracing your bed. It's a fertility pillow."

AJ screams and tosses the pillow back at me as if it were trying to bite her.

"What the hell is a fertility pillow?" Ryan asks, taking the pillow and examining it a little closer.

"You're supposed to position the pillow beneath her hips to help keep them elevated," Grandpa explains. "That position helps you get deeper, therefore shorten the length your sperm has to travel to reach the uterus and the descending egg."

"And Jaime is supposed to continue to lie on the pillow for at least twenty minutes after your ejaculation. It'll help keep her hips elevated and ensure gravity takes the spermies where they're supposed to go," Grandma adds

"Spermies?" Lexi whispers.

"Ejaculation?" Abby adds.

"I'm out of here," Dad hollers as he stands up and walks over to give me a hug. "Love you, girl. I'll talk to you soon."

"Night, Dad. Love you, too." He shakes Ryan's hand and kisses each of his other daughters before heading around the side of the house to his truck.

"Why exactly do we need all of this? We've lived together in our new house for about twelve hours. We're not trying to get pregnant."

"Hogwash! It's never too early to perfect the technique of baby makin'." Grandma smiles proudly across from us.

"I'm already a professional at that," Ryan quips, drawing laughter from my sisters.

"I'm sure you're not bad, but there's always room for improvement! When Orval and I were first dating, he would get all awkward and grabby, thinking everything was the equivalent of a stress ball. It took us a while to get into the groove of nookie together."

"Oh, God, she said nookie," Abby mumbles.

"What's this?" I ask, pulling out a leather strap and realizing instantly what it is, unable to retract the words or close my eyes quick enough.

"That's a flogger, sweetie! They used them in that Christian Grey movie. Grandpa and I like to reenact those scenes. They're super fun." Grandma smiles proudly as fire flickers in her eyes.

"I'm never getting that image out of my head. There isn't enough therapy offered in the state of Virginia to eradicate that," AJ groans.

"I don't understand why we need this. People have been getting knocked up the regular, old fashioned way without all the potions and stuff for a long time," Ryan says.

She gives him a pointed look. "We're just doing our part to ensure we get great-grandbabies. Soon."

"Wait! What about me? I'm the one who's married and has been trying to have a baby. Why wouldn't you give this to me?" Lexi asks. Her eyes are shining as if she's warding off tears.

"Oh, sweet girl, you don't need that. There's nothing wrong with your baby-making machine." Lexi looks devastated, and I suddenly realize that the subject of babies is hurting her way deeper than I originally thought.

"Well, thank you for all the...stuff. When we're ready, I'm sure we'll use...it...all."

Meghan grabs the bag and removes the contents, careful not to touch the pillow. "Don't wait to use this. Nothing says housewarming gift like a leather flogger from the grandparents, Jaime." Then she whips the tassels towards a smiling Payton.

"This might be the weirdest family gathering I've ever attended," Ryan whispers in my ear. "But I like it. And I love you."

"I love you, too," I reply moments before placing my lips on his, ready to see what our first night in our new home has in store.

Ryan

28

She's been in the bathroom a long time. Or maybe I'm just that excited to get her in bed that every second she's not out here is a second too long.

Her family hung around until eleven or so, chatting and telling stories like they always do. Jaime's grandparents didn't stay too long after giving us their weird housewarming gifts. Not that I'm against having a baby with Jaime in any way, I'd just prefer to get her down the aisle and have her wearing my ring before we're setting up a crib and buying diapers.

I wonder how quickly I can get her talked into marrying me?

The sound of the bathroom door opening to our bedroom has me forgetting my thought. The sight of her wearing a white lace negligee that barely covers her ass has me forgetting my own name. She's a goddess, a vision of every fantasy I've ever had all wrapped into one lace-covered package.

And fuck if that package isn't ten times better than any fantasy I've ever experienced.

"Come here." My voice is raspy and deep, laced with hunger and need.

Jaime struts over to the bed, a little extra swing with each step just for my benefit. The smile on her face lets me know she knows exactly what she's doing, toying with me like a cat and a string with each step she takes, seducing me further.

When she approaches the bed, Jaime climbs up and straddles me. My cock is practically clawing out of my briefs. Instantly, I'm assaulted with the scent of her arousal and the heat of her pussy. Glancing down, I realize she's not wearing panties. Thanks to all things holy I lost most of my clothes before I climbed in bed. My cock pulses in my briefs, begging to come out and play.

"Don't move," I tell her as I run my hands up her smooth legs, gently pushing the white lace up around her hips as I go.

Jaime sits atop my waist, her body already lined up perfectly for what's to come. I'll never tire of the way her body molds to mine as if they were made for one another, the way she sounds when she laughs and when she's coming, or the way my heart always kicks up a few beats when she's near. I'll never want another like I want her, like I *need* her.

"What do you think of our new home, Mr. Elson?" she asks, grinding her wetness against my throbbing cock.

"I'm not thinking at all right now, Miss Summer. I seem to be transfixed on one thing at the moment," I grit through my teeth, my entire body tense and taut.

"And what would that one thing be?" she coos, bending forward and letting her hair skim across my chest.

"You. Always you. And the way my body burns to be inside you."

I move my hands from her hips, since they seem to have a mind of their own, and grab a hold of her lace covered nipples, lightly tweaking and rubbing them until they're stiff. My mouth waters to taste those amazing little nubs. Jaime moans, her hands firmly planted on my chest as she continues to gyrate her hips against me.

Suddenly, I catch movement out of the corner of my eye just as my sex-induced brain registers pain. Intense, burning pain across my fucking chest that feels like someone doused me with lighter fluid and lit a match. I barely hear Jaime's scream as I swat away whatever in the hell just attacked me. Her eyes are wide as she looks between my eyes, my chest, and then across the room to where I flung the creature that tried to eat me alive.

"The fuck?" I holler, moving Jaime to the side to protect her in case Jaws decides to come back for round two.

I jump up, ready to kill whatever in the hell it is that attacked me and killed my hard-on, but when I look down, I'm certain my eyes are playing tricks on me. A little ball of yellow and white stares up at me from our bedroom floor. I start to get off the bed to see what in the hell it is, but Jaime grabs my arm and halts my progress.

"Awwwww!" she coos in one of those weird baby voices as she carefully climbs off the bed and picks it up. "Look at this cute little guy."

"What the fuck is it doing in our bedroom?"

"I don't know," Jaime replies softly, her face radiating happiness as she rubs the little feline fur ball against her smiling face. "Where did you come from, little sweetie?" she asks the kitten.

"Don't care where it came from. Only care about getting it out of here," I reply, looking down to examine the damage to my chest. Claw marks deep enough to draw blood extend for about six inches down my pecs, barely missing a nipple. "And put that thing down. It could be rabid or something. Look at what it did to me?" I say, but it falls on deaf ears.

When I glance back up at Jaime, she's standing there with tears in her eyes, grinning like she just won the damn lottery or something. The little ball of fur is tucked against her chest, sleeping soundly as if lulled to slumber by her beating heart.

Carefully, I step over and look down at the form in her arms. I'll admit, it's a cute little fucker, even if it did just try to maim me with the sharpest kitty claws imaginable. A slip of paper beneath his sleeping body catches my attention. Gently moving Jaime's hand, I reveal a folded note.

Here's the rest of your gift. Jaime's always wanted a cat, and I figured Ryan wouldn't mind a little more pussy. Litter box and food in the laundry room. His name is Boots, though Grandma wanted to name him Mammoth because of the size of his shlong. She also says not to neuter him.

Enjoy!

Love, Grandpa

"They got me a kitten?" Jaime whispers, her words laced with laughter.

"They got us a cat," I repeat deadpanned, unable to reach the level of excitement to match hers.

"You don't like cats? How can you not like cats?" Her wide, shocked eyes are focused intently on me.

"I didn't say I didn't like cats, per se, I just think they're shady and sneaky. And look what he did to my chest," I add, pointing to the little claw marks that are enflamed and puffy.

"Ahh, poor baby," she says, stepping closer until she's directly in front of me. "I'm sure he didn't mean to hurt you. He probably just thought you were hurting his mama."

I glance down at the cat, and I swear to God he's eyeing at me out of the corner of his shifty little eyes. "I wasn't hurting his mama. If memory serves correctly, I was doing the complete *opposite* of hurting her."

Jaime's eyes light up and a devilish little grin spreads across her face. "You would be correct. There was no hurting involved. It was only pleasure."

"Make sure you explain that to Freddy Krueger there. I don't want him attacking me or anything that dangles."

"Why don't you go grab a warm washcloth and wash up those scratches. I'm going to get Boots settled." And with that, Jaime turns and leaves the room.

My hard-on died a thousand deaths about ten minutes ago, but just the thought of climbing back into bed with Jaime and finishing what we started causes the blood to flow to one centralized location once again. In the bathroom, fortunately we unpacked the necessities and I'm able to find a washcloth quickly. I gently run it over the claw marks, wincing as the material brushes against the ripped flesh.

Damn cat.

Even though I'm anxious to get back in bed with the woman I love, I take a few extra minutes to use the head and brush my teeth. This is our first night in our new house, and I'm not about to let that beast ruin all the things I have planned to do to–*and with*–Jaime. Starting at her sexy red painted toes, I'm going to lick my way up her soft skin, all the way to her kiss-me lips. Lips that I wouldn't mind seeing wrapped around my cock.

Suddenly, more anxious than before to get back to Jaime, I turn off the light and head into our bedroom. She's lying on her side, facing where I will be very soon. There's an extra skip in my step as I make my way over to my side of the bed–or the side Jaime deemed as my side back when she started staying over at my place more than she was at her own.

When I round the corner of the bed, I stop in my tracks. "I thought you said you were going to get him settled?"

"I did. Grandma and Grandpa didn't provide a bed so I thought he could snuggle with us tonight."

"Put him in the utility room with his food and litter box."

"But there's no bed in there. Plus, it's his first night in a new place. What if he gets scared?"

"He's a cat. You know that, right? He can sleep anywhere."

"He isn't going to sleep just anywhere. He's going to sleep somewhere wonderful," she replies as the kitten burrows closer to her chest. A chest that is now covered in my old New York Yankees t-shirt.

Hey, Boots! Back off. Those are mine. I glare at the offending cat.

Climbing between the sheets, I swear he gives me the stink eye once more. It's as if he's keeping tabs on me, making sure I don't move in on his mama. Well, get in line, cat. She was mine first.

Lying on my side, I find my gaze locked on hers. Neither of us speaks, but we don't have to. Contentment and happiness radiates from her beautiful face, etched in each feature and around her upturned mouth. Happiness is the only thing I ever want to see on her gorgeous face. Never tears. Tears gut me, especially hers. I don't give a shit if I have to spend the rest of my life ensuring it, but my only goal is to make her happy. Whatever she wants, I will give her. Whatever she needs, it's hers.

Boots starts to snore. We both gaze down, and I can't help but smile. He's curled up against Jaime, mouth hanging open, and snoring like Grandpa after Sunday dinner.

"Look at us. Our first night in our new home and we're spending it together as a little family."

Even though I would much rather be balls deep between her legs, something settles deep in my chest when she says the word *family*. It spreads through my bloodstream, warming me as it passes, unhurried and systematic. Peacefulness fills the room and wraps around me like a worn blanket. Comfort. Ease. Home. All the things I've come to feel since Jaime stepped into my life. Maybe stepped isn't the right word, but whatever. Since Jaime appeared into my life.

"Thank you," I whisper, taking in the way her long brown hair fans across the soft blue pillowcase she picked out last week.

"For what?" she asks. Even in the darkness, I can see faint lines appearing between her brows.

Swallowing over the lump that rapidly developed in my throat, I keep my eyes plastered to hers and give her the most honest answer I can give. "For picking me. For loving me."

Jaime smiles that radiating smile that causes a fluttering in my stomach and reaches for my hand. "I believe you might have picked me," she chuckles.

"I might have spotted you and then pursued you like a cop chasing a law breaker, but you picked me, sweetheart. When you took a chance on a dirty carpenter who wears work boots with just about anything, you gave me the truest gift anyone ever could: Your heart. I know it wasn't easy or without fear, and I promise to treasure it–*and you*–the way you deserve. Because nothing is more precious to me than you."

"When you say things like that it makes me wonder what you see that no one else has before."

"I see everything, Jaime. You're everything. It doesn't matter who saw what before, because you were made for me. Plain and simple."

She smiles that soft little smile that I fucking adore. "I love you."

"I love you, too."

Without another word, I lean in and kiss her still-swollen lips. It's a tender kiss filled with adoration and compassion. One that will surely lead to bed-shaking, name screaming sex, if we let it. But it doesn't feel like the right time now.

Instead, I pull her in close, wrapping my larger body around her much smaller one. Boots is cradled between us, purring softly and batting his tiny paw in the air; probably dreaming about ripping my back apart in my sleep.

I watch as she starts to doze off, content to sleep in my arms. There's no better feeling. When I finally can't keep my eyes open any longer, I allow slumber to take hold and pull me under. My last conscious thought is of my green-eyed brown haired beauty curled up beside me in bed.

My love.

My forever.

Epilogue

Jaime

It's a Summer sister tradition that on the first Saturday of each month, the six of us get together. We take turns picking the location or activity, anything from margaritas and a movie to wine and painting classes at the small gallery uptown. One thing, though, is as certain as the sun rising over the Chesapeake Bay every morning; there will be alcohol involved.

Always.

We're gathered around the poker table at Abby's apartment, each of us with various stacks of chips before us. My stack is just a little shorter than the rest of my sisters. Okay, fine. My stack is non-existent. I'm one hand away from losing the twenty-five bucks I came with.

Empty glasses and chip crumbles litter the top of Levi's table that he brought over for us to use tonight. Since it was Abby's night to pick, she chose an activity she's been boning up on in her spare time: Five-card draw.

"Levi plays cards a lot at the fire station when he's working, so he's been teaching me to play," Abby says coyly as she pulls in another pile of chips from the center of the table.

"Teaching you to play? I'd say you've successfully hustled away just about everyone's chips, Miss Sweet and Innocent," Payton says.

"I call a hustle, hustler. You're hustling your own sisters for sport, hussy," Meghan adds while licking the salt off the rim of her empty margarita glass.

"You taught her to hustle, Levi! You should be ashamed of yourself," I holler into the kitchen where Levi sits with Josh and Ryan. They've been out of sight most of the night, but still close by for when we're ready to head home.

"I had no clue she'd be so good. I'm planning on taking my little ace to Vegas and see what kinda trouble we can get into," Levi says with a wink directed at Abby. Of course, no one misses the massive blush as she tries to ignore the implication made by her best friend. Implication that they'd get into some trouble or implication that he staked a claim by using a cute little nickname.

Take your pick.

What's even more interesting is that my dear eldest sister has received no less than six text messages that she refuses to acknowledge to any of us. Oh, she tried to be all sly and return a message under the table, but we caught her. Every time.

Right now she's leaning over her phone and the slightest of smiles plays at the corner of her mouth. Deep down, I'm hoping it's some guy who's working on swooping in and sweeping her off her tired feet. She works twenty-four seven at Blossoms and Blooms. The only adult interaction she gets (besides her deliveries) is Rachel, her employee, and her accountant. And from what I've gathered, he's been less than cooperative when it comes to scheduling her appointments after work hours and has been a complete thorn in her side since he took her on a few months back when her previous accountant retired.

"You about ready?" Ryan whispers in my ear before kissing the top of my head.

"I think so. I'm half drunk."

"Only half?" Ryan asks, amused.

"Yep, only half. I'm pretty sure it's my right side that's drunk, so we'll be good to go with the road head on the way home."

"Gross. At least wait until you drop me off," AJ chimes in, breaking my pre-blowjob, half-drunk, completely lost in lust haze.

"I'm riding with Josh and Meg now," Lexi says as she gathers up the empty glasses and takes them into the kitchen.

"You lost all of your money." Ryan helps me stand, but quickly pulls me into his strong arms. My favorite place to be.

"Yep. Hustled by the hustler."

"At least you didn't call me a hussy," Abby says, blushing all over again.

"You're not a hussy, sweet girl. You haven't been around the block nearly as much as AJ," Payton adds with a snort.

"Hey!" AJ crosses her arms and glares at the oldest sister. "At least I'm getting out and living my life."

"I live my life, thank you very much."

"Says the woman who practically sleeps in her office," Lexi retorts.

"Anyway, I think we're going to head out. Anyone need a lift?" I ask as Levi and Abby clean up the crumbs from the table.

"Not if you're giving road head," Lexi says.

"I'm good. Josh and Meg are only a few blocks from me so I'll catch a ride with them," AJ says.

"Me, too. I'm good," Lexi adds.

"I'm in if you promise to keep it zipped up until I'm out of the truck." Payton grabs her coat and follows me as we hug each of our sisters. Of course, with the added effects of the alcohol, the hugs last a little longer than normal.

Ryan escorts me to his truck, one hand on my lower back and the other holding the key fob. His touch sends warmth rapidly coursing through my veins and a fire to light in the pit of my belly. Is it bad that the first thing I think of is how quickly we can get rid of the pesky older sister? How is it that after six months of knowing him–being with him–I can still feel this way? Every. Time.

Heading towards Payton's place, I turn my attention towards my sister. "You know what you need?" I ask.

"I'm sure you're going to tell me, aren't you." It's a statement, not a question.

"I am going to tell you. You need a date. Someone who will pick you up at your house and take you to dinner. Maybe bowling or for a walk through the Botanical Gardens."

"We don't have a Botanical Gardens," she quips.

"No, but we should." Turning to face Ryan. "We should have a Botanical Gardens, babe. Don't you think so?"

Ryan glances at me with a smile before answering. "I agree."

"Of course he agrees. He wants to get laid. You could tell him your hair is blonde and the sky is red. Or maybe that OneRepublic is a good band, and he'd agree with you because you teased him with road head tonight and he wants to get lucky."

"I do want to get lucky," Ryan replies with a broad smile.

"See."

"Annnnnyway," I interrupt, drawing out the word as if I were intoxicated. Wait. Anyway. Anyway? That's a funny word, isn't it? Any. Way. Innnnywayyyyy. "My point is, you're not getting any older."

"You mean younger," Ryan whispers with a chuckle.

"What. Ever. You're getting old, Pay. And I don't want you to die alone with your cats."

"I don't have any cats. You're the one with the cat."

"Isn't Boots the cutest cat in the whole world? I mean, the way he scrunches up his face in disdain when Ryan kisses me is so stinking cute. Isn't it cute, Ryan?" I ask.

"Cute isn't the word I was going to say, but that'll work."

"Annnnnnyway, you need a date. Ryan, what's the name of that guy you worked with on that one job the last time?"

Ryan pulls his eyes away from the road only long enough to give me a curious look. "You mean Jimmy?"

"No, not Jimmy. The other guy."

"Chase?"

"YES! Chase! That's him! You should date him!" I yell. Why am I yelling?

"Um, babe, Chase is married," Ryan says as he pulls up in front of Payton's house.

"The fuck?! He's cheating on his wife?" I holler.

"No, babe. He's not cheating on anyone. You're the one who suggested Payton should date him. But he's married."

"Oh, Payton, he's married. Never mind."

"Anyway, this ride was super fun and completely educational. I'll see you both later," Payton says before throwing a kiss on my cheek and climbing out.

We wait at the street while she unlocks her door and lets herself in. When the light turns on and she gives a little wave through the curtain, we pull away, heading towards our house.

"He's really married?" I ask, completely stuck on that fact for some reason.

Ryan chuckles again. "Yes, babe. He's really married."

"Damn. I wanted to hook Pay up with him. He's cute with those gorgeous blue eyes and those dimples that make me want to lick them."

Ryan glances over again, a shocked expression on his face. "You want to lick his face?"

"No, I want to lick his dimples."

"Which are on his face."

"Why are you trying to start a fight? Do you *not* want road head?"

"I always want road head, but I kinda want to make sure that the next time you see Chase you aren't going to lick his dimples."

"I would never do that sober, sweetums. I prefer to lick only one head." And then, because alcohol makes me bold, I glance down and stare at his crotch so there's no question about what *head* I'm referring to.

Ryan pulls into our driveway and shuts off his truck. "Promise me you won't lick any of my employees, sober or intoxicated. Just the thought makes me want to rip off his dimples and beat him to death with them."

"That sounds…weird…but I promise to never lick another man. I was only teasing you, honestly. I really only want to ever lick you," I say, unbuckling my belt and climbing over the seat towards him, very ungraceful like.

His big hands slide beneath my coat as I move sideways across his lap, my neck at an awkward angle because of the roof. Ignoring the growing pain in my neck, I go in for a kiss. Ryan's lips are warm and perfect. It only takes a few seconds before he takes control of the kiss and works his hands beneath the layers of clothing I'm wearing to accommodate the early November night.

After several seconds that result in the steaming up of all the truck windows, he finally pulls away, breathlessly. My hands instantly dive for his buckle, a task that proves to be more difficult considering my lack of coordination and our positions.

"You do realize the last time we were in this situation we were both arrested?"

"Technically, *you* were arrested. I was perfectly decent when I stepped out of the truck to help you with the cop."

"True, but I believe you were very *indecent* moments before that cop arrived."

"True. We should give it another shot. I mean, we're in our own driveway so it's not like the owners are going to press charges," I coax by rubbing my hand across his erection.

"How about I take you inside and make love to you in our bed?"

"What about Boots?"

"Boots gets the boot for a bit."

"You can't make our baby sleep on the floor in the hallway."

"Yes I can. I can, and I will. Because getting you naked in bed without the voyeuristic cat watching is my solitary goal in life right now."

"I like your list of goals," I reply while he runs his hand up my side and pushes my top up as he goes. "Know what's on my list of goals for tonight?" I ask, teasing his earlobe with my tongue.

"What's that?" he whispers, his voice raspy and deep.

"Road head. As long as we're in the vehicle, it still counts."

"I love your list." His lips punctuate his words. They're hard and hot, and yet full of love.

His love.

Us.

Together.

Another Epilogue

Payton

I wave goodbye to my sister and her boyfriend. If they manage to make it home without ripping their clothes off I'll be surprised. I kick off my shoes and drop my coat on the chair. Sure, I should probably hang it up in the closet, but I'm too tired and a little too drunk to care tonight.

Besides, a few text exchanges have me a bit more preoccupied than normal.

Making sure the lights are off–all except the one above the sink– I slip back into my bedroom and rid myself of every piece of clothing I'm wearing. My favorite pair of soft, flannel pajama bottoms are sitting on the edge of my bed where I left them this morning, right next to the white button up shirt I've worn to bed the last three nights.

The shirt still carries his scent, one that's musky with a deep woodsy base. A scent that wraps around me in the night, comforting me with its familiarity and reminding me of the man who carried it.

A man who warmed my bed just a few short nights ago.

Nights that contained little sleep, but when it did finally come, vivid dreams replaying of our short time together.

I slip on the shirt and forego the flannel pants this evening. Maybe it's the alcohol. Maybe it's a way to get closer to him, to sleep in the exact same garments I slept in that night. Either way, it's comforting to wear his shirt, and only his shirt.

Climbing beneath the blankets, I snuggle into the pillow. It's not my pillow, but the one his head touched for a brief moment in time. I sigh deeply, one that signifies my exhaustion from working too many hours, as well as the onslaught of memories to come.

I reach for my cell phone, careful not to unplug it. His last text message still shows as a new, unread text. I haven't been able to talk myself into reading it, because as much as I've enjoyed the "I had a great time" and the "I'd love to see you again" messages, I just don't know where this could possibly go from here.

Truth is, it can't go anywhere.

So, for tonight, I'll curl up against the pillow, wearing the shirt he left behind, and not look at the message. I'll walk away before either of us has to because, sometimes, there's no other choice.

THE END

About the Author

USA Today Bestselling Author Lacey Black is a Midwestern girl with a passion for reading, writing, and shopping. She carries her e-reader with her everywhere she goes so she never misses an opportunity to read a few pages. Always looking for a happily ever after, Lacey is passionate about contemporary romance novels and enjoys it further when you mix in a little suspense. She resides in a small town in Illinois with her husband and two children.

Website: laceyblackbooks.com
Email: laceyblackwrites@gmail.com

Sign up for my newsletter so you don't miss a single sale, reveal or release!
www.laceyblackbooks.com/newsletter